SOULLESS:

Dead Bodies Don't BLEED

K. LAMAR

CONTENTS

Part III. Looking Down on Reality

ACKNOWLEDGEMENTS

To my first book critics: Dennis "Dime Bag" Tharp, Black, Mellow, Mill-Town Danny Boy, T-Mac, and O.G. Blake. Thank you for all of the valuable feedback.

To my boy, Solid: I don't know where you're at and I haven't heard from you in over sixteen years, but I've got nothing but love for you.

Lonnel "Black Rob" Harris: Man, Bro, you've always moved to the beat of your own drum and still managed to stick to the Original Rules without compromising your daily growth. If I had to pick one word to describe you, it would be *authentic*. I have nothing but love, admiration, and respect for you.

Leroy "King Lew" Lewis: You're one of the most knowledgeable and honorable men I've ever known. I've valued your insight and friendship over these last eighteen years. You already know that if you ever need me, I'm there, and I know that works both ways.

Derrick: Whether it was the last nutty bar or $1,000, we split it straight down the middle. Damn, we went through it all, never negotiated with terrorists, and always kept it one hundred with each other. That was the recipe that made water thicker than blood with us.

My homie, L.A., who's blacker than a thousand midnights (and I'm not talking about skin color): You're the last of a dying breed.

A'Kim Mack, a true sky-dweller: I appreciate all those conversations we had about life, this system, and especially the ones where you gave me insight on Islam.

Sonny Mack, a truly gifted young black designer: Don't let these streets sidetrack the vision.

Big Trev, "The Long Way": You already know how I fuck with you. There has never been a short way to it.

Stack Bundles: They better not ever say *Chicago* without saying your name!

Vision Marques: Man, Bro, I started working on Soulless like 16 or 17 years ago because I wanted to write the kind of book that I wanted to read—a raw, uncut story out of the Mil with no breaks whatsoever—but couldn't find out there. I stopped after a few chapters and let it sit on the shelf (even though everybody who read what I had written so far wanted me to finish it) because, deep down, I never truly thought it was possible for me to write a book. But then I got your first book—*Trap Zone*—in my hands. I was truly inspired in that moment. That's when I found you and hollered at you about my Soulless joint. There are times in a person's life when the words of another can help them see or keep them blind. I must say that it was that 15-minute conversation we had that gave me sight. Thank you for laying out the blueprint for me. I truly appreciate all of the TIME, GAME, and SUPPORT that you gave me without a hint of hesitation. I hope that I can be that kind of inspiration to someone else someday. [Check out these books by Vision Marques: *B's in Da' Trap*; *B's in Da' Trap Part 2: Reign of the German Princess*; and *She Did Dat*.]

I want to also acknowledge two young brothers who were taken from us far too early:

Devon Robinson, 1987-2007
and my little cousin, DaRon Coleman, 1990-2012

Rest In Paradise.

Dedicated to the woman who I hold nearest and dearest.
There are billions of women on earth, but none like you.
My bliss is attributed to your loyalty, your strength, your character,
your will, and your love.

PART I:

First-Hand Accounts

PROLOGUE

Solstice

"Goddamn, this mafucka is heavy," I muttered to myself as I grappled in the dark with the grated manhole cover I was trying to remove from the sewer. I started to question my own physical ability but quickly decided that it had nothing to do with me. I mean, I stood at five-foot-seven and a slim 160 pounds and was stronger than most niggas twice my size. Shit, I could probably slam a nigga on his head with no effort. This manhole cover was just some shit that the city had overproduced at the expense of hardworking taxpayers.

I thought about going to get my brother for help, but the nigga already thought he was stronger than me just because he was older. He had a habit of always trying to big brother me and I wasn't trying to hear that shit at the moment.

Fuck it, I thought as the mere idea of him showing me up yet again provided me just enough inspiration to do what I needed to do. I finally got the cover removed, but then realized that was only half the battle. The goddamn thing weighed a ton. It had to be a ton. It took me close to a minute just to slide it six feet behind a dumpster, where no one would be able to see it. Nevertheless, the plan was coming together.

One hour later...

I never understood it. Why would a mafucka circle a block twice before entering his house but not actually bother to observe his full situation? It was late at night and there were plenty of places for threats to hide but this dumb-ass nigga drove past my whip twice and didn't look my way either time. There I was, sitting behind the wheel, parked just two houses from where he rested his head. As I waited, I ran the flame of my lighter along my forearm, allowing it to sear my already desensitized flesh; this had become a practice of mine since I was a shorty. I had been stalking him so hard that I accidentally ran the fire across some fresh skin and the pain caused me to jump a bit.

It was in this moment that I realized just how accurate my notions of him were; he was a bitch nigga, not a gangsta. Nothing about him spoke to the character that he had manufactured. I knew of too many niggas like him, circling the block as if the act itself was some sort of proper precaution. There are very few niggas capable of understanding my displeasure with what this game has been reduced to. See, premiere street niggas are the last of a dying breed. Any time a fuck boy like this is granted allowance in the streets, there must be a deficit of real niggas who adhere to the original rules and work to keep order. Regulators are what we used to call them.

I loved the fit of my black Nike gloves so much and was anxious at the opportunity to use them. I began strapping them on and as soon as I heard him kill the engine, I grabbed my .357 Judge and climbed out of my Lexus.

—

The Kitty Korner is a knockout strip joint owned by a few hustlers from around the way. The bitches are subpar and the layout is minimalist. The main stage isn't complete and the champagne room is only partitioned by a large curtain. The bar is the best thing going there, aside from the high stakes gambles that take place in the back. The gambles bring out the ballers and where there are ballers, the bitches, snitches, jackers and thieves naturally flock.

It's nothing more than a failed business venture that serves more as a convenient way to launder drug money, but the Kitty Korner is a haven for niggas like me. I always walk through the door without getting patted. The owners fuck with my brother though. In less than five minutes, I can get myself a seven of loud, a bitch to fuck on, and a target to stalk.

"Soulless, where you been at?" Katrina, this thick, caramel-skinned cutie, asked as I entered the club.

She's bad. I fucked her once. She knew how to handle the dick, but I couldn't believe she thought she was privileged enough to inquire about my whereabouts. She's a bitch. She should only speak when spoken to. She should only come when called. I knew where this behavior came from, though—lame-ass niggas worshipping those bitches.

"Watch out, right fast," I said, removing her from my path.

As I made my way through the club, I saw Tango, a 19-year-old problem child who is walking mayhem with a lust for domination and asserting his will. He is the capo of Level Up, a crew run by Maserati. He has so much of a reputation for terrorizing and extorting veterans in the game that the streets refer to him as OG Killer. Tango spotted me and began moving my way.

I knew the boy looked up to me but I couldn't fully understand why. Part of my confusion came from not feeling like I can relate with niggas in the streets. They worship shit like cars and ho's—things that, to me, are a given in the game and nothing to brag about.

As young Tango approached me, I already knew what the gist of our conversation would be about. It was pretty much the same every time. I never minded the dialogue with him, though; I actually had more of a liking for him than the niggas my brother chose to fuck with.

"What's a king to a god?" Tango greeted as he extended his hand to me with a serious look in his eyes.

I clasped his hand with an even more serious look then embraced the young killer. "What's a god to a nonbeliever?" I responded.

Tango smiled, knowing that for me the ritual greeting served as more of a question of consciousness than a greeting. "How long you been here?" he asked.

"About five, six minutes," I told him. "Why?"

"Did you see Prince Ion when you came in?"

"Yeah, but we didn't speak. Why?"

"See, Soulless," Tango said before going into his pocket and pulling out a knot. He peeled off half and handed it to me. I took it and began counting as Tango continued talking.

"Big bro, you should have gotten that five to six minutes ago. As soon as that pussy-ass OG saw me, he made his way to me, talking about the nights on him before he slid me five bands. The real reason he did it is because he knows to pay homage when an elite steps into the room. He don't want to see me when the moon is out—I level up and transform into a different kind of creature with more hair and longer teeth."

By the time I finished counting the cash it was twenty-five hundred. I found Tango's metaphor a little bit funny, but I knew he was dead serious. I started to hand the money back to him but he stopped my attempt by pushing my hand back.

"Nah, that's you," he said. "You shoulda got more than that coming through the door. Look, big bro, it's time to level up. I respect your loyalty to yo' big bro, but you really need to rock with me and Maserati. I know Maserati pulled it on half the city and mafuckas been cryin' like ho's. This shit comes with the game. It was needed, man. There's a bigger picture to look at and I stand with him one hundred percent. He off in another time zone visiting the snowman right now but I know when he comes back we gon' turn this bitch upside down. We levelin' up and we skippin' from six to eight figures. So, the time to fuck with ya boy is now. Them OGs think they kings but we demigods."

I passed Tango his cash again. The shit didn't motivate me. I knew his conversation was based on his distaste for OGs.

"Let me tell you somethin', young Tango. I feel you one hundred percent. These veterans designed the rules to protect themselves. The only thing keeping *me off they ass is my brother. That said, I don't move without Theory. Take yo money, li'l bro."*

"Nah, nigga. That's you. Matter of fact, I'm drivin' on Prince Ion. He owe me another twenty-five hundred for not respectin' yo' slot as soon as you walked in. He five bands in the hole and I gotta go get my cash. These fake-ass OGs gon' learn to break bread any time you, me, or any other elite step into the room. Where that nigga Ion at? If he don't got the cash on him, I'm takin' that piece from around his neck."

"I'll take this cash, but I'ma leave you with this: I respect yo' approach. These niggas acquire second-hand principles without ever questioning the shit." I paused before tapping young Tango on the chest. "Yo' heart is hard and that's what makes you nobler than them."

I pulled a half blunt from behind my ear and lit it before passing it to Tango. "They abide by certain principles and practice certain mannerisms because they're weak."

As Tango passed the blunt back to me, I took a slow pull before continuing. "But you, young werewolf, you understand that exploitation, injury, and suppression are natural ways of life. Man, look around," I directed with my hand. "These niggas will never be able to comprehend that because they're strange, lame, and weak. The only real difference between me and you is that you way too public with yours. I'm a little more intimate. Think on that."

I noticed Prince Ion leaving the club as Tango and I embraced to say goodbye.

"What's a king to a god?"

"What's a god to a nonbeliever?" I responded before we parted ways.

Though I know a lot of niggas hate to see me coming, there are a few, like Tango, who recognize and respect the real and embrace me with smiles and hugs. I know there are rumors out there surrounding certain moves I pulled on niggas, certain unsolved homicides that I was liked for. It is what it is. One thing is for sure: none of these niggas want to take a chance on fuckin' with me and I don't give a fuck. As far as I'm concerned, the certified niggas are safe from my gun. It's the underserving who gotta worry about me.

As I moved deeper into the club I reached a gamble taking place on a pool table in the back.

"Bet anotha hunnit," Li'l Greg dared as he raked up cash. "You niggas know what it is."

As the dice came out, I noticed there were a few familiar faces standing around. When it comes to the stones, I can't resist. I've been gambling since I could leave the porch. In my eyes, it was a hustle, never a gamble. I had to make my way over.

Li'l Greg seemed to be amused as I dropped a bill onto the pool table. Usually, I'm able to read men well, but I was not prepared for what came out of his mouth next.

"What it do, Soulless? You must be tryna re-up with that light-ass hunnit. This the bankroll section over here. They pitchin' quarters in the alley, nigga. Take yo' ass out back."

As a few snickers and giggles went out, I felt a slight burning in my chest. Li'l Greg is a bitch. He's from a side of town that doesn't produce real niggas. Who was he to joke with the real ones?

"Fuck it, I'll take yo' li'l coins, right fast," Li'l Greg decided. "I break you bum-ass niggas so easily that I'm startin' to wonder if y'all out there pitchin' packs for me."

"Shoot this money and stop talkin', nigga," I said.

"Fuck you mean, nigga? Yo' li'l bum ass ain't in no position to give orders. Nigga, ya lucky I'm givin' you a chance at it. I do this shit for fuck-off paper. You doin' it to feed ya bitch and gas that standard-ass Lexus outside."

Li'l Greg continued to talk shit as he passed time after time. I was down damn near six hundred and felt like the bitch-ass nigga was committin' a soft robbery.

"My son got mo' assets than yo' po' ass, Soulless."

Niggas were beginning to giggle a bit too much. This nigga was really trying to make a spectacle of this. "Aye, watch yo' mouth, pussy." *I pointed into his face to make it clear that I was serious.*

He eyed me as the dice passed once more and there continued to be a sense of bravado about him. I knew he was a bitch, but he was a master of impression management and these niggas believed in the theatrics. I wanted to hit him in his mouth. Who the fuck did he think he was talking to like that? The least he could do was show me some respect while he took my cash.

"What, you mad now? I only hit you for like six hunnit. Real niggas don't miss the peanuts, broke-ass nigga."

Did he just try to tell me what real niggas do? What the fuck does he know about real?

"I told you once," *I reminded him.*

"Shut the fuck up and watch my dice, nigga."

As he shot the dice, I could feel myself growing impatient.

A full minute went by without anything being said. I could tell there were a few cats who knew he was out of his mind because they knew how I get down.

Li'l Greg eventually crapped out on a side bet and I began to collect my paper. He spoke again.

"You ain't got the hand for this shit, li'l nigga. But, I'ma let you try to win some of this shit back."

Am I trippin', I thought? The fluency with which the arrogance rolled from his tongue told me that he has been given a pass for this shit too many times before. This nigga shouldn't even have felt comfortable lookin' me in the face. I had to hit this nigga in his shit.

Nah, fuck that. Certain niggas were lookin' my way. That nigga was thinking money is what makes him real, but I was going to show him what real looks like. I was going to strip his bitch ass and then kill him. Yeah, that's exactly what I was going to do. I would take his shit and then kill him.

"What the fuck is you grinnin' for, nigga?" he asked me. "You down. I'm the one who should be grinnin'."

"You know what?" I said as I flung the rest of my knot at him. It wasn't much, close to a band. I was going to get it all back anyway. "There go some more cash for you, since you got it all anyway, rich nigga," I told him as I started to walk off. "I'm outta here."

As I made my way to the door, Jessica, a 23-year-old bitch with a fat ass and cute face, walked up to me. She always reminded me of Lauren London and I knew exactly what she wanted. She liked to ride and listen to music while I let her suck my dick and hold the heat. I had twenty minutes to spare.

———

"Man, the cash in my pocket. You can have this shit," Li'l Greg spoke with his hands in the air as the mouth of my Judge flirted with the back of his head.

"Shut the fuck up and invite me in, bitch nigga."

He complied, looking around the block as if he were hoping for a neighbor to notice his distress. Even if the police were called, I didn't give a fuck. They could get it too. I only needed a few swift minutes anyway.

The moment the door was open, I shoved him inside, causing him to lose his footing a bit. He wanted to try me. I knew it. We were moving toward the kitchen as I thought about poppin' him. As we entered the kitchen, he turned back to get a look at my face. It didn't matter. He was dead either way it went. He frowned as if he were somewhat fearful.

"Come on, Soulless," he said, dropping his hands as a wave of realization seemed to overcome his temperament. "You salty about that shit earlier for real? I just be talkin' shit, my nigga. You know that. It did look like you hurtin' a little though. If you been hurtin' that bad you coulda just come to me and I woulda straightened you out. I coulda gave you a pack. Or, since I know how you like playin' with them pistols, I coulda gave you a door to watch."

This nigga really has me fucked up, don't he? I thought. As I stood there with my gun now trained on his nose, I wondered how delusional he must be to believe he was going to proposition his way out of this jam. As he continued to lob insults at me, I found myself thinking that a bullet to his face would be a disservice to my ego.

"You broke one of the original rules, pussy" I explained.

"TAH! Bro, when players get together, we talk shit. That's just what we do."

SMACK!!

Without even thinking, I had put down my Judge, snatched a small cast-iron skillet from the stove, and cracked his shit. Bits of caked-on grease flew off the skillet and onto the sleeve of my varsity Pelle Pelle. Li'l Greg stumbled backwards with his arms flailing. It seemed as if he were trying to fight back and almost looked like he tried to hit me as I stayed right on his ass. Maybe he was trying to grab me for leverage. Either way, I wasn't feeling it. I stared at him for a second as he struggled to gain his footing. He stumbled backwards a couple more steps until he backed into the kitchen counter.

The blow to his head had almost put him out of it. He leaned back against the counter for stability and lifted his arms by his face and head in a weak attempt to protect himself. The first swing had caught even me by surprise but it was all I needed to get to it.

"You think the RULES–DON'T–APPLY–BITCH–ASS–NIGGA?!" With each word, I brought the skillet down on him with one hand as I held him up by the shirt with the other. I began pounding in his bottom lip, causing his fronts to tear through the flesh. It was as if the lip had disappeared entirely, exposing nothing but the blood-covered platinum and diamonds. When I realized that the bottom of the skillet was only blunt enough to push his forehead in a little, flatten his nose, split his mouth, and remove a few fronts, I raised my arm and, with a flick of my wrist, turned it on its side before going back to work on his ass.

I aimed the side of the skillet at the part of his face that was already pushed in a bit and came down hard. *CRACK!*

As I continued driving the brim of the skillet into his face, I took satisfaction in seeing that the smug expression had disappeared. There were sounds coming from his mouth and I couldn't tell if the nigga was trying to say something or if it was just the moist sound of tissue and bone fragments blending. After two more strikes, his face finally cracked, pushing blood and gray matter out the top of his skull. There was a section of skull hanging from where his eye had been before I began to mince it.

Before I knew it, we had collapsed to the floor and I was kneeling in front of some shit that I couldn't even recognize. Where the fuck had his eyes gone? Nothing was left but his jaw line. I found myself salivating at the sight of this pussy-ass nigga, lying before me in deformed shame. My heart was racing. The feeling was one of complete thrill. The power I felt was intoxicating.

As I stood to my feet, I could tell that I had ejaculated in my jeans while I was beating him. It had only happened like that a few times in my life but I hated it every time. The first time it happened was during an incident when I was 15 years old and I never had any control over it.

"Damn!" I cursed, kicking Li'l Greg's lifeless torso. "I shoulda told yo' smart-mouth ass that if you turned me on, it would be hard to turn me off."

I looked around the kitchen and remembered that I had no clue where in the house he kept his stash. I stared at him and laughed. This bitch made me break one of the original rules: get the money first.

Since I had caught him just as he was getting home, I knew I would at least be able to get my money back from the gamble earlier, in addition to any other winnings he had on him. I searched his pockets and came out with eleven thousand. I put the money in my pocket then began walking around to assess the interior of his house.

I first reached the threshold that separated the kitchen from the living room and noticed that there was a hallway to my left. It was dimly lit by what looked to be a trail of LED lighting. I stepped back into the kitchen to retrieve my Judge before continuing my stroll.

As I started walking down the hall, I noticed that the lights were actually TVs lining the walls. There were three on each side, bearing screensaver images of Li'l Greg and his homeboys in various club sets. This nigga truly believed in his own prestige. It didn't surprise me at all that he had actually done some shit like this. It was almost comical. I began knocking the shit off the walls as I moved through the house searching for a safe or other valuables.

With only two rooms to choose from in the modest ranch-style house, I quickly picked one and ransacked it. Aside from a few bands, an ounce of soft, and a jar of pills in the nightstand, there was really nothing else worthy of my time. I added the few grand to the eleven I had just retrieved. The second room had a closet full of designer apparel and expensive furs. I knew it must be Li'l Greg's room. I took a moment to look out the front window and I smiled as I saw that the night was still silent. I had all day in this bitch.

I started with the dressers, pulling out the drawers and flipping everything on its face as I conducted my search. I came up with a yellow-gold Breitling sprayed with yellow diamonds as well as a pair of large, canary-yellow diamond earrings. My brother loved shit like this. It would be his.

I scanned the room and looked toward the pile of pillows resting at the head of the bed. A little piece of something sticking out from under one of the bottom pillows caught my eye. I reached under and pulled out a compact .40. This made me pause and become more thorough in my search. I shoved the pistol in the waist of my jeans then snatched up the pillows one at a time, inspecting each one before tossing it to the side. Finding nothing else among the pillows, I lifted the mattress off the bed and shoved it to the side, revealing a gray and white tundra-camouflaged AR-15.

"Oooh-weeee," I said, as I gently scooped up the rifle and handled it like a newborn baby. "Come here, you pretty bitch." I knew it had probably been more of a fashion accessory than a tool for a nigga like him. I took a pillowcase off one of the king-size pillows, put the rifle, the .40, and the other valuables in it, and headed back to the kitchen. I had a body to deal with.

When I reached the kitchen, I put the pillowcase with my new merch on the counter and started looking for supplies to assist with my cleanup. During my search, I came across the bloodied cast-iron skillet I used on Li'l Greg and tossed it in the pillowcase.

I eventually found a roll of large, black garbage bags and a roll of duct tape in the kitchen pantry and began ripping some of the bags apart at the seams to turn them into big sheets. I laid out several of the sheets on the floor and taped them together, creating one giant sheet. I rolled Li'l Greg's corpse into the middle of the sheet and wrapped him like a present, securing the package across the top with more duct tape.

When I had it all wrapped up, I tried a test lift to see if I could pick up the body, but I couldn't get enough leverage. I tried dragging it, but it became obvious that the goddamn trash bags were creating too much friction against the floor and weren't going to be quite strong enough. There was no way I could get his body to my car without ripping the plastic. I needed something stronger and with more glide. I walked around the house a bit and found one of those long, clear protective mats people put on their floors to protect the carpet from high-traffic areas. Perfect.

I took the mat into the kitchen and laid it on the floor, parallel to the wrapped corpse. I lifted the top part of the body and carefully pulled it onto the mat so the garbage bags would stay secured. I then did the same with the bottom half of the body. When the body was centered on the mat, I tried another test drag and could tell the mat had given me the durability and glide I needed. I was good to go.

Thinking ahead, I didn't want to have to go back into the house after getting Li'l Greg in my car so I grabbed the pillowcase with the merch, placed it on top of his body, and secured it with just enough duct tape so it wouldn't slide off. I then started dragging the body through the house. The thick plastic of the mat made it a smooth transition as I quickly transported Li'l Greg out of his house, down his walkway, and to the passenger side of my car.

I opened the front door, grabbed the couple items off the seat—the Draco I always kept close and my favorite book—and tossed them in back. I went back to Li'l Greg's body, unfastened the pillowcase, and threw it in the back seat as well. I then commenced laboring to lift the body, along with the plastic mat, into the car and positioned it in the front seat. When I finally got it in, I reclined the seat and closed the door. I didn't even bother to check my surroundings as I made my way to the driver's seat and hopped in.

Some of the garbage bags had come loose around Li'l Greg's head as I wrestled to get him in the car and I looked over at what was left of his face as he sat low in the passenger seat. I fired up the blunt that I had in the ashtray and started my whip. I scrolled through my music to Brotha Lynch Hung's "Situations" and absorbed the lyrics.

There was something about this ghetto classic that always gave me an adrenaline rush. I could recall my brother playing this shit every night as he would prepare for school the next morning. It was these kinds of songs that raised me. I lived this shit for real, which made it more of a soundtrack to my life.

I shouted the lyrics out while storming up the block and looked over to Li'l Greg. "This how gangstas ride, bitch-ass nigga."

As I floated up Atkinson pulling the smoke into my lungs, I realized that I hadn't eaten shit all day. I always forgot to eat. I dipped through a few blocks in our old neighborhood to see if any familiar faces were out. I never stopped for these niggas. It was just something that I did to make it known that I was still out there. Most of them were just tight with my brother and I knew that they only kept it cool with me so that I wouldn't come through on some terrorist shit. Cool or not, if I wanted them, I had no problem with taking a look at them. The problem was that I knew how it often disappointed my brother when I did shit like that. Out of respect for him, I left anyone affiliated with him alone. The moment fallout occurred, though, they were lunch meat. It didn't matter what the circumstances were or how much history they had with him.

I made my way to the sewer drain I had uncovered earlier, pulled up to it, and parked so that my passenger door was adjacent to it. I leaned over and opened the door before pushing the body in the seat next to me out of the car. The head and torso slid out and smacked the pavement, but the legs were still inside my ride. Despite my best efforts to aim the body at the gaping hole in the ground, it became clear that it wasn't going to fall in as smoothly as I had hoped.

"Damn," I cursed, stepping from the whip and making my way around to the passenger side. I pulled Li'l Greg out the rest of the way, stuffed his ass into the sewer hole and listened as his body crashed at the bottom. I then threw the plastic mat down as well.

The sound of the sewer grate scraping against the concrete as I dragged it back to the hole started to piss me off. The mothafucka seemed heavier than it had been the first time.

After finally getting it positioned back over the hole, I climbed into my shit and collapsed before grabbing the blunt out of the ashtray and relighting it. This was a lot of work for one bitch-ass nigga. "Even in death, you's a bitch, Li'l Greg."

I sat there for a minute, smoking my blunt as I started my track over and stared out the windshield. I was tired now, but high as a bitch with the munchies. I thought about the skillet inside the pillowcase in the back seat and it hit me: "I'm finna make me some mafuckin' eggs."

1 | HOME

Calico

"**B**oy, grab that wood and take it to my truck—that's good firewood."
My father and I had been working on building a playground
in the yard of his church. In the few months since I had returned home from
the penitentiary, he had been working the shit out of me.

I knew he had good intentions and was only trying to prevent me
from getting back into any trouble, but, little did he know, I was becoming
irritated with all of this hard work. I've never been the type of individual
who took kindly to a nine-to-five. There were a lot less complicated ways
to obtain work in the world without slaving or dirtying up my hands. But,
I was trying with everything in me to put all of that aside.

I gathered the wood from a tree we had cut down and carried it over
to my father's truck. I was in the process of loading the wood in the truck
bed when my father yelled to me.

"Hurry up! I have to get home and get ready for work." Outside of
ministering, my father had a second job as a bus driver.

"Yes, Master!" I yelled back. He hated when I called him this, but
anyone who worked for him knew that he gave out orders as if he were the
master and they were the slave.

I continued piling wood into the truck as fast as my body would allow
me. I was tired. I was worn out. My father came out into the alley and stood

next to the truck. I had one more piece of wood to load then my father could be gone about his business.

As I loaded the last piece, he asked, "Do you want to stay to get some more work done, or do you want me to take you home?"

"I'm stayin' here. I'm tryna finish cutting down the trees so we can start building the playground tomorrow."

My father handed me seventy-five dollars for my work and the keys to the shed.

"When you finished, boy, lock up my tools in the shed and catch the bus."

I gave Master a hug and told him that I would see him tomorrow.

As soon as his truck disappeared, I wasted no time gathering the tools, tossing them in the shed, and locking up. I would straighten up the shed later and think of an excuse to explain to my father why I didn't end up cutting down the rest of the trees. At that moment, I just needed some time to myself, away from scrutinizing eyes.

I double-checked the church's yard to make sure I didn't leave any tools lying around. We hadn't had a chance to build a fence around the yard to protect it from trespassers. The last thing I needed was some kids to wander around the church and find something that could hurt them or someone else.

After I had everything locked up, I made my way to the liquor store. I was in desperate need of a high. As I was walking, a custom black Chevy Tahoe sitting on some nice rims pulled alongside me. It seemed to be coasting along at the same rate of speed that I was walking, which told me that any occupants had their attention on me. I could feel my pulse quickening as a million possibilities ran through my head. Milwaukee had become somewhat of a hazard in that innocent civilians were often vulnerable to violence and harm. Being far from innocent, I didn't like my chances at that moment. How would this night end? Was the reaper here to collect on the debt that all men must pay?

Damn, I wish I had a pistol, I thought to myself. Just as I was preparing to take flight, the passenger's window came down, exposing the face of one of the occupants.

"Damn, my nigga. Whattup? Long time no mothafuckin' hear. What, you too good to holla at ya boys?"

It was Theory. Theory had been one of my roll dogs before I got jammed up six and half years ago. That was the last time I saw him.

———

We had been at a house party that King Lew from our block was throwing. We were inside the party having a good time—drinking, smoking weed, fucking with ho's. I had been off to myself, dancing with Tammy. And man, did that girl know how to move her body. She'd do one of those pop and lock rotations with her hips and ass in that little pink sundress that'd make any man's blood rush to his penis.

Theory approached me and pulled me to the side.

"You brought yo' bitch wit' you?" he asked.

"I never leave home without her."

"Can I hold ya ho' down while I run to the store to get some cigars?"

I willingly handed him my ten-shot, lemon-squeeze HK, model four-five, considering that I didn't feel a need for it at the time. I hadn't had any drama with anyone for awhile. Theory had lost his pistol in a drug raid, along with everyone else in our clique. They had been selling cocaine out of a house, when a neighbor called and complained to the police. The police ran in and confiscated four ounces of cocaine and seven pistols. They were seven of our finest pistols. Theory went to jail, but he ended up getting released four months later on a small technicality. We all went without a pistol for about two weeks, which exposed us to more threats than we were comfortable with. Theory and Five-Seven had been robbing any and everybody in the city so the thirst for revenge against them was real and we were more than vulnerable during those two weeks.

This female that I had been fucking with during that time had gotten into it with a group of girls and they jumped her. After that, she started carrying a .45 lemon-squeeze that she had taken from her daddy. But, the end result was me taking it from her, under the guise of looking out for her best interests and not wanting to see her get into trouble. My finesse game had been on point that day.

I still carried that .45 and handed it over to Theory, then went back to grooving with Tammy—man, could that girl dance.

"If you ever in yo' life grab my dick like that again I'm going to break your pretty little hand." I told her as we danced.

"Okay, Daddy, do you want me to give it a kiss like I did last night and make it feel better?" she asked with a flirty smile, then turned around and began poppin' her soft ass on my dick.

We were having a blast. That lasted until we heard shots being fired into the crowd. Everyone in the party broke for the door, me included. When the shooting started, I forgot all about Tammy. Oh, well.

Later on that night, I was sitting at home watching the news when there was a knock at the door.

"Who is it?"

"It's me, nigga—Theory—open the door."

I opened the door and Theory was standing there smiling, as if nothing had taken place. He came in and sat on the couch.

"What went down at the party?" I inquired.

"I caught them niggas," was all he would say.

"What niggas?" We were into it with some of everybody. Personally, I had no beef, but my association alone made their drama mine.

"Don't worry about it," Theory responded.

He handed me back the .45.

"How did it feel when my bitch bust her nut?" I asked playfully.

24

I checked the clip of the gun: it was empty. This nigga had fucked my bitch to death. She was dry and had no more nuts to bust. I took the gun into my bedroom for a refreshment. I loaded it back to its capacity and tucked it into my waist.

When I got back into the living room, Theory asked me to walk with him to the gas station to get a blunt.

"I thought you went to the store to get some blunts back at the party?" I questioned.

He just sat there, smiling.

"Come on, nigga," I said. "Let's go—you crazy." I cut the TV off and checked to make sure that all the doors in the back of the house were locked. I didn't want anyone coming into the house on moms and pops as they slept.

As we stepped onto the porch, I turned to lock the front door. The moment I secured the lock, Theory yelled, "Five-O!"

I turned around to see my house surrounded by cops with their guns drawn. The police yelled for us to freeze.

Theory looked to me and said, "They done gone crazy."

The next thing I knew, Theory's feet were slapping his ass. He was gone, running for dear life with a few of the cops chasing him on foot. I thought about the pistol that was tucked in my waist and considered trying to get rid of it, but knew I'd probably be a goner if I tried. I wasn't about to take a chance like I just saw Theory take. I didn't know about him, but I knew I loved life. I threw up my hands in surrender.

In no time at all, I was sitting in the Milwaukee County Jail, charged with two counts of reckless endangerment. I would learn later that Theory was able to outrun the cops who chased him. Even though I was caught carrying the weapon that Theory had gotten down with earlier that night, the police knew that I wasn't the gun man. Detectives held me in interrogation for three days, trying to get me to turn state on the shooter. I couldn't. I couldn't swallow that amount of pride to rat out one of my niggas, a nigga who I had known since childhood. Of everyone in our circle, Theory and I were the closest—or so I thought. He had no problem letting me take the fall.

During the six and a half years that I sat in the penitentiary, I never received a single letter, visit, or money from Theory. Still, I took his case with pride. I felt honored to have taken the rap for one of my niggas. Even made men felt compelled to turn rat when they found themselves under pressure.

"Where you comin' from?" asked Theory, staring at my attire. It was clear that he did not approve.

"I just got finished helpin' pops cut down some trees for the playground he buildin' at his church."

"Why you ain't get up wit' me as soon as the bars broke?"

It was funny how he was able to feign concern all these years later. I wish he would've cared that much when my commissary was low. He was bogus. He knew he was bogus, but I managed to reserve all ill feelings that I had for him. "I really ain't had time for nobody. I been trying to get myself situated."

"Where you headed?"

"I'm going to the liquor store to get something to drink."

"Save yo' li'l cash. I got some weed and drinks in the truck."

Theory motioned for me to climb into the back seat of the Tahoe. I hopped in and saw that my big homie, Five-Seven, was in the driver's seat. Five-Seven was the OG of the clique. He was a 33-year-old gang banger from Chicago, who was rumored to have a massive body count back home. He came to Milwaukee after the police started liking him for certain murders and had not been back home since.

Five-Seven looked into the back seat at me. "Whattup, Calico?"

Everyone in the truck spoke to me, except Soulless. He was on his phone talking to someone as if he had not even noticed that I had gotten in. I knew he didn't like me. The feeling was mutual. There was something about him that never quite settled with me. He always seemed jealous of anybody being too tight with Theory. There had been many occasions where I felt it necessary to beat his ass, but he was my guy's little brother, and it was on this principle alone that I spared him. I was sure I wasn't the only one in the clique who saw it. The boy was off. It was a wonder that he had managed to survive all this time.

"Aye, Five-Seven, drive me back to my pop's church for a minute." I knew I better go back to straighten up the tools in case I didn't get another chance before my pops saw that I had just thrown his tools in there without putting them in their proper place.

It was then that Soulless looked at me through those lifeless eyes of his and I could sense his venom. Why he was mugging me was unclear. He was acting as if I *had* ratted on his brother, rather than doing six and a half years for him.

We pulled up to the church and Theory climbed out with me. We went into the shed and he started helping me straighten up the tools inside that I had tossed in there earlier.

"So, you on some born-again Christian type shit, huh?" Theory asked me. I wasn't sure where he was getting his information but clearly he had heard from someone that religion had become important to me while I was down.

"Hell, nah. I don't draw from those signs. I practice Islam."

Theory looked to me before smiling. I sensed the condescension in his demeanor. "Oh, my bad, Farrakhan. You just threw me off, 'cause you ain't got the bowtie and bean pies. So, you down with them niggas that killed Brother Malcolm, huh?"

I knew that there were going to be those who were not open to my new way of life, but the digs that Theory had been tossing my way were almost enough to make me feel foolish. Almost. But, at the end of the day,

I knew that it was just Theory's attempt at lighthearted fun. I still felt the need to clarify, however.

"That's the Nation of Islam, Theory. I practice orthodox Islam."

Out of nowhere, he slid a thick, folded knot of cash into my shirt pocket.

"What's this for?" I asked.

"It's for being a real one."

I could not in good conscience accept the cash from Theory. After pulling it from my shirt pocket, I held it out and tried explaining why I could not accept it.

"Check it out, Theory. I know that you feel gratitude towards me for how shit played out. But, if I'm being honest, I have to say that I didn't keep my mouth shut for you. I did it for me. There was no way that I would have been able to live with myself knowing that I had turned rat. It could have been my worst enemy and I would have done the same thing."

Theory nodded his head and for a second it almost seemed as if he was rocking an expression of complete appreciation. He pushed my hand away from him, making it clear that he was refusing the money. "Either way, you a real one, and that's rare in this game."

We had finished straightening up the tools so I locked up the shed again and we made our way back to Five-Seven's truck. For most of the day, we rode around, drinking, smoking weed, and talking shit as we reminisced about old times. After the weed and liquor began to settle, I started to realize what exactly had been going on. I was slowly falling back into my old ways. No good could possibly come from hanging with Theory, Five-Seven, and Soulless' slithery ass. I asked Five-Seven to drop me off at my baby momma's house.

Theory seemed to be down with the idea, probably because he had never seen my son. Little Cal was born seven months after I landed in jail and was now 6 years old. As we made our way, Soulless was still on his phone and, other than mugging me, had yet to acknowledge me. I could feel the animosity. Being cut from my particular cloth, I tried breaking the ice. "What it do, Soulless? You don't fuck wit' ya boy no more?"

Soulless stopped his private conversation in midsentence and stared at me viciously before replying. "Fuck you and yo' life, Cal."

Initially, I was floored. Five-Seven seemed to think that the shit was funny, though. Theory said nothing. Then, I realized that Soulless was not done speaking.

"But, shit ain't what it seems. I just got a lot on my plate right now."

"Ho' trouble?" I asked.

"Naw, I ain't you. This money gon' come, these ho's go, and problems are just a part of the game," Soulless said more to himself than me.

When we pulled up to my baby momma's house, everybody climbed out and headed towards the door with me. I rang the doorbell and Tammy answered with a look of surprise on her face.

Theory must have read her expression. "Calm down, li'l momma. We just came to see the baby."

"What a disappointment, 'cause he's at school," she responded. "He's not expected home for another hour."

"How's li'l Calico doing? He need anything?" Five-Seven asked Tammy.

"Nah, he's got everything he needs. I just took him shopping for some school clothes."

Five-Seven took a knot of money from his pocket, peeled off a hundred and handed it to Tammy. "You didn't say anything about shoes."

"Nah, I'm cool," she declined. "I got him."

"That's still my nephew," Five-Seven returned. "I ain't got the chance to do nothin' for him since he was born. So, let me try to be there for him when I can."

Tammy paused for a moment before looking at me for assurance. When I nodded my head, she obliged.

"Thank you," she said, putting the money into her pocket.

Theory gave me a hug and told me that he had some business to tend to. He asked for my phone number so he could get up with me later and I gave it to him.

After the fellas pulled off, Tammy stepped to the side, letting me into the house. As soon as my son heard my voice, he came running to me, screaming.

"Daddyyyy!"

I gave my li'l man a hug before kissing him on the forehead. Tammy then directed him to go upstairs to his room. I could tell she had something on her mind.

"Daddy will be there in a minute," I told him.

"Promise?"

"I promise, baby."

As soon as Calvin disappeared from view, Tammy began grilling me.

"What are you doing, Calvin? Did you forget that quickly where you just came from and who put you there? So, you don't give a fuck about us, right? I can't believe yo' dumb ass finna get back out here fuckin' with these niggas—the same niggas that couldn't even buy a stamp to send you a letter when they were out here driving Escalades and Tahoes. The same niggas who couldn't come by to see if yo' son had a fresh diaper to put on his ass. Now they wanna come throwin' money around, like I'm supposed to be grateful.

"My son needs a father, Calvin. You see how crazy he is about you. I'll be damned if I let you hurt his feelings again. He not gon' get used to coming to a fuckin' prison again to spend time with you. I'm not doing it either. You forget that I was the only one holding you down while you were in there. I could've easily been out here fuckin' and god knows what else. But I stayed down and I kept our love real. Not them, *me*!"

"Tammy, Tammy, Tammy—slow down, baby. You got the wrong idea about what you just saw. Trust me. I'm not fuckin' with them dudes. I was on my way home from working with pops at the church when they rode down on me. You know how I hate that nasty-ass bus, so I got a ride. That's it, that's all."

"You shouldn't have yo' ass around them at all, Calvin! You are on *papers*! I'm not trying to control you or make you miserable. I'm only telling you this because I love you—*we* love you—but we tired of missing you. They don't give a fuck about you. *Trust me.*"

As I looked at her, I could see the sincerity behind her words. It was in her eyes. She truly had my back. There was no way that I could argue with her.

"Okay, okay, baby, I understand your pain. I do, and I respect it to the fullest."

She started again. "If you understand, then you—"

I turned and headed for the stairs, leaving her standing there in the living room. I loved the girl with everything in me, but I was not up for another one-on-one with her. She was about to fuck up my high. I had just conceded to everything she said and she was still looking for combat.

I went into the room with my son and fell onto his bed. He was sitting on the floor playing a video game. He asked me to play the game with him, but I was just too worn out. I lay there watching him play the game until I could no longer hold my eyes open.

When I awoke later that night, Calvin was lying on his bed next to me, balled up. As I got out of the bed, I stepped on my shoes. I wondered if Tammy or Calvin took them off me while I was asleep. I was grateful to Tammy for nurturing the relationship between my son and me. She was good about bringing him to visit me while I was locked up. Without those visits, my son wouldn't even know me.

I walked around to the side of the bed where Cal was sleeping and gently straightened his small body as I got him under the covers. I tucked him in and just watched him sleep peacefully for a minute before leaving his room.

I made my way into Tammy's room and slid underneath the covers with her. I could feel the warmth of her body and she didn't resist as I pulled her closer to me. I wanted badly to have my way with her, but I was too tired. Before I knew it, I was back asleep.

I was awakened sometime later by the music of Tammy's phone ringing. I looked at the clock on the nightstand—it was two-o'clock in the morning.

"Hello?" I answered sleepily.

"Calico?"

"Whattup? Who dis?"

"This Theory, nigga."

"Whattup, Theory? What's goin' on?"

"Calico, I need a favor. I need to borrow that axe I saw in the shed at yo' daddy church."

"What?" I climbed out of the bed, careful not to wake Tammy. "What axe?"

"Nigga, the axe I put away."

"Bro, that wasn't an axe. It was a hatchet."

"Axe, hatchet, just let me use the mafucka."

"At two-o'clock in the morning? Come on, Theory. Get real. What the fuck you need a hatchet for?"

"I'll let you know when I get there."

"Hold up, Theory. I'm in bed with the family. I'm not tryna make no moves tonight."

"Cal, Cal, Cal, I'ma straighten you out, bro—that's my word. I just need this one favor."

The only thing I could think of at that point was the look on Tammy's face if I were to get jammed up again. "Theory, you know I'm on papers. They can't wait to lock me back up."

"Cal, it ain't nothin' like that. I just need to use the hatchet. I'll be there in about twenty minutes. I'ma blow when I'm out front."

"Nah, nah," I spoke, thinking about Tammy. I didn't need her in my business at this point. "Don't blow."

Theory ended the call without replying. *Allahu Alim what this brotha is up to,* I thought. But, what choice did I have? This dude was determined to get his hands on that hatchet and I didn't need him waking up the whole damn house. I would never hear the end of it.

I was still exhausted so I continued lying in bed for a while before getting up. I had slid into bed with my clothes still on so when I did finally get up, all I had to do was go grab my shoes out of my son's room.

I took my shoes into the living room and was tying them up when I heard the horn blow. Theory had not listened to a word I said. It was funny how he just assumed that I would agree to whatever dumb-ass idea he had come up with. I had just gotten back up with Theory earlier that day and he was already beginning to irritate me.

I grabbed my jacket and left the house, locking the front door on my way out. He was parked out front in a teal Jaguar XE sedan. I climbed into the passenger's seat and he smashed off.

"You gon' tell me what's good, or nah? The last time I let you hold somethin' I ended up in the pen for six and a half."

"Come on, Cal. You know I'm sorry for all that. But, you know how that spur of the moment shit be. I mean, I was bogus for not looking out for you or the shorty, but I'm finna make it all right. You really think you the only one in the city with a hatchet? I'm comin' to you because I know you need a blessing. I'm gon' hit yo' hand for letting me use it."

"One man's blessing is another man's curse," I told him.

"Man, come the fuck on wit' all that higher consciousness shit, Cal. I'm 'bout to put some money in yo' pocket. Li'l Cal can't learn how to do salat if he hungry, my nigga. Now, you can't tell me that you gon' deny renting me the hatchet for a second."

No matter how much I wanted to protest, something in me would not allow me to stop him. I had no way of knowing if it was loyalty or the unassailable logic that I really did need a blessing. I could only hope that I was not stupid enough to be loyal to a person who had no real loyalty for me.

Before I knew it, Theory was parking in front of my father's church.

"Tell me what it is that you're about to get me into, Theory. What the fuck are you planning to do with a hatchet at three in the morning?"

"Cal, just grab the hatchet right fast. I'ma run it all down to you."

"Whatever, man," I said under my breath as I got out of the car.

There was no way I could trust this man's judgment and I knew it. Still, I felt compelled to ride it out with him and headed for the shed in the back of the church.

Had I been thinking, I would have told Theory that I no longer had the key to the damn shed. It was funny that I was now beginning to think of excuses to give him, as if I was not a grown-ass man capable of making the word *no* a complete sentence.

I had a second mind to keep it moving past the shed and walk my tired ass back home. Instead, I grabbed the hatchet and made my way back to the car. I tossed it into the back seat as I climbed back in.

Theory was talking on his phone as he pulled off. It seemed as if he were talking to a female. I noticed that he was driving in the opposite direction of my house. I figured that maybe he had become too preoccupied with his conversation to notice.

"Turn around and take me back to the crib, Theory."

"Chill, Cal," he said, lowering the phone. "I'm only gon' need the hatchet for a hot second, so if I use it right fast, I can just take you to drop it back off, and then run you home."

"What's a hot second, and what the fuck is you finna do with it?" Deep down, I knew that Theory's mind was not all that creative. That meant that there were only a few options regarding his use of the tool.

Theory acted as if he didn't hear a word of what I said. He just continued talking into his phone. As the blocks began to become more foreign, I realized that he was driving us into the boondocks. We were in Brookfield. A few minutes later, we were pulling into a rather posh area before coming to a stop in front of a very nice, modern-style ranch home. There was a red Genesis GV80 in the driveway next to an 8 series and X5 BMW. From the looks of things, these dudes had been doing quite well for themselves these days.

"Grab the hatchet and let's go," he said after killing the engine and climbing out of the car.

It was not until we got to the door and I watched him ring the door-bell that I noticed he was wearing gloves. It was becoming more and more apparent that I was not about to walk into the ideal situation. Still, I ignored my better judgment, choosing to believe that it was all good, as promised.

I was surprised to see another one of our guys, Glock, open the door. As we made our way inside, I heard music playing. We entered the living room and found Soulless and AP sitting around, smoking weed, drinking, and talking shit. They seemed very lively for so early in the morning.

The crib was plush. There was a 110" screen TV on the wall, white Indian leather furniture, music blaring from different parts of each room, and a fireplace. There was also a huge aquarium with what looked like baby sharks swimming around. Someone had some serious cash. It was not until AP got up from the white leather chair that I noticed the red stain. Immediately, I knew what it was.

As he walked over to shake up with me, I noticed the small bits of spatter along the contours of his face. Something told me not to say anything. I needed to pretend as if I were ignorant to what was going down. I took the blunt that he offered me and had myself a seat in one of the chairs. There was some bullshit-ass TV show on the screen, some shit that no one was actually watching. Theory seemed preoccupied with something and left me in the living room as he disappeared deeper into the house.

As I looked around the room, I noticed that shit seemed to be rather casual. I knew these dudes were up to something but I had not been able to gather many context clues.

Before long, Theory reappeared in front of me.

"Follow me, Cal. Bring the hatchet wit' you."

I did as directed and followed him, AP, Glock, and Soulless, who was talking on his phone, as usual. Soulless opened a door that seemed to lead to the basement. Everybody walked through the door and down the stairs. I had taken up the end of the line since I wasn't familiar with the house.

As I descended the stairs, I saw that there was a pool table off to the left side of the banister. I began to wonder a million different things. Still, I was not going to ask a damn thing. I may have been trying to turn over a new leaf, but I was still from the streets. It wasn't going to take me long to put two and two together. While I was confident in my ability to peep game, I had not been expecting the situation to make itself as blatantly obvious to me as it became in the next few seconds.

"What the fuck?!"

2 | COMPLICIT

Calico

My life flashed before my eyes. What I saw in front of me was enough to make anyone nauseous for a number of different reasons, but my main feeling at that moment was fear—fear of the vision I had of myself back in that cold jail cell. I recalled the mental anguish of hopelessly waiting for mail call, only to realize that I had been forgotten by the world and the self-torment of running to the phone to dial numbers that had been restricted from accepting my calls for years. I remembered the depersonalizing process of being strip-searched at random points by the wandering eyes of racist, backwoods country types who saw me as nothing more than a way for them to feel better about their own fucked up lives. There was much more to prison than the time. There was also the mental trauma that men like me could barely stomach. I was not going back.

I stood there at the bottom of the basement stairs, shocked and dazed. The shit seemed so far out of the realm of reason that I found myself laughing in my mind. There was no way that I had just walked in on this. I had to be dreaming. But it was no dream, it was reality.

The entire basement was covered in blood. Five-Seven was squatting down next to the pool table, slicing away at a decapitated body. He seemed to be having trouble slicing at the leg with the butcher knife he was using. Soulless, finally off the phone, seemed to be completely indifferent to what was going on as he stood next to Five-Seven conversing about some chick he had knocked earlier in the day. I seemed to be the only oddball out of the bunch. My legs wanted badly to turn and jet out of there, but my instinct told me that these dudes were not about to allow me a peaceful exit after what I was seeing. The best thing for me to do in the moment was pretend as if none of it bothered me.

Suddenly, Theory called for me. "Let me get the hatchet, Cal."

As I remembered the hatchet was in my hand, it became clear to me that they intended to use my father's gardening tool to commit unspeakable acts. There was no way I could allow this. My hand practically turned to stone as I stared from my father's hatchet to the dead body in the center of the floor. I had not even noticed that Theory was trying to grab it from me.

"Relax," he said as my mind snapped back to my surroundings. I could sense that there were a number of eyes on me. Theory seemed to be the most reasonable person in the room at the moment.

"Cal, it's good, baby," he coaxed. "Just give me the hatchet."

It took everything in me to communicate what I was feeling in that moment, and though I knew it would not be accepted, I had to speak it. "I want nothing to do with this madness, bruh."

As a few of the fellas began to groan and murmur in reaction to my words, Theory seemed a bit disappointed. This was a selfish mothafucka, if I ever saw one. He could have easily dropped me back off to my child and my lady and I would have never known about any of this. It was almost as if he needed me to be there to share in the experience with him. I was beginning to see a whole new monster from the one that I had parted with six and a half years earlier.

"Cal, right now ain't the time for all this shit. You here already. I mean, what you gon' do, leave and go home, pretend none of this ever happened? You party to the crime, baby boy. Now give me the mothafuckin' hatchet so we can *all* get the fuck up outta here."

"Nah," I said, heading for the stairs. I could not bring myself to sit around and watch as a creation of Allah was destroyed so heinously. Before I could even consider climbing the steps, Soulless had a gun stuck in my face.

"Bitch-ass nigga, you can either release the hatchet and stand down or we can add a body to the workload."

I stared in his eyes as he stood there with that same fucking grin on his face that he had since we were kids. It had always been his tell and we knew when we saw it that nothing good was going to come out of the situation. Even though I knew he was capable of dropping me right there on the spot before going back to the conversation that I interrupted, I still did not have it in me to cower. I stepped to the heat and eyed him. The way I saw it, I was more than likely going to die anyway.

"Is that a threat or a fairytale, Soulless?"

Before he had the chance to react, Theory pushed Soulless' gun out of my face. "Chill the fuck out, bro. You outta pocket for pullin' a pistol on one of the fellas."

Theory placed his arm around my neck before escorting me off into another area of the basement.

"Calico, you ain't the same nigga I remember, man. You makin' me look bad in front of the guys. I vouched for you. I told them that you was the man for this shit."

"Fuck what you told them," I spat, still feeling played from the gun that had been shoved in my face.

"Don't trip," he said in a silky tone, as if I was some stripper he was trying to hook up with. "After tonight, none of this ever happened. Now, relax ya hand, baby. This me—ya boy—Theory. Give me the hatchet."

What choice did I have? Soulless made his point clear that if I didn't help these dudes, I would surely end up on the floor with my head removed. I knew when I saw that grin that he would have taken my life from me and laughed about it the next day, like it was just the funniest thing. I had grown up with the little savage. I knew that he had no qualms with killing. I obliged, releasing my grip on the hatchet.

"Yeah, that's the Calico I know," Theory praised me like I was some sort of dog that had just performed well for him. "*By Any Means!*"

By Any Means was something that we all used to scream back in the day, back when we were as thick as they came, back when no one would have even considered pulling a gun on the team at any time.

Theory grabbed the hatchet from my hand and directed me to wait where I was standing. Five-Seven's face came to life the moment Theory walked over and handed him the hatchet. He then looked to me and nodded but I could tell it wasn't genuine. At this point, I didn't trust any of these niggas. Had it not been for Theory, Soulless would have painted the walls with my brains. Theory made his way back over to where I was standing.

"Let's leave these niggas to it, bro. I need help countin' this money."

I followed Theory over to a small bar and we sat down. It was clear that, before they had gotten hold of this place, it was a pretty decent spot. There was really no way to go wrong with a crib in Brookfield. The basement was laid. There were two pool tables, a few dartboards, a cigarette machine, the small bar, and another mini bar. They even had a jukebox, old school style. Had I not been trying to grapple with the reality of the corpse not even twelve feet from me, I would have been down with entertaining myself. But all I could see at this point was Tammy making countless trips to visit me in Green Bay or Waupun Correctional.

I looked to the bar and saw that there were several stacks of money lining it, along with a few gold Hublots, four Patek Philippes, some diamond necklaces, and a bunch of gold coins. I was so fucked up by everything around me that I didn't even think to ask for my share of the split.

"What kind of coins do you think these are, Cal?" Theory asked, holding up one of the coins.

I looked to the coins before looking back to Theory. "I don't know what the fuck that is, man. Stop askin' me stupid-ass questions, Theory."

Theory laughed off my comment and started counting the money. Time felt like it stood still as I watched him.

After about twenty minutes of silence, Five-Seven's voice boomed throughout the basement.

"Come here, Cal!"

I walked over to Five-Seven and the body he had been chopping on only to notice that it was no longer a body. It was more like puzzle pieces of limbs and blood. The torso was cut down the middle with the entrails spilled out onto the floor. The moment I was able to distinguish the small intestines from the large, I knew I was reaching my threshold. The smell of carcass alone was far too horrifying for me to focus on anything else. I knew what their objective was: no body, no case. Still, they were out of their minds.

Five-Seven handed me a shovel and a rake and said, "Help AP clean up the bodies."

I looked to AP, who had been standing there, staring back at me with a lit blunt in his mouth to keep from inhaling the evil odor. He kneeled to grab a garbage bag from the floor and opened it. I knew what Five-Seven was doing. He needed to ensure that I wouldn't run to the cops. He was literally looking to get blood and dirt on my hands. I maintained my composure, knowing that now was neither the time nor the place to display weakness.

It wasn't until I began raking up the body parts that I realized why Five-Seven had said *bodies*. I noticed a second body just outside the room. It was clear that it was female remains. As expected, Soulless was on his knees over the body, seeming to enjoy himself far more than anyone else. He had one of the female's severed arms in his grip, flailing it about as if it were simply an inanimate object that had never sustained life. He made my blood boil as I stared at him, carrying on as if this shit were all good.

"Five hunnit I can chop this bitch's hand off with one swing," he said to Five-Seven, who had handed off the hatchet to Soulless after he was done using it.

It was clear from the look on Five-Seven's face that he was tempted. "Bet," he said, folding his arms and leaning against the wall to watch.

Without hesitation, Soulless raised the hatchet in one hand as he held up the arm in the other and chopped through the poor girl's wrist like it was nothing.

Never had I seen such a wicked and depraved bunch in my life. I could not believe the heinous acts that were taking place before my very eyes. A continuous pattern of chills ran through my body as the smell began to permeate my senses. The whole scene made me think of someone like Jeffrey Dahmer. These men were not able to see just how depraved they were.

I finished shoveling the body parts into the garbage bag before consciously tossing it at AP, who tied it and carried it out of the basement. Still certain that I was an implied kidnap victim, I began looking for the furthest corner to escape the shit that was happening around me. There was none.

Soulless had begun to obsess about how good the hatchet felt as opposed to the knife. The way he was describing it, you would have thought he was selling Wonder Mops on the shopping channel.

Choosing the lesser of evils, I made my way back to Theory, who was now standing behind the bar as he finished counting cash. He shoved part of the pile my way.

"Help me count this shit, Cal."

"I thought you counted it already," I said.

He looked at me as if I was becoming a nuisance.

"I never count just once. Now, grab a stack."

As I went to grab the cash, I noticed that there were also two large blocks of oily, dark brown heroin. I knew for a fact that none of it was there when I had walked away. I continued not to ask questions. The quicker I got out of there and the less I knew, the better.

"A lot of shit changed since you been gone," Theory said, as if the shit was not clear enough already. "We eatin' in a major way now. Wait 'til you see the Range I just sent to the paint shop. Eights on that boy."

"Fuck all that," I spoke, unable to hold back my resentment any longer. "What the fuck makes you think that we not gon' address this big-ass elephant in the room, Theory. Mothafucka, you bogus, and that's all there is to it. What part of the game is you honorin' by bringin' me here?"

Theory looked to me through eyes of steel as he fixed his mouth to speak.

"Nigga, you ain't shit like the Cal I remember. All you do is cry about shit. I said I had a lick for you. Did you think we was finna go steal some bikes out somebody front yard or somethin'?"

"I never agreed to no lick," I growled through gritted teeth. The reality was that, without Soulless around, I was free to speak my mind to Theory. I probably would have done it anyway.

"You mothafuckas can't even see that y'all are out of y'all minds," I continued. "Then, you let yo' morally insane, retarded-ass brother pull a gun on me."

"Calm down, nigga. You know how Solstice gets. Quit actin' like this shit is new to you. We *been* talked about the shit that made him the way he is."

"*You* helped make him the way he is, Theory."

The moment it rolled from my tongue, I began to feel remorse. But, the shit had to be said.

"You enable that shit by continuing to create fucked up situations for him. Go in there and look at what yo' li'l brother is doin' to that body. Better yet, go in there and give him a hand. You can't, because you ain't got the stomach for that shit. Yet, you keep him around and pretend that you and yo' homeboys ain't usin' him for his psychopathic ways. Five-Seven is doin' that shit as a countermeasure. Soulless looks like he's havin' a blast. AP and Glock haven't looked at that puddle in the middle of the floor since it got here. You ain't never tried to correct yo' brother. You feedin' that monster because he's just as much an instrument for you as the hatchet that I gave you."

I could tell I was striking a nerve and I was sure I was pushing my luck. Theory never allowed for anyone in or out of the clique to speak ill of Soulless. To my surprise, the conversation remained civilized.

"Look, nigga, I keep him with me because I know what he can do if left to his own faculties. The li'l nigga has no filter and no real sense of right and wrong. You see him choppin' up a body and say that he's being influenced. I see him choppin' up a body and say that he's just doing what he do."

The back-and-forth went on for a while before I began to sense the heat emanating from Theory's tone. He could have tried to rationalize it a million ways but I was not buying it. Soulless was headed down a dangerous path and, while he may have been a killer, I was certain there were a number of niggas in the streets whose fear of him had turned into motivation to get the threat out of the way.

An hour passed before Soulless and the crew finally managed to get everything cleaned up. They all headed over to where Theory had stacked the money in neat piles. We all stood there for a brief moment, staring at each other. Altogether, there was $469,000, not including the value of the drugs and jewelry.

Theory counted out eighteen g's from his cut and handed it to me.

I would be lying if I said that the cash in hand was not a good feeling. Shit, I was fresh out the joint with practically nothing.

"What's this?" I asked.

"It's for the hatchet," he said then also tossed a Rolex my way. "That's just for being my manz."

"What the fuck do I want with a hot-ass Roley?"

"What? That Rolex ain't hot. It belongs to the cat who owns this house. He used to rob his own jewelry stores just to collect the insurance money. Only him and his thot knew about it. This shit comes with no worries. They burned down the store after they robbed it so there's no paperwork for any of this shit."

I put the money and watch in my pocket. As good as the money felt in my hand at first, I was starting to feel played by the evident shortchange. I was now just as culpable as the rest of them and felt I should have gotten my proper chop. However, I supposed that the alternative was having pieces of me stuffed into a garbage bag by a more than willing Soulless. There was a time and place for everything. I was confident that Theory would listen to reason, if I were able to catch him alone.

I guess they figured I was just some sort of bitch now or something. Here I was, awakened at an ungodly hour, strong-armed out of my father's hatchet, and compensated with a mere eighteen bands from almost half a mil. I wanted to flex, of course, but I had no win. I knew them too well. Had I been strapped up, the night would have gone in a completely different direction.

In the split, Theory, Glock, Soulless, and AP each got $93,000. Five-Seven, being respected as the OG that he was, was given an extra four g's and came out with $97,000. I laughed to myself as I stood there looking like a bitch while these niggas broke bread like it was the last supper. It made me wonder if Judas had been played as badly as I had. I couldn't stand there a minute longer as they laughed and embraced one another, making it clear that I was no longer a part of the crew.

"I'ma be in the car, Theory," I said. "Is that okay wit' you, Soulless?"

Soulless seemed to be a bit less tense as he looked at me through bloodshot eyes. I could tell that the split had changed his mood. "Aye, look, you betta stop playin' wit' me and get on up outta here with that cash before I take it and ya life. That eighteen g's got you lookin' like a free meal, boy."

"Yeah, what the fuck ever," I said, walking up the stairs and leaving the house without looking back. As I made my way to the car, I noticed just how far out of our element we were. These were not average cribs. I was willing to bet that there was some sort of neighborhood watch system in place. Like all dumb-ass criminals, I began taking measures to hide my face from view, as if I had not been seen coming through the door. Paranoia was a bitch. I climbed into the passenger seat and closed the door. Seconds later, I was pounding the dashboard. My frustrations were beginning to get the best of me. "Allah, is this your plan for me?"

Then it hit me—FINGERPRINTS. I took off my shirt and jetted back into the house. I used my shirt to wipe down everything I could remember touching before simply wiping shit down for the hell of it. Theory was not sending me back to prison a second time.

I went back into the basement to wipe down the rake and shovel I had used. My prints were not about to be left anywhere.

I said nothing to anyone as I did what I had to do before heading back out to the car. My thoughts ran wild as I found myself back in the passenger seat, wondering if I had covered my tracks well enough. I thought about the hatchet. I knew I couldn't get it back from Soulless and, for some reason, my father's reaction when he found out it was missing was the only thing constantly nagging at me at that point. I was the only person ever allowed to use his tools. I knew that after he discovered it was missing, he would make it out to be this great betrayal. All the responsibility rested on me.

That wasn't all I had to worry about though. I also had to prepare for the up-and-coming stress brought on by Tammy. It's always hard for a person who doesn't like to lie to tell a lie. The fact that I am lying always seems to seep through my pores. I begin to reek of my lie. There was no way around her. I had to face her.

The sun had already beat me home so I knew that she would be up already. Neither her nor my son would understand that I had been a victim of circumstance. Her argument would be that the moment I made a conscious decision to get out of bed for Theory was the very moment that it all fell on me. She would not have dreamed of allowing me to shift blame.

Theory finally came walking out of the house carrying a Louis Vuitton gym bag in his right hand. He climbed into the car before tossing the bag into the back seat. He said nothing. He just started the car, pulled off, and fell into traffic. When his phone rang, he stared at the screen before throwing it onto the dash.

"You know I just got treated like a bitch, right? Do I look like I got a pussy between my legs or some shit?"

He laughed without even looking my way. "Cal, I told you. What's done is done. Ain't shit you can do to change it."

"Man, fuck them mothafuckas in the garbage bags! There's a much bigger principle at hand. I'm talkin' about you and me."

"What about you and me, nigga?"

"You know exactly what the fuck I'm talkin' about! I got out of bed to come and assist you because I thought you was in a bind. You bring me into a fuckin' double homicide worth over a half mil and you hit me with eighteen g's, like I'm the peon? What? Y'all split that cash five ways. You think I don't know math, Theory? You couldn't even give me the odd fo' g's? Five-Seven got it."

"Hold fast, nigga," Theory started.

"Make that yo' last time callin' me a nigga, BROTHA," I interrupted.

"First of all, NIGGA, why you think you deserve more than what you got? Did you go in there knockin' mafuckas' heads off? Hell, nah! You was at home snuggled up with yo' face all up in that bitch's ass. I could've gotten a garden tool from the hardware store for ten bucks. I called myself looking out. All yo' scary ass did was stand around, lookin' stupid. You didn't put in no work. I gave you that because I felt like you had it comin'. Now, be thankful that I'm such a real nigga, and quit cryin' like a bitch."

"Bitch, huh?"

"Yeah, nigga—bitch."

"Theory, you need to take all that authority out yo' voice because the shit that's extending from yo' tongue don't stand for shit. You owe me, mothafucka. I gave up six and a half years on the strength of love. You ain't even reach for me. What if I was in there fucked up? You niggas left me for dead in there. No money, visits, or letters. I could've easily turned rat. All I had to do was open my mouth and you was dead. You owe me, Theory. Eighteen bands just ain't gon' cut it."

"Nigga, you ain't finna guilt trip me into paying you. What the fuck is this, some sort of soft extortion attempt? I'm a street nigga, dawg! You didn't open yo' mouth because you wasn't supposed to. What the fuck you need a reward for? Real niggas do real shit. Period. It sound like you threatening to go to the police on some revenge shit. I'd hate to have to put you down, bruh."

I could've slapped blood from his mouth in that moment. This was my manz. We had practically come from the playground together. I couldn't believe the shit coming out of his mouth.

"Theory, take me home, and from this point forward, disassociate ya'self from me."

"It's like that, Calico?"

"My name ain't no damn Calico. It's Al Karim. Stop callin' me that dumb-ass shit. And, you mothafuckin' right it's like that, if you think my freedom was only worth eighteen thousand. You'd kill me for less than that. I'm lookin' at another bit, a life bit, for some shit that you forced me into, and you give me eighteen bands?"

"Whatever, Mister Holy Man. I see them holy-ass pockets is bulging from that light eighteen too. Holla at me when you ready to get yo' mind right."

We drove the rest of the way in silence. When we pulled in front of Tammy's house, Theory extended his hand as if to show me some love. I looked at it as if it had been struck by the plague before climbing out of the car. He smiled before smashing out, burning rubber up the block.

As I was walking up the walkway, something clicked in my head. Theory had called me on Tammy's phone but I hadn't given him her number. I had given him my phone number. As quickly as the thought invaded my mind, it was gone. The front door to the house swung open and just beyond the threshold stood a barely five-foot-four demon lady. It was Go Time.

3 | FALLOUT

Calico

"**N**IGGA—"

"Tammy, before you even get started, I don't care what you refer to me as. Just don't call me a nigga."

She folded her arms and shifted her weight to one leg as she mugged me. "Nigga, what? Shut the fuck up. You been out there fuckin' with them triflin'-ass niggas."

I walked right past her and into the house, but it did no good. She was on my heels.

"Nigga, I just did a whole prison term wit' yo' ass. I refuse to go through that shit again. I'm tired of nothin'-ass niggas… You don't give a fuck. You don't give a fuck about me, Calvin… Stupid, stupid-ass nigga. What, do those niggas fuck better than I do? Has being in prison turned you the fuck out? You did six and a half years around niggas then you come home and be around niggas. You must be like one of them niggas on the downlow like Oprah talked about… Nigga, I put my life on hold for you, but do you appreciate it? Hell, nah! You come back out here doin' the same shit as before you went in. What, does prison make you stupider? Or am I the stupid one for believing in you, for putting my life on hold for you, for wanting to be a family? Nigga, we just had this exact same conversation yesterday and here we go again. I can't deal with this. I just can't deal with it, Calvin. I don't think we should be together anymore, at least not until you can get yourself together. Get yo' shit outta my house and go—"

Before she could continue, the doorbell rang. She went to answer it.

"It better not be them niggas," she yelled.

I didn't even care who it was, as long as it wasn't the police. I went into the bedroom, grabbed some clean clothes and headed for the shower. I could hear her voice as I was getting undressed.

"He prolly in the bathroom. I think he finna take a shower."

Next thing I knew—BAM, BAM, BAM!

"Boy, you in there?"

"Yeah, pops. I'a be out in a minute."

"Boy, why you just now decidin' to take a shower? You knew when I was coming."

"I'm comin', pops. Just give me a minute."

"Alright, boy. Where's my grandbaby?"

"I don't know, pops. You gotta ask Tammy."

I noticed that I had some dried blood on my Nikes. I threw the shoes into a corner and climbed into the shower. I washed my entire body as if I were cleansing myself of all sin. I had flashbacks of Soulless placing the girl's head on the ground after cutting it off. It was nearly unrecognizable. Skin had been torn from the bone and the little flesh that did remain was battered and bruised. I hated to think about what they could have done to the girl to cause such destruction. He was actually talking to her head as he carved her body. It was disturbing how vivid it all was in my memory.

"If I would've caught your thick ass before all this, a mafucka might've gave you a shot of this dick," he mused as if the frameless head facing him was somehow able to comprehend his words. It was then that I began to realize the depths of his depraved mind. This nigga had been possessed by a jinn of Satan. The shit caused me to shiver under the scalding-hot water.

I had another man's blood under my fingernails. I felt like filth. As I was cleaning my nails, I heard the bathroom door open and shut.

"Nigga, I'm not through wit' yo' lousy ass. Do you even care what happened in this house this morning? Your son came into my room looking for you, crying. He thought yo' gay ass was back in jail."

"Tammy, I've had enough of the gay talk."

"What else do you call it when a man—oh I'm sorry, a boy—chooses another boy over a female."

"Over a female? See, this shit ain't even about my son. It's about yo' selfish ass. You feel played. My son ain't got shit to do with this."

"You know what," she said, making it clear that she had no real response for me. "I'm through dealing with this shit from you, Calvin. I'ma put a stop to it before it even begins."

"Stop all that cussin'," my pops yelled at us.

Tammy lowered her voice, but only a little. "Your son loves you, Calvin. He looks up to you. And, I'm not gon' lie, I do feel played. I love you too. But, my baby ain't finna be watchin' the way you live and try to walk in yo' footsteps. You his role model, Cal—a fucked up role model to have—but you are. What you need to do is get yo' priorities straight. Be a man. Be a leader and not a follower. A man who stands for nothin' will fall for anything. It's pretty obvious that you don't stand for shit because you're falling for everything under the sun. I'm not gon' be the one to have to tell my son that his daddy chose the streets over his family and now he's dead or back in jail. I'm not about to tell him no shit like that."

I got out of the shower to dry off and get dressed.

"Do you hear me, Calvin? Do you hear me or is what I'm saying going in one ear and out the other?"

"Tammy, listen. Understand something. I know what I did was bogus and I definitely didn't intentionally try to hurt you or my son. Believe me, that's the last thing I wanted to do. Theory and them don't mean shit to me.

I couldn't care less about them. It's you that I love. It's you and my son who turned Calico into Calvin.

"As far as choosing the streets before my family? Naw, that doesn't pertain to me at all. You have the wrong suspect for your line-up. Everything that I've done since I've been home has been for my family. Yeah, I had a relapse and fell back into the wrong crowd, but that doesn't change the fact that I'm aware of what I've been through and what I have here in you. Do you have any clue what I had to go through last night to cut off official ties from them brothas, to let them know that I had disassociated myself from them?

"It's real fucked up to know that you hold all of these ill feelings towards me. Yeah, maybe it's best that we separate because you don't know me. The person you dressed my character up to be is not me. You spoke your mind. You said what you felt needed to be said. You want me out of your house? I'm gone. I'm outta your hair. One less worry. I'll send somebody to get my shit."

With that said, I gathered up my clothes and shoes and walked out of the bathroom, leaving her standing there. I took the clothes into the kitchen, dug into the pants pockets and retrieved the money, watch, and my other belongings. Then, I put the clothes inside a garbage bag. I intended to send them up in flames as soon as I got the chance.

My father had been impatiently waiting for me in the living room. He had a lot he wanted to get done at the church before he had to get to his other job.

"You ready to go?" I asked.

"Yeah, boy, I *been* ready—long time ago."

I yelled back into the house to let Tammy know that we were leaving and I didn't bother waiting for a response. After I climbed into his truck, I fought to keep my composure.

"Boy, what's gotten into y'all that can cause you to walk out on yo' family all of a sudden?"

"Nothin', pops. She just woke up this morning with the germ."

"What is you talkin' about, boy? What germ?"

"It's her time of the month, pops. She's bleeding."

"Then say that, son. Don't Islam teach y'all proper English?"

I didn't respond. I felt that he had asked me an ignorant question, so I sat silently. He must have felt my unease.

"Son, there's something that I've really been meaning to talk to you about and it's been bothering me for the longest. Haven't I always taught you to be a God-fearing man?"

"I am a God-fearing man, pops."

"Then why are you aligning yourself with terrorists?"

"If you want to know why I became a Muslim then ask respectfully. As far as this terrorist theory, show me a religion without extremism and bad seeds and I'll show you a scam. Nothing is beyond good and evil in this world, pops. You should know that better than anyone."

"What I know better than anyone is that my son was not raised to believe in anyone other than Christ, our Lord and Savior."

"Look, pops. I had a cellie who practiced it. I became curious and asked him about it. He began to explain to me the tenants of Islam and its teachings and I ended up studying deeper."

"What would possess you to dig deeper into a world that directly contradicts your own?" he asked, barely able to navigate the city and focus on me at the same time.

"A lot of what I heard him talk about sounded fascinating to me. I found a lot of truth in it too, dad. I made my way to the library and picked up a Quran. I found it logical and fascinating and the style of expression touched my soul."

"Christianity is the only way to reach the soul, boy."

When I saw the way he was looking at me, I realized there was no winning this one. He eyed me with a contempt that almost made me feel as if I had lost my mind.

How could I tell him that other religions seemed to be full of grotesque and ridiculous ideas that suggest only a far-fetched mood of spirituality? They have nothing to do with real-life situations. Islam, on the other hand, is a practical religion, which guides man along on his trek of life. Commandments of the Islamic religion lead a person to the right way—not only in the hereafter, but also in the world. Islam embodies all the good aspects of the world's social trends.

I could not allow the conversation to die without further elaborating. I guess a part of me felt bad because I knew that his disappointment rested in the reality that he felt he had failed me.

"Dad, when I picked up the Quran, I felt something in my spirit— something that I didn't feel when I picked up the King James. I used to feel your sermons and I know there is always truth in what you say, but I felt something from the Quran that even you could not give me. It's hard for me to accept a religion that was forced upon us. It's hard for me to accept a blonde-haired, blue-eyed god. So, in the end, I had to trust in what I felt."

"Boy, the devil is a lie. Do you understand what that means? That means that he is good at being a lie. So, when you say that you felt something, you need to dig deep and search your soul for what it is that you actually felt, because that damned devil is a master of trickery. But, if you open your heart and just reach out for the only truth there is, that truth shall make you free. God shall grant you the kingdom of heaven and everything in it, son."

What was I thinking? He had begun an entire sermon right there in the car as we coasted along Sherman Boulevard. I thought I was listening to WNOV on a Sunday morning.

I sat there, blocking out his rants, allowing my thoughts to take me back to the night before. I knew there was a chance that I was wanted by the police. Every time I'm around Theory, there is always some bullshit in the game. Now, I was looking at possibly spending the rest of my life in someone's prison.

Reality hit me when the car came to a halt outside of the church. When my father asked for the key to the storage shed, I dug into my pocket and gave it to him, careful not to let him see the money I had in my pocket. He would have had a million and one questions about where I had gotten it. We climbed out of the car, and I followed him around to the back of the church.

"Boy, I thought you said you was gon' cut the rest of these trees down yesterday after I left for work."

"I know, pops, I'm sorry. I didn't realize how tired I was yesterday and I ended up leaving shortly after you left."

"Well, let me grab the chainsaw then so we can finish cutting them down now."

While my father went to the shed to get the chainsaw, I waited nervously by the trees, anticipating his discovery of the missing hatchet. To my surprise and relief, he returned with the chainsaw and didn't say a word about the hatchet. He simply revved up the chainsaw and we got to work.

My father and I worked for a few hours in the churchyard. We cut down the rest of the trees, loaded the wood into his truck, and started some rough work on the playground.

"I was hoping to get more done today, boy, but I have to get to work. Go empty those bags of sand into the sandbox while I put away the chainsaw and lock up."

I did as my father ordered and headed over to the sandbox.

As I was dumping the last bag of sand, the moment I had been dreading arrived.

"Boy, where is my hatchet?" my father asked as he charged toward me on his way back from the shed.

"I don't know, pops. I haven't used it today and I locked it up with everything else before I left yesterday."

"So, I guess it just got up and walked off on its own then. I don't see it, and I didn't see legs growin' out of it the last time I used it."

I walked over to the shed and pretended to help look for it. I knew damn well that it wasn't there, but I had to play it off. If he found out what had been done with his hatchet, I would have been praying for the police to come and arrest me.

"Where is it, boy?"

"I don't know, dad. I put it in here yesterday."

"Boy, you's a lie and the truth ain't in ya. That's that damn Islam, got you behaving in such a manner."

"Pops, I've had enough of people insulting my religion. I have never in my life disrespected you or any of your beliefs. Please treat me with the same respect. And, as for the hatchet, I coulda sworn I locked it up yesterday when I finished but I may have absentmindedly left it lying out."

I carefully took a hundred dollars from my pocket and handed it to him.

"Here, take this and buy you a new one."

"Where did you get this money from? Are you out here sellin' that poison again? Huh? I rebuke you, in the name of Jesus!" he said, tossing the money back into my face.

"I don't want your dirty money," he continued. "That's Satan's money. You think I'm stupid, boy, like I don't know what you're doing out here? I done been around the blocks that you tryna go around. Boy, you ain't learned nothing. You just got out of jail for shooting somebody... When are you going to grow up? I didn't raise you to live this way. You chose the streets, the streets didn't choose you. I taught you better than that... Fix your face, boy. Why you lookin' all silly? Go on, boy—go on back to prison. You think you a man and can manage on your own. We'll see how you manage in the cell with Bubba... You a disgrace to this family... Go on and get out of my face. You better off in prison."

"Hold on, dad. I hear the sincerity in your words and wonder how you could find it in you to speak to your own son like that. You really think I belong in prison? And, while we're on the subject of prison, let me break it down for you."

"I don't need you to break nothin' down for me, boy."

This was the first time that my father made me mad enough to raise my voice at him. I couldn't hold back any longer.

"Well, stop talkin' like you know what I went through in there. You have no idea what it was like for me. You never even took the time to sit down and talk to me about it. You're so busy puttin' me down in order to boost your own self-esteem that me and my situation became irrelevant to you. The only thing that kept me motivated in there was knowing that I had a son out here who needs me... Every day I lived in the belly of the beast—in torment—and you stand here, wishing that I go back through it? In my heart, I believe that if I didn't have a child, I would have given up a long time ago. But, because of him, I continued to fight."

"That's what you supposed to do," he shot back at me. "I raised you to be a man. You made the bed. You had to lie in it. It's called accountability, boy."

He had no clue that I had gone down for a crime I didn't commit, but he was not the kind of man to sympathize with the codes and folkways of the streets. Even if he believed I was innocent—which was a long shot itself—he would have simply held me accountable for the crowd that I chose to clique with. In all honesty, it was the truth, but my father had no appreciation for gray areas.

"That was the worst time of my life," I continued. "I was being held in a cage, like a wild animal. I was in a whole 'nother county, away from any familiar faces, and no one close to me even bothered to send me two words of encouragement. It's so hard to remember who you are in the midst of that kind of depression and dysfunction. The stress of being released became unbearable at times and it was as if I had been left to face it alone."

My father stood there, staring at me as if he had not been moved by a word I spoke.

"Boy, you talkin' like you was a prisoner of war. You went to jail for a crime, not for social activism. It wasn't on us to feel sorry for you."

I could do nothing but shake my head at him. He acted as if I was asking for a pity party.

"Y'all have no idea what goes on in there. Everyone can say that they understand the loss of freedom, but it's a whole different feeling to be deprived of your humanity. The psychological and emotional toll that comes with a prison sentence is indescribable. We were treated no different than livestock—herded to be fed and washed—while constantly being berated and antagonized.

"Imagine being held under the care of people who care nothing about you while your family ties and relationships are destroyed. It's enough to make a man go insane even before he grasps the full scope of what he has been sentenced to. Without speaking the words, a judge uses his authority to remove a vital part of the family structure out of the picture with a few strokes of his pen. Next thing you know, you're shipped off on a bus to God knows where. Then fear sets in when you realize that you are being sent to a place that you have no desire to go and you don't have a clue how long you'll be there, or if you'll even come out alive.

"Without warning, you're introduced to a system that is designed to promote submission and humiliation, beginning with the first order: 'Strip off your clothes!' This is followed by: 'Bend over, spread your ass—'"

"Watch yo' damn mouth!" my pops demanded, forcing me to check myself before continuing.

"Excuse me: 'Bend over, spread your *butt cheeks* and raise your scrotum sack.' Soon, you're introduced to prying eyes and probing, unfriendly, gloved hands. Your sense of power is transformed into helplessness, with dignity being a thing of the past.

"You're told that you can purchase a comb or a brush. If you happen to fall to the mercy of your humanity by making a simple mistake, you are subject to time in a box, with little to no human interaction and only four walls to stare at. Meanwhile, people around you are losing their minds, banging on doors, and screaming at the tops of their lungs at four-o'clock in the morning.

"You are forced to endure the actions of children dressed in corrections uniforms, ordering you to go one way or another to get your cell assignment.

Your community is now concrete and steel, surrounded by razor wire. The eyes that greet you upon entry are filled with hate so thick that it can be felt in the very core of your being. Your eyes scan quickly, hoping—in vain—to see a familiar face. Confronted with the question of what to do next, you wonder where to sit and which bed will be yours. During all of this, you can feel yourself crying on the inside, but you're determined not to let it show on the outside.

"Instinct tells you that it isn't the time or place to display any weakness. Soon, you even discover that performing ordinary bodily functions is difficult to do. Before you're placed in a cell, using a toilet in the intake area is like going to the bathroom in the middle of your living room among the chaos of twenty strangers who are watching you, screaming obscenities at each other, and sounding as if they're going to kill someone. Even after you get assigned a cell, it's still hard because you literally have to defecate and urinate in front of a complete stranger.

"When meal time comes, you try to take it in stride as you look at the cold, greasy substances on the tray. Out of necessity, you learn to eat it with your plastic utensils, no matter what it may look or taste like. If you don't, you'll literally starve to death."

"Boy, you wasn't starvin'. We sent you money," my father interjected.

"Fifty dollars once a month?" I questioned. "To be honest, fifty dollars can only get you through about three days. I just never told y'all how messed up I was because I didn't want to be a burden. But, the reality is, without money to eat, you are barely able to make it from one day to the next. You begin to find a liking for sustenance that you would have never even considered ingesting under normal conditions. Every minute of every day is spent knowing that you are living in a kind of hell that so few *truly* deserve to endure. Seeing others around you doing their time as comfortably as possible makes you more aware of the reality that no one is in your corner. You accept it because you have no choice, but it takes a strong man to keep his head up when his entire situation is telling him that he is worthless because the next step down is death. Tension, confusion, and noise are an ever-present part of daily life that must be tolerated until late at night, when tense muscles and frayed nerves finally give way to a fitful sleep, plagued by nightmares. The nightmarish existence of the waking day spills over into the chaotic sleep of night. It is only then that you are able to devour small bits of peace, as if they were delicacies.

"Contact with the outside world is limited to letters that you may never get answers to. Phone calls only happen for those fortunate enough to have a person who will accept collect calls. Visits, which are considered a luxury, come few and far between, if ever, for most men there.

"The tough part is that every aspect of prison existence is controlled by a group of people who have no clue of what human relation skills are. Many of them are straight out of high school and still live with their parents. These are the people who are handed authority over grown men and your only choice, other than death, is to accept it.

"That isn't something that I would ever allow myself to get used to, no matter how many times I'd been incarcerated. The dehumanizing initiation process remains virtually the same. Could it have been worse? Yes. Am I grateful that it wasn't? Yes. Does that knowledge make it any easier to deal with? No.

"And this is only a glimpse of what my reality was like. Answer this, dad—is being loyal to someone who you love a sin? Before you judge me, put yourself in my shoes and try to view the world through my eyes. For once, try to see what I've been through and what I'm currently going through.

"I'm a disgrace to your family, pops? Well, then no longer consider me a part of your family."

I had nothing else to say to my father. I turned on my heels and walked away. I needed a drink.

I walked down to the liquor store and bought myself a fifth of Hennessey. I needed a place to go—somewhere I could get away from everyone and be myself. I was tired of every individual in my life, except my son. They didn't give two fucks about me, let alone one. All they cared about was insulting and putting someone down, just to uplift their own spirits.

I crossed the street from the liquor store and stood at the bus stop. I was going to buy myself a couple bags of weed and find someplace where no one could reach me.

I caught the bus back over by Tammy's house to stop at my young guy's house next door. I knocked on the door and a voice came from inside.

"Who is it?" Li'l Larry asked.

"It's Calico."

I heard Li'l Larry removing the wooden two-by-fours he kept in the brackets fastened to the other side of door. The door then popped open and Li'l Larry appeared.

"What's up, Cal?"

"What's up, Li'l Larry? You got any weed?"

"How much you want?"

"Just a couple dime bags."

Li'l Larry motioned for me to step inside the house. Once inside, he locked the door and secured it again with the two-by-fours. The house didn't have much furniture. There was one raggedy couch, a space heater, and a TV that had a Play Station connected to its back.

I dug into my pocket to retrieve twenty dollars for my purchase. So much had occurred since my last encounter with Theory that I had almost forgotten about the money. Li'l Larry's eyes fell to the knot in my pocket.

"Damn, nigga. Who you done robbed?"

I smiled at his comment but didn't say anything. I knew he had made the comment in jest, but little did he know, there was some truth to what he said.

"Instead of the two dimes, give me an ounce," I told Li'l Larry.

"Cal, you know I got a couple pistols for the low, right?"

"Oh yeah? Let me check 'em out," I requested, mostly just to be saying something.

Li'l Larry walked over to the couch and pulled a gun from underneath the cushions. He walked back over to me and handed me the gun.

"That's a classic, baby," he said. "And I got an extra clip."

The gun was a gray and black 9-millimeter Smith & Wesson. It was beautiful—so beautiful that I found myself getting an erection. Damn. Was this shit in me for real? Maybe my pops was right. I knew Li'l Larry was prepared to throw some outrageous price at me. He had seen the knot in my pocket and he knew he could get any price he asked for if I wanted a pistol bad enough. I would pay in full.

"I need fo' hunnit for the heat, bro. The clip gon' run you another fifty."

I peeled $800 off my knot and handed it to him for the gun, the extra clip, and the weed. Li'l Larry took the money and walked off towards the back of the house. I pulled the clip out of the gun to check the magazine. It was full to capacity. I tucked the gun into my waist and waited for Li'l Larry to return from wherever he had gone.

Moments later, Li'l Larry came back into the room and handed me a sandwich bag full of weed and the extra clip to the gun. I told Li'l Larry that I appreciated him extending his hand to me and I showed him some love by shaking his hand. He tried to force my hand into some kind of gang sign, but I overpowered his hand into a ball.

"My fault, Calico. I forgot you don't get down like that…but you need to come on home."

"Good lookin' on this shit," I told him as he opened the door to let me out. I didn't even respond to the shit that was coming out of his mouth. "I'll be back to holla at you when my weed gets low."

I walked a couple of blocks to the creek. I knew no one would find me there. Back when I was little, about seven or eight years old, my friend Tommy and I would go there whenever our parents made us mad. Sometimes we would sit out there all night and go home and get our asses whooped the next day.

I found a nice shaded spot under a tree. I sat down, twisted the cap off the Hennessey and took a big, long gulp. I sat the bottle down on the ground, took the weed out of my pocket, and rolled some blunts. I was ready to get high.

I sat by the creek for hours just thinking and smoking blunt after blunt. The Hennessey was gone before I even opened the bottle. I was stressed the fuck out and I knew that once my high vanished I would have to return to reality, a reality that I didn't care too much to go back to. I was tired. I was sick and tired of living life on this here planet in my shoes. I was living in the world alone. My bitch had left me over a situation that she knew nothing about. I was a victim, just like the people Soulless and Five-Seven had murdered in that basement. My father wouldn't accept me because I refused to follow in another man's footsteps and be the man that he is. He didn't understand that a man had to be his own man. I couldn't be like him. I had my own destiny.

As if all that wasn't bad enough, I was on my way to spend the rest of my life in prison. All it would take was for one person to get caught up and give the police my name.

While I was in prison, I saw so many dudes who had been falsely accused of crimes. The person who actually committed the crime would get caught and put the crime off on one of his guys. I'd be damned if I would ever be caught inside the belly of the beast again. Fuck that—death before dishonor.

I had been called a loser so many times by people who claimed to have love for me, that I had actually started to believe I was a loser. I was starting to feel as if everybody would feel better if I was dead, no longer a cancer to them. And, even though I knew my son loved me, I also knew it was a reality that when a woman decided that she no longer wanted to be a part of her baby daddy's life, that decision was made automatically for their child as well. I'd seen it happen so many times.

"Allah, why me?" I asked. "Why must I face so many trials throughout my life? I remember you saying that with every difficulty, you'd grant relief. Where's my relief, Allah? I guess it's on me to find my own relief. I see a lot of brothas who are influenced by Satan daily and they live with hardly any complications. But I try to do right, I try to follow your guidance and walk in your path, yet I still live in difficulty every day. Why do the good suffer and the bad prosper? I can't take it anymore, Allah. Even the strongest men become weak at some point."

I reached down to my waist and grabbed the 9-millimeter I bought earlier from Li'l Larry. I aimed it at my head and prayed.

"Our Rabb, have mercy on my soul. I repent before you all of my sins. O Rabb, the greatest, have mercy on my soul, for you are the cherisher and sustainer of the world and all that's in between. Accept my soul as of those whom you associate, O Rabb. Rabb, accept me as you accepted Prophet Muhammad Sallallahu Alayhi Wa Sallam and those followers of Muhammad Sallallahu Alayhi Wa Sallam. I believe that there is no deity except Allah Subhanahu Wa Ta'Ala. Allahu Akbar."

I pulled the trigger.

4 | THE PLAN

Theory

My doorbell was ringing like crazy. I had been laid out in bed, next to this thick-ass redbone who I had met at the club the night before. I called out for her to wake up, but the bitch didn't move. She was dead to the world. I had put it down on the bitch, fucked that pussy into a deep sleep.

I slid on my boxers, got out of bed, and went downstairs to answer the door. I looked through the peep hole and saw my guys—AP, Glock, Five-Seven, and my brother, Solstice—standing on the porch. I opened the door to let the goons inside. They looked as if they hadn't been to sleep since we left the club. They were still smoking, drinking, and acting a damn fool.

"Where the fuck yo' keys at?" I asked Solstice.

"Man, fuck all that," he said, pushing past me. "What the fuck was you in here doin' that took so long to answer the door? That's what I wanna know."

"Straight up," AP echoed, knowing that he would do nothing but incite a scene from my little brother. "You runnin' around the crib in yo' boxers and shit like you got a bitch somewhere."

I knew that these were the sort of niggas to scare a bitch away. The last thing I wanted to do was allude to the fact that I had a bitch in the room. "I just woke up. Damn."

Before either of them could inquire more, I headed back upstairs to my bedroom, closing and locking the door when I got inside. Seconds later, my boxers were back off and I was back in bed with my new bitch. It amazed me that she didn't wake up from all of the noise downstairs.

I was ready for round four with her and wanted her good and wet so I started rubbing her clit to try to wake her up. Gradually, I moved my fingers down and started working my middle finger in and out of her pussy. She started to rouse and squirm a little in response to my finger sliding in and out of her so I added my index finger and started fucking her slowly with two fingers. When I felt her pussy start melting on my fingers, I worked in my ring finger as well and fucked her until all three fingers came out dripping and she was moaning softly.

I knew the bitch was ready so I reached over to the nightstand for another condom. I rolled it on then pushed her onto her side so her back was against my chest. I wedged my leg between her legs to open them up then navigated my dick to her pussy. She woke up the rest of the way as my dick spread her open and slid inside. I grabbed her leg and held it up as I pushed deeper into her tight walls, climbing inside of her hot-ass pussy and giving her long, pitiless thrusts. She started moaning louder and moving with my thrusts, bouncing against my pelvis with her ass. The tip of my dick began pounding the tight ring of her cervix, sending jolts of ecstasy throughout her body.

"Fuck this pussy," she moaned and starting pushing herself harder onto my dick, as if she were trying to crack her own body in half by impaling herself with it.

I grabbed her by the waist with both of my hands and quickly flipped her onto her stomach. I then gripped her hair and pushed her head into the pillow. I directed her to raise her ass up a little so I could see her pussy and, after she raised it and presented the target, I began stuffing her pussy with slow, hard thrusts. She begged me to fuck her faster but I made her wait and continued with singular assaults.

I gradually increased my pace and allowed her some faster, even rougher strokes—until she sounded close to coming—but then I slowed it back down again. She whimpered from frustration and begged me to fuck her faster again. I delivered my thrusts faster, then slower, then faster again, subjecting her to the agony of delayed ecstasy combined with the fear of the next assault.

Her arousal reached its pinnacle when I started thrusting hard and fast and commanded, "Make that pussy cum on this dick!" She came hard, her pussy flooding my dick as she opened her mouth wide and screamed my name. It gave me pause when I heard my name—I realized that I didn't know hers.

She immediately collapsed all of her weight onto the bed, not yet aware that I wasn't done. I pulled out of her, removed the condom from my dick and replaced it with a fresh, lubed one. I could tell that she had begun to settle into the bed, but I had something else for her. I grabbed her ass cheeks before spreading them and taking aim at my new destination.

"Ooh…Whatchu doin'? Wrong hole."

As she tried raising her head to look back at me, I calmly placed it back into the pillow. As long as she had not expressed her desire to be done, I was going to have my way.

"Theory, take it slow, okay? You can't beat up my ass like it's pussy."

"Yeah, okay."

I gradually worked my dick into her ass and she took the invasion with a soft moan. I gave her ass a hard slap, making those meaty, brown cheeks wobble. Her hands clutched the pillow as I fed her with more dick. The feeling of my nuts slapping against her warm, wet pussy was amazing. Her ass was jiggling in rhythm with my pipe game as she asked for permission to cum again.

Once I gave her the okay, she reached between her legs and began playing with her pussy, lost in the sensation of my dick massaging the inside of her soft ass. I gripped those fat, smooth, soft cheeks as she rubbed her pussy and clit. She looked back at me with a fuck face that made me finish with a cry. "*DAMN!*"

I jammed myself home, knocking the wind out of the bitch's body. She began to rub herself harder. I could tell that she was close to another orgasm and she came within seconds. I could feel her ass clamp tighter onto my dick, squeezing the last of my nut into the condom. Before I knew it, the bedroom door flew open. So much for locks.

"What the fuck?" asked Solstice as he walked over to the bitch's head and pulled it up by her hair to get a better look. Once he was satisfied, he dropped it back onto the pillow before pulling out a wad of hundreds and carelessly flinging the bills onto her back and all over the bed. He then began undoing his pants and pushing me out of the way. "Watch out, nigga. You know rule number twelve: no ho' savin.'"

Somehow, Solstice had organized our original rules by number, but it was a rule nonetheless. I had to honor it.

I looked to the door and saw that AP, Glock, and Five-Seven were also staring and commentating.

"Uhn-uhn, boy," demanded the girl as she turned over onto her back and pushed the money off of her and onto the floor. "I don't fuck around like that. I don't need yo' money."

"Man, fuck all that," Solstice insisted, pulling out his dick before attempting to tease her lips with it. "Bitch, how much it gon' cost me to get a shot a that pussy or some head?"

When she turned her head away from him, I knew that she was either not down with the shit or simply fronting because of my presence.

Because I was loyal to the original rules, I made my way out of the room. I was confident that, if she were to get down for the fellas, their chances would be better with me out of the picture. At the end of the day, I had already gotten what I needed.

I made my way into the bathroom and began to run the shower as I thought about how crazy my little brother was. The shit was funny to me. He felt like we needed to share everything. Bitches were no different than jeans, sneakers, or a whip. The only girl that he had ever shown even a modicum of respect for was my main dip, and that was only because of me. But, she too was nothing more than an object of pleasure in his eyes.

I undressed and climbed into the shower. About a minute later, I heard the bathroom door open and close. I looked out from behind the shower curtain and saw the bitch standing there in one of my T-shirts. She must have held up under the pressure. Either way was cool with me. I figured this was my first and last time seeing her anyway.

"You got me fucked up, Theory, for real. Why did you leave me in there with them thirsty-ass mothafuckas?"

"My bad," I told her, realizing just how beautiful her lips were. Perfect for sucking dick. "I thought you was right behind me."

She rolled her eyes then pulled my T-shirt off and stepped toward the shower. I couldn't understand why she thought it was okay for her to shower with me, but I did want to find out what those lips felt like so I let her in. As soon as she stepped in, I began trying to push her head towards my dick.

"Boy!" she snatched away and stared at me as I continued to push her to her knees. This time, she obliged, but was still eyeing me as if appalled by my advances. "Do I look like some kind of ho'?"

The question had not been a full second from her lips before my dick was inside of her mouth. Immediately, she began to eat it as if she had been waiting all morning for it. She closed her eyes as her warm and wet flesh folded around it. I started feeding her the dick deep, in and out of her mouth, holding the back of her head with my fingers locked in her hair as I fucked her mouth. I began thrusting my pelvis back and forth, forcing my rod down her tight throat. She began playing with her big brown nipples as she moaned on my dick. She thought I was going to cum in her mouth, only to feel my hand lock tighter onto her hair. I pulled her wet mouth off of my dick and took my shaft into my other hand, jerking it hard and releasing nut right into her face. Her mouth came open right on time and I finished by coating her pink tongue. I held her tight by her hair as I pushed the tip back into her warm lips and let her suck the last out. If I had to answer her last question, I would say that she was definitely some kind of ho'—some kind of ho', indeed.

There was then a knock on the bathroom door. It was Five-Seven, letting me know someone was on the phone for me. I got out of the shower and threw a towel around myself, completely disregarding the bitch as I opened the door and grabbed the phone from Five-Seven. When I put it to my ear, I heard a lot of people in the background on the other end. I was so busy being nosy, trying to figure out what was going on, that I forgot to say anything to the caller.

"Hello?" the voice on the other end checked.

"What it do? Who dis?"

"It's me, nigga! Don't play dumb with me, Theory." It was Angela, my number two bitch. I would have been lying if I said I never had feelings for the bitch. She was down in more ways than I could count. The problem was that she had been around a few corners in her lifetime and it was hard for me to say with full certainty that she would not have tried with me the shit she had tried with niggas in her past. But, she always had a baller for me and my niggas to move on and she was willing to slang that iron if it ever came to that. Plus, the pussy was insane. The bitch knew how to fuck.

While she knew about Kim, my li'l Alverno College ho', being my main dip, and happily played her position as mistress, she also could not stand my number one. She often went out of her way to remind me of Kim's past as a stripper. I knew she only did it in an effort to taint my image of the girl, but I was a street nigga; that kind of shit never bothered me. As long as Angela was down for me and my best interests, I allowed her space to vent every once in a while about how she deserved to be number one. The bitch would have done whatever for me, even if it meant settling for only a fraction of me.

"Whattup, baby? I just got out the shower. I'm about to get dressed."

"We still gon' holla at ol' boy, right? I can't be laid up with that nigga no more."

"Most definitely," I assured her.

"You clear on how it's goin' down, right? When I call yo' phone and order a pizza, that means we at the crib and it's a go."

"All that ain't gotta be discussed over the phone, Angela. We already went through that. Don't trip... Just do what I told you to do and I'll take care of the rest."

I ended the call without giving her the chance to reply. She was a street-savvy bitch, but sometimes forgot certain parameters of the game, like not discussing details over the phone.

I had met Angela about a year ago at a concert downtown and she was cool as fuck. She was from Chicago but spent a lot of time in Milwaukee because she had a nigga here—a nigga who was supposedly having some serious cash. According to her, her dude had been running a nice amount of heroin through Milwaukee. She told me that the nigga owned at least three jewelry stores and that he would have the stores robbed in order to collect the insurance money. She said he was worth $500,000 on a bad day.

This dude had one of the baddest ho's around, yet he was fucking off on her. Angela was beautiful. She looked just like Halle Berry. The only difference was that she was much thicker in the chest and waist.

She had been the reason for her boyfriend's success. She had used $125,000 from a $200,000 settlement she received from a bad car accident to help him open up his first jewelry store, but she got none of the benefits. After he got what he wanted out of her, she was useless to him. He began lying, cheating, and beating on her. These were the very things that turned good women into devious, dirty bitches. For this reason, I never truly closed my eyes on the bitch.

One night, while we were at the movies, she told me that she was tired of his shit and that she wanted me to strip him for everything that he owned.

"Mafuckas don't realize what they have until it's gone," she had said. She proceeded to tell me all of this shit about how he kept close to a half million in cash, as well as his heroin, at the house. She said she didn't need all the money or the drugs; all she wanted was the $125,000 back that she had invested in the first jewelry store. She explained that she would only be able to get me in the house. The rest was up to me and my team.

I didn't know how serious she was until she called me that day and gave me the details to set the plan in motion.

I got dressed in some black 501 jeans and a black beater. Knowing I wouldn't be returning home until after it went down, I grabbed my pistol and hoodie before heading into the bathroom where the bitch was still trying to freshen up. I rushed her along and then we headed for my truck with the goon squad on our heels. We all piled into the truck to drop what's-her-name off. She stayed somewhere deep on the east side in a neighborhood I wasn't familiar with. When we pulled up outside of her house, I asked for her number. The bitch had some good pussy and I'd be damned if I'd just let it slip away. I had plans on hitting that ass again.

Five-Seven and I switched seats after I dropped the bitch off. He was the only one of us with a valid driver's license. We all knew that if we were to get stopped by the police with me behind the wheel, it would bring unwanted scrutiny to all of us and we'd probably all go to jail.

I think what we were more afraid of, however, was the reality that my little brother would probably take the situation into a direction that none of us wanted it to go. He had never been inside of a cell and he had his mind made up that he would die in the streets before he went to jail. Even I couldn't talk him out of this one. While I knew my brother would have never intentionally placed me in harm's way, I was sure that he had no idea what he was going up against when it came to the cops. In his mind, he was certain he would be able to get us out of any jam by way of his gun. And, when it came to me, he believed it would be more irresponsible to allow me to get cuffed.

It was a nice, warm, sunny day, so we drove around for a few hours checkin' for bitches. Most ho's who were out prowling were nothing more than motorheads. In Milwaukee, it was as if the ho's were more willing to fuck the cars than the niggas driving them. I started scoping out this bad-ass little bitch. I couldn't see her face, but from the back, she had it. My attention was directed at her big, bodacious ass, which was wrapped in leggings that revealed all of her personal assets.

While I was scoping out the bitch, I noticed my nigga, Calico, walking down the street. I had heard that he was out, but was staying low. I couldn't be mad at him for that, but I hadn't seen him in ages. He had been in the joint for a case he had taken for me years ago. Keeping it real, I had completely forgotten about my nigga while he was away—outta sight, outta mind.

"Pull this mafucka over 'Seven. That's that nigga Calico right there."

Ironically, my little brother was in the back seat on the phone with Calico's baby momma, Tammy. Solstice had been fucking on Tammy for like seven months before she even met Calico; so, in Solstices' eyes, she belonged to him. Whenever he had the time, that is.

I didn't have an opinion about the shit one way or the other. The way I saw it, bitches were not to be trusted. That was just the real. I explained to Solstice years ago that bitches like Tammy needed a soft-ass nigga like Calico to stand on. Otherwise, she was dead out here. Real niggas knew how to treat a bitch like Tammy, though, and Solstice had been doing just that.

I could tell Calico was a bit nervous as we pulled up alongside him. I lowered the window.

"Damn, my nigga. Whattup? Long time no mothafuckin' hear. What— you too good to holla at ya boys? Where you comin' from?" I asked, staring at his attire. He was looking average.

"I just got finished helpin' pops cut down some trees for the playground he buildin' at his church."

"Why you ain't get up wit' me as soon as the bars broke?"

I felt a little bit fucked up, acting as if shit were all good between the two of us.

"I really ain't had time for nobody. I been trying to get myself situated."

"Where you headed?"

"I'm going to the liquor store to get something to drink."

"Save yo' li'l cash. I got some weed and drinks in the truck."

I motioned for Calico to jump in the back seat and he got in.

"Whattup, Calico?" Five-Seven asked him after he got in.

I could tell that there was some tension coming from Solstice's side of the truck. He was still on the phone and wouldn't even take a second to speak to Calico when he got in. All I could hope was that Solstice was not in one of his "fuck the world" kind of moods.

"Aye, Five-Seven, drive me back to my pop's church for a minute."

Five-Seven turned around and we headed back to the church.

As we pulled up to the church, I decided to climb out with Calico. There were some things that I had to get squared away with him. I followed him into the shed and started helping him put his father's tools away and lock up.

"So, you on some 'born again Christian' type shit, huh?" I asked him.

"Hell, nah. I don't draw from those signs. I practice Islam."

I tried to hold it in, but the shit was starting to take a comical turn. I just hoped that he had not noticed my tone. "Oh, my bad, Farrakhan. You just threw me off, 'cause you ain't got the bowtie and bean pies. So, you down with them niggas that killed Brother Malcolm, huh?"

"That's the Nation of Islam, Theory. I practice orthodox Islam."

I was not there to debate with him on world religions and shit. My only concern at this point was righting my wrong. The one thing I knew for certain was that, no matter what God a person worshipped, the "game god" imposed his will on all who had no respect for the rules. I had stepped outside of the original rules by not holding my mans down the right way after he took my case and I had to make it right. Even though I knew Calico was not the type to ever mention it in life, I also knew that I owed this debt. Nothing was left to be said about it. I went into my pocket and gave him the eight bands I had.

"What's this for?"

"It's for being a real one."

"Check it out, Theory. I know that you feel gratitude towards me for how shit played out. But, if I'm being honest, I have to say that I didn't keep my mouth shut for you. I did it for me. There was no way that I would have been able to live with myself knowing that I had turned rat. It could have been my worse enemy, and I would have done the same thing."

The shit was something that I had no choice but to respect. He had kept it all the way honest. Did this mean that he deserved the cash any less? Fuck no! It had done nothing but illuminate the fact that he had some authentic polish on him. I pushed his hand away as he tried to hand me the cash back.

"Either way, you a real one, and that's rare in this game," I told him.

We made our way back to my truck. For most of the day, we rode around, drinking, smoking weed, and talking shit as we reminisced about old times. After the weed and liquor had begun to settle, Calico asked us to drop him off at Tammy's.

I had not seen Calico's little man yet so I was actually eager to head over there. I was just not quite sure how it all would play out with Solstice in the ride. As if on cue, Calico began establishing contact with Solstice.

"What it do, Soulless? You don't fuck wit' ya boy no more?"

"Fuck you and yo' life, Cal," said my brother. I was a bit thrown by it, but I had plans to check him for it. Before I could say anything, he recovered. "But, shit ain't what it seems," my brother continued, "I just got a lot on my plate right now."

"Ho' trouble?" Calico asked.

"Naw, I ain't you. This money gon' come, these ho's go, and problems are just a part of the game."

We pulled up to Tammy's house and everybody climbed out and headed towards the door with Calico. After he rang the doorbell, Tammy answered with a look of surprise on her face.

Out the gate, I was able to read her expression. "Calm down, li'l momma. We just came to see the baby."

"What a disappointment, 'cause he's at school," she responded. "He's not expected home for another hour."

Five-Seven asked Tammy how little Calico was doing and if he needed anything. Tammy told him that she had just taken the little nigga shopping and that he had everything that he needed. Still, Five-Seven dug into his pocket and gave Tammy $100 to buy little Calico some shoes.

I wasn't about to stand around there mingling with those mothafuckas. I told Calico I had some business to take care of and to give me his phone number so that I could get up with him later. Calico gave me his number and I walked back to the truck so we could hit it.

Later that evening, as the boys and I were driving around tyring to see what we could get into, my cell phone rang.

"Hello? I'd like to order a large pizza with everything on it." The voice paused before continuing. "My address is 4317 West Stone Brook."

"Okay, Angela, your pizza will be there in forty-five minutes," I said as I wrote the address down.

After I hung up the phone, I passed the address to Five-Seven and told him to head to Brookfield. I explained to everyone in the truck what was about to go down and that I had a lick for $500,000 or more. Before I could continue, I was interrupted with some questions about who, when, and where. I just ignored their questions and continued with what I was saying before I was so rudely interrupted. I explained that this bitch I had been fucking with turned me on to her nigga—some nigga who supposedly owns some jewelry stores and supplied a good percentage of Milwaukee with boy. I told them that it was the bitch who had just called me, giving us the go-ahead.

"The bitch is the one who gon' get us inside the house," I explained. "This is how it's going down: when we get in there…."

I broke everything down for the squad as Five-Seven drove us to pick up supplies. A few minutes later, he pulled up to a drugstore and went inside.

The rest of us stayed in the truck, quietly contemplating getting our hands on half a million dollars. Solstice broke the silence.

"Man, if this lick is some bullshit, I'm poppin' that bitch and burning her body up for jeopardizing our lives."

I remained quiet, still thinking about what I was going to do with the money when I got my hands on it. I was really hoping for this lick to go through. We already had money, but to me and my boys, we could never have enough.

When Five-Seven got back to the truck, he had gloves for all of us. We left the drugstore and headed for the house.

5 | EXECUTION

Theory

Although it was dark, I could tell we had arrived in a nice-ass neighborhood with big houses and big lawns. Five-Seven pulled into the driveway of a modern-style ranch house and the two of us got out of the truck first, just as planned. We made our way up the walkway and pressed the doorbell—three times.

"Who is it?" a voice asked from inside the house.

"It's the pizza delivery guy," I answered.

Moments later, Angela was standing in the doorway.

"He's laying in the living room on the couch," she informed us.

I grabbed Angela by the back of the neck. Five-Seven shut the door and hurried to walk in front of me. The living room was decked the fuck out: a big 110" screen plasma TV connected to a surround sound system; a fireplace; a big-ass aquarium with an array of fish in it, including a baby shark, which took up a whole side of the wall; white Indian leather furniture; and a crystal table. This dude was living in luxury, yet had no idea of what was in store for him.

We approached him from the blindside—he didn't see it coming. Five-Seven's big, strong, cocky ass reached from behind the couch and brought dude up by his neck, finally giving me a good look at this dude Angela had been telling me about. He didn't look like shit to me. He was Black but looked to be part Native American or something and had an average build—maybe a bit on the heavy side.

I walked into the living room with Angela by the hair and threw her to the floor. Hands still around dude's neck, Five-Seven threw him to the floor, next to Angela. At that moment, the goon squad walked into the living room, pistols in hands.

Five-Seven spoke up.

"Let's make this as uncomplicated as possible. In case you haven't figured it out, this is a robbery. You can keep your house, cars, jewelry—hell, your credit cards. All we want is the money."

Solstice walked right through us. He picked the nigga up off the floor by his ponytail and slapped him with the pistol.

"Nigga, I'm not gon' play with you. These niggas gon' play, I'm not." Solstice shot into the floor. "You have less than a minute to tell me where the money is."

"Alright, alright. I'll take you to the money," he said as he carefully stood up and surrendered his arms in the air. "Just don't hurt me."

"What about the girl?" I asked.

"Uh, her either."

Angela shot a cold look at her man from the floor. I picked her up off the floor and we all followed ol' boy as he led us into the master bedroom from the end of Solstice's gun, as if he were on a dog leash.

"Well, where is it?" Solstice yelled.

"Take that picture from the wall," the dude directed.

Solstice walked over to the wall and removed a portrait of Angela, revealing a safe. He turned around.

"Jackpot," he said. "Now, get your bitch ass over here and open this safe up."

The dude walked across the room to the safe. Solstice rested his pistol on dude's temple.

"If you even *look* like you 'bout to try anything—pow."

While he was across the room opening up his safe, Angela whispered to me that it wasn't the real safe. The safe's door popped open and Solstice threw dude to the bed and bum rushed the safe to see what was in it. "Nigga, how much money is this?"

"About seventy. Now, get the fuck out," he told my brother.

I was about to ask Angela where the real safe was when Five-Seven rushed to the bed and shoved his pistol into the nigga's eye.

"What the fuck is you doin'? What you reachin' fo'?"

Glock walked over to the bed and picked up a pillow. There lay a .44 Desert Eagle. Glock grabbed the pistol.

"You mighta just signed yo' own death warrant," Five-Seven told him. "Didn't I tell you we came here in peace? You's a stupid-ass nigga."

While Five-Seven was talking to dude, Angela whispered to me again. "That's just a dummy safe. The real money is in a safe in the basement but I don't know the combination and there's no way he's going to give that one up as easily."

I let go of Angela and walked over to the dummy safe. The money inside wasn't bundled in any way. It was just an unorganized accumulation of what looked to be mostly hundred-dollar bills.

"Solstice, grab a pillowcase," I directed my brother.

He snatched a pillowcase off one of the pillows on the bed and brought it over to the safe. As he held it open, I started grabbing handfuls of the loose bills and stuffing them down into the bottom of the pillowcase.

"Now this is a nice start, bro," Solstice said as I dropped in the last handful of cash. He then twisted the top of the pillowcase to close it and secured it with one of dude's ponytail holders he found on the dresser.

I walked over to Angela's boyfriend and started pistol whipping him, then pointed my pistol at his chest.

"No, please don't kill me. I'll…I'll give you whatever you want. Just, please don't kill me."

"Go into the kitchen and get me a butcher knife," I instructed Glock. I wasn't about to waste any more time—we'd already been inside for too long.

Glock went into the kitchen and returned to the bedroom, carrying the knife.

"Okay, homeboy," I said to dude. "Enough bullshittin'. Where the real money at? I know there's another safe in this house. Tell me where it is and give me the combination."

"Man, you already got the money. Y'all got everything I have."

He must have thought I was some kind of fool. I grabbed the knife from Glock's hand.

"You got ten fingers, but you only got one minute to tell me where the other safe is at before I start chopping them off," I threatened. "Sixty… fifty… forty… thirty… twenty… ten… Seven, hold that nigga down."

Five-Seven grabbed him and pinned him to the bed. I took a hold of his hand and sent the knife slashing down across his thumb. He yelled out in pain. Angela screamed right along with her man.

"The money is in the basement," she cried, "Puleeze don't kill him… please. I'll show you where the money is."

Five-Seven yanked the nigga off the bed by his arm, leaving his thumb behind. I grabbed Angela by the arm and commanded her to lead us to the basement. As we walked out of the bedroom toward the basement, Solstice yelled from behind us that he and Glock were going to take a walk outside and put the pillowcase with the seventy g's in my truck.

Angela led us through the basement door and we started making our way down the stairs. When we were about halfway down, we heard a gunshot ring out through the house. I felt Angela's muscles tense up through my hold on her arm. I let go of her and told her, Five-Seven, and AP to continue into the basement with the dude. All I could think about was my little brother.

I ran back upstairs and as I was turning the corner to go back to the bedroom, I heard more loud blasts. My reflexes made me jump back behind the wall. My heart was pounding a thousand times per minute. Next thing I heard was my little brother yelling.

"Stupid bitch—you almost shot me!"

I turned the corner to see what was happening. Solstice had dropped the pillowcase and was stomping and kicking a corpse that lay on the floor. It was the body of a young female and he was calling her every name in the book—except a Jezebel. My brother was a lost cause. There was no talking to him until he had taken out all of his anger on the corpse.

Glock stood in the middle of the hallway, looking at Solstice like he had lost his mind. The gun Glock was holding was locked back. He was the shooter.

"What happened?" I asked Glock.

"I don't know. Me and Soulless was walkin' out the bedroom when the li'l girl came out of nowhere and took a shot at us."

"Oh, well," I said. "Just come to the basement when Solstice is done beating the shit out her body."

I grabbed the pillowcase with the money and returned to the basement. I tossed the pillowcase on the pool table near the bottom of the basement stairs and got back down to business.

"What happened?" Five-Seven asked me.

"Some li'l bitch took a shot at Solstice and Glock knocked her head off."

"That's my little sister, man! She's only nineteen years old!" Angela's boyfriend yelled.

"Not anymore, she's not," I said, then turned my attention directly to Angela.

"Bitch, why didn't you tell me that there was someone else in the house, huh? What are you trying to pull?"

Angela's eyes widened. "Theory, I didn't know she was here—I swear to God. We had just came home... We had been gone all day... I swear, Theory. I didn't know."

Angela's boyfriend shot her a look with hate so thick that it made me think about who I might be fucking with. But, who was I kidding? This nigga could be no more of a killer than we were.

At that moment, he took off after Angela. "YOU PUNK-ASS BITCH! YOU SET ME UP!"

He only made it a couple of steps before Five-Seven slammed him against the wall, still hollering.

"BITCH, I SWEAR ON MY MOMMA, YOU A DEAD HO'! I'MA KILL YOU, YO' MOMMA, YO' SISTER, AND THAT FAT BITCH YOU CALL YOUR GRANDMA!"

Angela ran up to me as if she was hoping to be rescued but I found it more agitating than anything. I pushed her away from me and towards the pillowcase on the pool table.

"Bitch back up off me! Grab that money and take my truck back to Chicago. I'll use your Jaguar."

Without a word, Angela grabbed the pillowcase and started walking up the stairs. Even after she had disappeared from the stairs and was walking toward the front door, her nigga continued to yell after her.

WOMP!

"Shut the fuck up," Five-Seven demanded as he delivered a room-quaking slap to the dude's face.

At that moment, Solstice came down the stairs dragging the girl's body by the legs. He stopped in front of Angela's boyfriend and let his sister's lifeless body rest on the floor in front of him. Man, that girl was fucked up. As if being shot wasn't bad enough, Solstice had beaten the skin from her face. Whoever she had been the day before, even a mother couldn't identify what Solstice had made of her. She looked like she had been thick though. She had some big-ass titties.

When the dude finally recovered from the slap across his face and saw his sister lying in front of him, he went hysterical—crying, yelling, cussing, launching threats, and punching the basement floor. I motioned for Solstice to hold him down before I cut off two more of his fingers, reminding him that I still wanted that combination. He was yelling in pain, but he still wouldn't give me what I wanted.

"Fuck that. He ain't gon' talk," I concluded. "Five-Seven, you still got that address Angela gave us? Let me see it."

Five-Seven handed me the piece of paper with the dude's address on it and I handed it over to Solstice.

"Go get his momma, li'l bro," I bluffed. "If she resists, I want you to wreck her mothafuckin' ass. I'm not about to keep playin' with this nigga."

"That bitch gave you my momma's address?"

"That's right. You should really learn how to treat a bitch. You can't bite the hand that feeds you—it might bite back."

I grabbed the piece of paper from Solstice and flashed it in front of him, just fast enough for him to see that it was an address. I handed the paper back to Solstice.

"Go get the bitch," I instructed, sure to keep a cold stare on Angela's boyfriend.

Solstice moved for the stairs.

"Hold up… If I give y'all the combination, is y'all gon' leave me and my family alone?"

"Yeah," I assured him. "That's all we wanted from the beginning. You killed your sister, not us."

"Five-zero-six-two-zero," he revealed, finally giving up the combination.

Five-Seven entered the numbers into the safe—*click*. The door popped open and I walked over and looked inside. Jackpot.

As I was looking at all the money in the safe, gunshots suddenly blasted behind me. Startled, I turned around to see what the fuck was going on. My little brother had shot the dude three times in the back of the head. I was beginning to question myself for involving Solstice in the robbery. I knew he was a savage. Deep down, I also knew that once we were inside of the house, there was only about a one in ten chance that we would leave without him killing anyone.

Sometimes, even I wondered if the boy had a soul. As much as I hated to admit it, the boy was a ticking time bomb, ready to explode at any moment. What was I to do? He was my little brother; he was all that I had.

I cringed at the name *Soulless* every time I heard it and I cursed Five-Seven to his face for giving him the name. At the same time, I knew that Five-Seven had a point. Solstice had been this way since we were kids. I stood up for him then, and I would always stand up for him, even when he did stupid shit like this to piss me off. To keep it honest, we were going to have to kill the nigga one way or another. The problem was that Solstice had not even considered checking with me before moving. It was my lick, and he had already executed two people without my orders.

Five-Seven and I started taking stacks of money out of the safe and stacking them on the bar. Yeah, this was the real safe. With all the money we took out, it had to be $500,000 or better—that bitch Angela wasn't lying. Under the money, we found watches, gold coins, and a couple of bricks of what looked to be heroin.

After we had everything out of the safe, I looked over to my little brother and that stupid-ass nigga was down on his knees trying to cut up the bodies with the butcher knife I had used to cut off dude's fingers.

"What the fuck are you doing?" I questioned.

"Nigga—no body, no case," he explained. "Now, get your ass over here and help me chop this nigga up."

Five-Seven looked to me and said, "The li'l nigga got a point, Theory."

I conceded. "Then what the fuck y'all gon' do with the bodies once they're all chopped up?"

"Acid," answered Solstice. "Now, come and help me."

I knew they weren't going to get anywhere trying to cut up those bodies with a knife. That's when it hit me—Calico. I remembered seeing an axe at the church when I helped him straighten up the shed.

I went into my phone to call the number Calico gave me earlier, but it wasn't in my contacts. I must have forgotten to save it after I entered it. I turned to my brother.

"What's that bitch Tammy's number?"

"What for? What you need my bitch number for? Find yo' own pussy."

"Man, don't nobody want that li'l funky-ass bitch. I need to get up with Calico. His daddy got an axe at the church."

Solstice looked at me with an icy mug. I knew he was not cool with the reality of Calico laying up with Tammy.

"Man, fuck that nigga Calico. If you got love for him, you bet' not invite his ho' ass into this shit. You see I'm already two for two."

I smirked. Even though he was serious, he knew that I laid law, and he would not have dared to go against my word.

"Li'l bro, you bet' not kill my boy. We gon' fight behind him."

"We gon' fight then," Solstice challenged, only half-jokingly.

"Nigga, what's the number?"

"Hold up," he said, standing to show me his phone as he eyed the rest of the team suspiciously. "I ain't finna say it out loud around these niggas," he said, trying not to laugh.

"Man, knock it off," Five-Seven laughed.

I got the number from Solstice and headed up the stairs.

"Someone come lock the front door after I leave. We don't need anyone wandering in here."

I made my way out to Angela's Jaguar as I dialed Tammy's phone number.

"Hello?" Calico answered sleepily.

"Calico?"

"Whattup? Who dis?"

"This Theory, nigga."

"Whattup, Theory. What's goin' on?"

"Calico, I need a favor. I need to borrow that axe I saw in the shed at yo' daddy church."

"What? What axe?"

"Nigga, the axe I put away."

"Bro, that wasn't an axe. It was a hatchet."

"Axe, hatchet, just let me use the mafucka."

"At two-o'clock in the morning? Come on, Theory. Get real. What the fuck you need a hatchet for?"

"I'll let you know when I get there."

"Hold fast, Theory. I'm in bed with the family. I'm not tryna make no moves tonight."

I was not about to let him off the phone without at least getting him to let me come and grab the keys to the shed. It was easy to finesse Calico into doing shit that he disagreed with.

"Cal, Cal, Cal, I'ma straighten you out, bro—that's my word. I just need this one favor."

"Theory, you know I'm on papers. They can't wait to lock me back up."

"Cal, it ain't nothin' like that. I just need to use the hatchet. I'll be there in about twenty minutes. I'ma blow when I'm out front."

"Nah, nah. Don't blow."

After I said what I had to say, I hung up on that nigga. He was starting to piss me off. He thought that just because he had been to the joint, he
wasn't hood anymore, like he was better than the rest of us or something.

—◆—

When I pulled up outside of Calico's house, I honked for him to come out.
I knew he didn't want me to blow, but I did anyway. I could not have cared
less about the bitch, Tammy. A real nigga would have had her in her place.
He came out and climbed into the car. He started right in with the questions.

"You gon' tell me what's good, or nah? The last time I let you hold
somethin' I ended up in the pen for six and a half."

"Come on, Cal. You know I'm sorry for all that. But, you know how
that spur of the moment shit be. I mean, I was bogus for not looking out for
you or the shorty, but I'm finna make it all right. You really think you the
only one in the city with a hatchet? I'm comin' to you because I know you
need a blessing. I'm gon' hit yo' hand for letting me use it."

"One man's blessing is another man's curse," Calico responded.

"Man, come the fuck on wit' all that higher consciousness shit, Cal. I'm
about to put some money in yo' pocket. Li'l Cal can't learn how to do salat
if he hungry, my nigga. Now, you can't tell me that you gon' deny renting
me the hatchet for a second."

I didn't even wait for him to respond as I pulled into traffic. I had no
time for the bullshit games. This shit was happening.

In a matter of minutes we were pulling up in front of his father's church.
I parked the car and waited for him to exit.

"Tell me what it is that you're about to get me into, Theory. What the
fuck are you planning to do with a hatchet at three in the morning?"

"Cal, just grab the hatchet right fast. I'ma run it all down to you."

I could tell that he wanted to continue protesting, but how could he?
The nigga had nothing. And, with a bitch like Tammy, I knew he was going
to have to start producing cash soon.

"Whatever, man," he said, climbing out of the car as he uttered something else, something about trust.

I hated what he had become. He was so uptight now. It was as if he had checked his dick in at the door for a pussy. Calico had changed. He wasn't the Calico I had known. This Calico was some fake-ass impersonator.

When I saw him making his way back to the car, I picked up my cell phone and acted as if I was engaged in a serious conversation. It was my way of avoiding the millions of questions that I knew he would be asking.

I could tell he was beginning to grow antsy as I drove in the opposite direction of Tammy's crib.

"Turn around and take me back to the crib, Theory."

"Chill, Cal," I said, lowering the phone. "I'm only gon' need the hatchet for a hot second, so if I use it right fast, I can just take you to drop it back off, and then run you home."

"What's a hot second, and what the fuck is you finna do with it?"

I placed the phone back to my ear, pretending I didn't hear a word he was saying. I held that fake conversation with myself all the way back to Brookfield.

When we arrived back at the location, I checked the area to make sure no nosy neighbors were onto us before I killed the engine. I told Calico to grab the hatchet and follow me.

He got out reluctantly and followed me to the porch. I rang the doorbell and Glock eventually opened the door for us. These fools had made themselves at home. They were drinking, smoking weed, eating, and watching TV.

AP said the pillowcase with the seventy g's was missing and asked me if I knew where it was. I told him I gave it to Angela as her cut. He then showed Cal some love by shaking his hand and passing him a blunt. I made my way into the basement looking for Five-Seven. I hadn't seen him anywhere in the house when I came back in. I found him bent over the bodies trying to cut them into pieces with the butcher knife. I went back upstairs and told Calico to bring the hatchet and come with me. We all made our way into the basement.

Calico stopped when he reached the bottom of the stairs, wide-eyed and with a look of horror on his face. I knew what was coming next. The nigga looked as if he were hyperventilating or something. I went to grab the hatchet from his hands. I was ready to bounce. We had been inside of that house for too long. I knew Calico was going crazy in the head, his mind running every which direction. I patted him on the shoulder.

"Relax, Cal, it's good, baby. Just give me the hatchet."

"I want nothing to do with this madness, bruh."

"Cal, right now ain't the time for all this shit. You here already. I mean, what you gon' do, leave and go home, pretend that none of this ever happened? You party to the crime, baby boy. Now give me the mothafuckin' hatchet so we *all* can get the fuck up outta here."

"Nah," he protested once more and turned for the steps. Solstice could not wait to get on his ass.

"Bitch-ass nigga, you can either release the hatchet and stand down, or we can add a body to the workload," Solstice said as he shoved a gun in Calico's face.

I knew that my brother was crazy, but Calico was far from a bitch.

"Is that a threat or a fairytale, Soulless?"

I could not afford for the shit to go any further than it already had. I stepped between the two of them to quell the heat. I felt the same way Solstice was feeling at this point, but I could not allow Calico to know this. I had to play it smart. I turned to my brother. "Chill the fuck out, bro. You outta pocket for pullin' a pistol on one of the fellas."

I placed my arm around Calico's neck and escorted him off into another area of the basement. "Calico, you ain't the same nigga I remember, man. You makin' me look bad in front of the guys. I vouched for you. I told them that you was the man for this shit."

"Fuck what you told them."

"Don't trip. After tonight, none of this ever happened. Now, relax ya hand, baby. This me—ya boy—Theory. Give me the hatchet."

He obliged, releasing his grip.

"Yeah, that's the Calico I know," I praised. It was a shame I had to baby the nigga, but it had to be done. *"By Any Means!"*

I didn't want him bitching up on me again so I began to direct him towards the bar. "Let's leave these niggas to it, bro. I need help countin' this money."

As we both took a seat, I noticed that he was eyeing the cash and jewels sprawled across the bar top. I smiled inwardly. He may have preached that Quran, ham, salami, bacon shit, but when that money was on the line, even Allah couldn't deliver the nigga from sin. I knew the nigga was itching to know what his portion would be, so I decided to lay it on thick for him. I picked up one of the gold coins and held it in the air.

"What kind of coins do you think these are, Cal?"

"I don't know what the fuck that is, man. Stop askin' me stupid-ass questions, Theory."

I just laughed and grabbed a stack to start counting. After about twenty minutes of silence, Five-Seven called Calico over to where he was. As he walked off, I began to think about just how dangerous Calico could be to what we had going on. With all of this high and mighty shit, there was no telling if he had it in him to run to the jakes on us.

By the time Cal made it back over to me at the bar, I was just finishing the count. I pushed half of the pile his way. "Help me count this shit, Cal."

"I thought you counted it already."

The constant questioning was beginning to become a problem for me. "I never count just once. Now, grab a stack."

"A lot of shit changed since you been gone," I informed him, as if the shit was not clear enough already. "We eatin' in a major way now. Wait 'til you see the Range I just sent to the paint shop. Eights on that boy."

"Fuck all that," he spat, placing me on edge immediately. "What the fuck makes you think we not gon' address this big-ass elephant in the room, Theory. Mothafucka, you bogus, and that's all there is to it. What part of the game is you honorin' by bringin' me here?"

"Nigga, you ain't shit like the Cal I remember. All you do is cry about shit. I said I had a lick for you. Did you think we was finna go steal some bikes out somebody front yard or somethin'?"

"I never agreed to no lick. You mothafuckas can't even see that y'all are out of y'all minds. Then, you let yo' morally insane, retarded-ass brother pull a gun on me."

"Calm down, nigga. You know how Solstice gets. Quit actin' like this shit is new to you. We *been* talked about the shit that made him the way he is."

"*You* helped make him the way he is, Theory."

The moment it rolled from his tongue, I began to feel my blood cooking. I felt my body tense with anticipation, hoping he would give me a reason to leave him right where he sat.

He continued, "You enable that shit by continuing to create fucked up situations for him. Go in there and look at what yo' li'l brother is doin' to that body. Better yet, go in there and give him a hand. You can't, because you ain't got the stomach for that shit. Yet, you keep him around and pretend that you and yo' homeboys ain't usin' him for his psychopathic ways. Five-Seven is doin' that shit as a countermeasure. Soulless looks like he's havin' a blast. AP and Glock haven't looked at that puddle in the middle of the floor since it got here. You ain't never tried to correct yo' brother. You feedin' that monster because he's just as much an instrument for you as the hatchet that I gave you."

I wanted badly to smack the nigga in his mouth for disrespecting, but I knew it would be all the fuel my little brother needed to put Calico's lights out. He acted as if he didn't know how we grew up as kids. On the one hand, I knew I didn't owe Calico's comments a response, but, on the other hand, I still found myself needing to explain to him.

"Look, nigga, I keep him with me because I know what he can do if left to his own faculties. The li'l nigga has no filter and no real sense of right and wrong. You see him choppin' up a body and say that he's being influenced. I see him choppin' up a body and say that he's just doing what he do."

As far as I was concerned, there was nothing left to be said after that. There was no room for rebuttal, or debate. He was my brother and I knew what was best for him. Fuck what anyone else thought.

An hour passed before Soulless and the crew finally managed to get everything cleaned up. They all headed over to where I had stacked the money in neat piles. We all stood there for a brief second, staring at each other. Altogether, there was $469,000, not including the value of the drugs and jewelry.

I counted out eighteen g's and handed it to Cal.

"What's this?" he asked, as if he could afford to be picky.

"It's for the hatchet," I said, then tossed a Rolex his way. "That's just for being my manz."

"What the fuck can I do with a hot-ass Roley?"

"What? That Rolex ain't hot. It belongs to the cat who owns this house. He used to rob his own jewelry stores just to collect the insurance money. Only him and his thot knew about it. This shit comes with no worries. They burned down the store after they robbed it so there's no paperwork for any of this shit."

I knew that it would be some bullshit once he saw that the rest of us had spilt the cash evenly. What could he have had to complain about? He had just been handed a free eighteen thousand.

"I'ma be in the car, Theory. Is that okay wit' you, Soulless?"

Solstice looked from me to Calico before responding.

"Aye, look, you betta' stop playin' wit' me and get on up outta here with that cash before I take it, and ya life. That eighteen g's got you lookin' like a free meal, boy."

"Yeah, what the fuck ever," Calico said as he walked up the stairs and headed out to the car.

AP, Glock, Soulless, and I all got $93,000 a piece. Five-Seven got $97,000. We figured we would let him get the extra $4,000 since he never hesitated to look out for us. After all, he was the OG of the clique. After hitting Calico with eighteen bands, my share of the cash came up a little bit short. I had that $70,000 on its way to Chicago, though. With Calico out in the car, my nerves had eased a bit. I had love for him and I wished he would stop playing games with Solstice. The boy was certainly off his rocker and Calico often acted as if he had no clue of what my little brother was truly capable of.

We were loading our shares when paranoid-ass Calico ran back into the house wiping down his fingerprints. I could tell from his silence that he was salty. I didn't give a fuck.

"What's our next move?" I asked Five-Seven.

He looked to Solstice and AP. "No time for acid, Solstice. We'll just dump the bodies and torch the house. Let's use the Beamer outside to get back home so we ain't ridin' so deep in one car."

"Well, I'ma drop Calico off and meet y'all back at my crib."

After making sure that everybody was good, I made my way out to the car. I climbed in and threw my bag of money into the back seat. As soon as I got in, my phone rang. I looked to the screen before tossing it onto the dash.

Calico started in with all of his talking, of course. He was saying how he felt like a bitch for allowing himself to accept such a small amount of the cash and blah, blah, blah. I went back and forth with him for most of the ride. The shit even got a bit heated as both of us starting feeling like our minds were not being respected. After a while, I was no longer trying to hear what he was saying. I had gone off into my own little world thinking about what I was going to do with my money. I didn't hear a word he was saying. When we pulled outside of Tammy's house, I extended my hand to show him some love, but he left me hanging. When he got out of the car, I smiled at him and burned rubber on his ass.

As I was in traffic, I thought about Angela on her way to her place in Chicago with a bankroll and a hell of a lot of incriminating information. She was a cool chick, with a nice shot, and she had looked out by putting me onto the lick, but if she wanted to, she could bring down my entire team. One of the original rules to the game was *no witnesses*. So, who was I to go against what I knew I had to do?

I grabbed my phone from the dash and called my man, Five-Seven.

"Yeah?" he answered after the first couple of rings.

"What it do, big homie? Let's take a trip."

"Where?"

"Chicago," I offered.

"You read my mind," he replied.

As we ended the call, I smiled, knowing that we had been around each other too long. We had the tendency to think just alike.

"Is this the block?" I asked Five-Seven a few hours later as he turned left into a small, somewhat sketchy-looking apartment complex.

"Yeah," he replied, surveying the area. "This it."

I clutched the ten shot .357 automatic that rested near my abdomen, unsure of what to expect from the locals. I was not a big fan of the Chicago scene and I knew Five-Seven had not been home since the last time he had to swing through to clean up some unfinished business. While many of the older niggas might have known who he was, the chances of the late heads recognizing his face card were slim. Putting one of these niggas under was not beneath me at the moment. I was hoping, however, that we could just do what we came to do and then get right back on the highway and head home.

Five-Seven killed the engine to Angela's Jaguar.

"Let's get it," he said as he opened the door and climbed out. I followed his lead.

As we made our way to the door of the apartment building, I noticed that no one was really paying us any attention. Everyone seemed to be focused on doing them.

"I got that loud pack," a young hustler said from the small stoop where he stood.

Five-Seven pulled the rolled blunt from behind his ear and held it up.

"We just got some, li'l homie. Good lookin' though."

Inside the building, I began to see just how different shit was here. This mothafucka looked like a dog kennel with wooden doors. The floors were solid concrete, like some shit that I remembered from the movie *Candy Man*. I could hear music blaring from different apartments and the smell of piss and weed flirted with my nostrils. I found myself studying Five-Seven's mannerisms to try to get a feel for where he was mentally. He seemed to be at home. It was then that I realized that I was practically at home as well. Every ghetto was the same in my book.

We reached the apartment number that Angela had given me and I knocked on the door.

"Who is it?"

"It's me, baby."

I could hear the sound of a few latches and deadbolts being released before the door finally cracked open.

"I didn't know you was bringing company," she said, hiding behind the door as she allowed us entrance.

"You know I ain't comin' alone," I said as I peeked behind the door at her. Just as I had imagined, she rocked a pair of emerald green lace boy shorts with the matching bra. Her feet were covered in a pair of plush bunny slippers as she tried to make a break for her room.

"Hold up, bitch," I said, grabbing her by the wrist before she had a chance to get away. I had told Five-Seven how bad this bitch's body was and I wanted him to get a good look at it before we dumped the bitch down.

I pulled her in for a hug before turning her around so that her back was to the big homie. Then I grabbed a handful of her ass and began to shake it. After kissing her on the neck, I looked to an impressed Five-Seven before smiling. "I told you, nigga. Kim K. all day."

"Stop playin'," Angela pretended to protest.

I needed to get to business. "Bitch, where the money at?"

Angela walked me to the kitchen where I found that she had bundled the money into seven ten-thousand-dollar stacks and had them lined up neatly on the table for me. On top of the middle stack was a fat-ass blunt, rolled and ready to burn.

"I know you gotta bust a couple moves with this first," Angela said. "Just give me my $125,000 whenever."

"Turn this shit up," Five-Seven said, heading towards the stereo where a Chief Keefe track was playing. As he turned the track up, I knew what he was on.

"Give me a hug," I requested, pulling her close once more as she smiled. "Baby, you did a good job, and I want you to have a safe trip. You'll always have a special place in my heart."

"What?" she asked, taking a step back. "Where the fuck am I supposed to be goin'?"

"Seven," was all that I said as my mans got to work.

He upped a .22 revolver that had a crazy looking silencer on it. The shit looked like something from a YouTube DIY video.

POP!

The bullet crashed through the side of Angela's pretty face, sending her toppling over onto one of the kitchen chairs. Her arm hit the table so hard on her way down that it knocked the blunt off the stack of cash. My reflexes caught it before it hit the floor.

"Man, where the fuck you get that In-the-Heat-of-the-Night-ass revolver from?" I asked as I stuffed the cash into a plastic bag that rested on the edge of the table.

"I know a white boy that know a white boy," he said, "This mafucka worked better than I thought it would."

After the cash was secured, we made our way for the door. Just as I was about to walk out, I noticed the keys to my truck hanging on the key rack by the door. "Oh yeah, I almost forgot about these," I said and tossed them to Five-Seven as we made our exit, leaving the music blasting as Angela's brains spilled out onto the floor. "Follow me."

Out in the hallway, I quickly looked around and realized that no one else was in it. We were in the clear.

"Aye, Sidney Poitier, call that white boy and tell him to get you four more of them silencers."

6 | ESCALATION

Calico

I pulled the trigger. Nothing happened. I checked the gun to see if there was one up. There was. I emptied the chamber and cocked it again to load a fresh bullet. I continued in my attempt to erase myself from the face of the planet. Without thought, I put the gun to my head and pulled the trigger a second time. Again, nothing happened. I figured Li'l Larry must have sold me a bogus 9-millimeter.

I picked up the bullet off the ground that I had disengaged from the chamber. As I was putting it in my pocket, I felt the Rolex and remembered Theory telling me that the watch was worth some money. Maybe there was another alternative, other than suicide. If I could get enough money from selling the watch, it might help me start fresh.

I decided to give Theory another try and see if he would be willing to buy the watch from me. While leaving the creek, I aimed the pistol at the sky and pulled the trigger—POW! *Ain't that about a bitch*, I thought. I sent another one up to the sky and the gun fired again. I realized then that the gun wasn't bogus at all. Allah had spared me.

As I made my way to Theory's house, I praised Allah for his glory in that moment. I had clearly not fallen completely from his merciful grace. Perhaps there was a purpose for me still. What it was, I did not know but I was sure that my understanding would be made clear sooner, rather than later.

I had become so caught up in communicating with my beneficent master, that I had not even realized that I was standing in front of Theory's house—or the house that I remembered him staying in with his mother before I was incarcerated. It was dark and getting late as I looked around for his truck or the Jaguar he had been driving the night before. I didn't see either. Still, I went up to the door and pushed the doorbell. After no one came to answer, I pushed it a second time. Just as I was about to leave, Theory's black Chevy Tahoe came pulling into the driveway.

"Well, look what the cat dragged in," Theory said as he got out of the truck.

"What's up, Theory. I need to holla at you."

"Holla at me?" he asked sarcastically. "I don't have any holla back for you until you show me some love. You know I'm sensitive, Cal. You hurt my feelings when you left me hanging this morning."

I extended my palm to show Theory some love.

"That's more like it," he said, disarming the alarm before leading us into the house. "Now, I feel better."

As we entered the crib, I immediately noticed the large painting hovering over the couch. It had to be at least six feet wide and three feet tall. It portrayed Theory and his younger brother, Soulless, on their front porch. Theory was standing as Soulless sat against the banister, staring out into the distance. The surveying sharpness of it made it hard to look away. I could tell that Theory had paid a nice amount of cash for it.

What really captivated me was the glassy image of their mother, standing just outside of the doorway as she smiled warmly in Theory's direction. The transparency of her image was almost ghostlike. I don't know what it was about the translation of her, but the shit was mystifying, devilish even. Whoever had captured her image had perhaps done so in a light that was unfavorable to Soulless. The portrayal was eerie. I could see straight through her.

"Who the fuck painted this shit, bro?"

Theory looked to the painting before looking off.

"You know li'l bro be fucking with that shit."

I had forgotten how good the boy actually was. There were times when we were shorties that Soulless would disappear for days with those brushes and paints. Had it not been for Theory exposing his talents to us, we would have never known that he even had any talents at all. I had told Theory once or twice that he needed to foster the boy's growth, but I don't think he ever listened. If only he knew the kind of talent he possessed. This gift was not his to keep to himself; Allah had blessed him with it so that he could share it with the world.

"Where's moms, Theory?"

"She passed away from psoriasis of the liver four years ago. I never moved because this house is pretty much all I have to remember her by. The doctors told her to stop drinking, but she couldn't shake it."

"I'm sorry to hear that."

Theory's cell phone rang. He answered it and I assumed it was a female from the way he was talking to whoever was on the other end. I headed for the bathroom to empty my bladder. The liquor from earlier was still running through me.

The bathroom looked the same as when his mother had lived there. It was done in mostly black with white accents. Even the floor tiles were black, along with the toilet cushion, shower curtain, floor mat, and clothes hamper. After I handled my business in the bathroom, I washed my hands and made my way back into the living room.

The living room, unlike the bathroom, looked totally different from when his mother was alive. He still had the same black and white furniture, but the plastic coverings were now absent. The white carpet that, as children, we were not allowed to walk on without first taking off our shoes, had been replaced with brown carpet. A large, white projector screen had replaced what was once a TV. CDs were no longer scattered everywhere, thanks to streaming media and digital downloads.

Theory was sitting on the couch, still talking to whoever it was on the other end of the phone.

"Nobody…my guy, Calico," I heard him say. "Remember when I told you about my nigga who took the case for me?"

Theory paused before going on to say, "Yeah, he a real one." He paused again. "Hold on," he told her. Theory aimed his phone at me.

"What the fuck are you doing?" I asked him as I instinctively tried to shield my face.

"Taking a picture, nigga."

"Man, you trippin', homie. Don't be sending pictures of me to people, bruh. I don't even know who that is on the other end of that phone." I knew that he would send the picture regardless of what I said. He was dismissive like that.

"Chill out, nigga," she wants to see what you look like," he said before placing the phone back to his ear. "Back to the subject at hand. I don't wanna hear no more about you droppin' out of school. Bitch, don't tell me I'm wasting my money on tuition for nothin'… Well, then you better hit those books."

A few minutes later, he finished his phone conversation and hung up. "Whattup?" he asked me.

"Nothing…I'm just here to trade a favor."

"What kind of favor?"

"I need you to take this watch off my hands so I can carry out some business I have planned."

"Nigga, why you think I owe you something, because you took that li'l bullshit-ass case for me? That's law, nigga. You were supposed to keep yo' mouth shut. You didn't do shit that was worth a cookie. I woulda done the same for you if the situation were vice versa. That's why we call each other niggas… But, yeah, I'll take the watch off of you. Let me check it out."

I didn't argue with him because in many ways he was right. I doubted that he would have done the same for me, however. I handed him the diamond

Rolex and he started to walk off toward the stairs. I followed him upstairs to his room and he went into the closet. He came back out and handed me a thousand dollars.

"That should be enough for yo' Muslim oil, nigga."

"Theory, you brothas are gon' stop all this disrespect towards me. I never disrespected you, so why you feel the need to disrespect me?"

"Aw, nigga, shut the fuck up with all that sentimental-ass bullshit you be talkin'. You think that because you found some fake-ass religion to worship in prison that you better than the rest of us."

"Theory, I didn't come over here to draw up a confrontation with you. I came over here to see if you would buy the watch from me."

"Whatever, nigga. You sold yo' li'l bitch-ass watch, so what the fuck is you still standing around for?"

"I told you how I feel about you calling me *nigga*. I hear you using that word a lot. Do you even know what it means?"

"Yeah, nigga. I know exactly what it means. 'Pac couldn't have said it better: Never Ignorant Getting Goals Accomplished."

"Yeah, brotha, if you believe that shit, then you are a real nigga—as real as they come."

"Nigga, miss me with all that goofy-ass shit. This ain't the chow hall. You ain't finna be wasting my day with all that 'Message to the Blackman' shit. We ain't in the slave era."

"How come we ain't? Check it out—here's some game for free. Just because you so-called niggas are out here rockin' whips and chains, don't mean that you ain't bein' held captive by whips and chains. It's just become too sophisticated for you to recognize it for what it is."

"Nigga, are you finished?" he interrupted before I had the chance to go any further. "Now, get the fuck out my crib with all that shit."

I was so mad by the way he had been treating me that I no longer wanted any dealings with him. I flung the money that he had given me to the floor.

"All right, I'll leave. Just give me back the watch."

Theory looked to the cash on the floor before looking back to me.

"Pick my money up off the floor and hand it to me, like I handed it to you."

I ignored his demand and was reaching to grab the watch off the bed when I was blindsided. Theory had punched the hell out of me; he had hit me in the jaw. It took me a few seconds to come back to the reality of what had happened. He stood to the left of me in his bow-legged stance, fist clenched tightly. He took a second swing at my head, but this time I saw it coming. While he was mid-swing, I side-stepped his blow before trying to knock his mothafuckin' lights out. I was going for his chin, but I misfired and connected with his eye. I saw him struggle, trying to maintain his balance. I decided to take advantage of the situation and rushed him, planting hard, stiff blows to his face and upper body. It was going to be an ass whooping that he'd remember for the rest of his life.

Theory fell to the floor. I would have stomped him into a bloody pulp if he hadn't once been my guy. He had been, though, so I didn't put my feet on him. I just continued raining blows down on his face until I heard a cracking sound, as if his jaw bone had split.

"Theory, don't ever put your hands on me again."

With that said, I walked out of his room and down the stairs toward the front door. I would figure out another way to sell the watch and get the money that I needed in order to leave town. I was stepping out of the front door when I realized that I had left the watch in his room.

When I went back up to grab it, I didn't see Theory in his bedroom but noticed his closet door had been left open. I took a careful step in to grab the watch and heard a gun cock. Theory had been inside the closet grabbing his gun. The man intended to kill me. Reflexes made me reach inside my waistband, grab my pistol, and extend my arm, aiming my pistol at the closet door.

"Theory, what are you doing, brotha?"

"Nigga, you still here? I'm 'bout to wreck yo' mothafuckin' ass."

What took place next would change my life forever. Theory came walking out of the closet. At the sight of the shiny black metal clutched in his hand, I squeezed my trigger.

POP! POP!

His eyes widened in surprise. He looked down at his chest and found two spots of blood soaking through his yellow Polo.

"Damn, Theory! Look what you made me do... Accept Islam before it's too late, brotha. Do something right in life."

Theory still had enough strength to try to raise his pistol toward me. I squeezed a third time and the bullet hit him smack in his forehead. His limp body collapsed to the floor. I stood there, dumbfounded, arms outstretched, looking down at the three separate holes in Theory's body. *Oh, God! What have I done?* I thought. "Damn, Theory! Look what you made me do."

I don't know how long I stayed there looking at Theory's lifeless body lying on the floor. My mind eventually told me that it was time to get out of there. I immediately began looking around for the cash. When I went into the closet, I saw a white and gray assault rifle and a blue steel pump leaning up against the wall. I bypassed them and found the large Louis Vuitton bag that Theory had from the robbery. I looked inside, saw the cash, and snatched up the bag without hesitation.

As I entered the hall in a frantic state, I thought about the fact that Soulless, too, had been in on the lick. I was sure I was going to be on the run for murder this time so I needed all the cash I could muster. I made my way down to the basement, where I knew Soulless always had his bedroom.

When I got to the basement, I noticed that it had been redecorated. There were even more paintings lining the walls. Some were originals, others classic replicas that Soulless had painted himself, like a Basquiat, and the album cover of Eric B. & Rakim's *Paid in Full*. Then there was a large painting of Jesus' Last Supper, in which Soulless had ironically replaced the image of Judas with that of his own. This fool had the audacity to paint himself kissing Jesus. It just went to show how narcissistic and self-absorbed he was. Still, the painting amazed me.

He had a mini library of a few hundred books on shelves next to his bed. On his bed, I noticed two books spread open, as if he had been in the midst of studying them. There was a well-used *King James* version of the Bible, as well as Dante's *Inferno*, both lying face down, yet opened as if he were saving a page in each. On the nightstand next to the bed, there was a third book—*Beyond Good & Evil*. I had heard of this particular title when I was in the joint. It was a heavy read and it surprised me to see that this jinn had a taste for it.

As I turned to search the room, I was caught off guard by the realism of one of the paintings—a lion's eye bearing the reflection of a gazelle as if it were stalking its prey. The shit looked like a poster, and the eye looked like glass. *Damn this boy could have really been something great,* I thought to myself. He had even painted the iconic portrait of Malcolm X holding the AK as he stared out of the window. He had named the piece *I See Death Around the Corner*. To think that the sheistiest person in the city had the ability to provoke this level of thought was ironic to say the least. Unwilling to lose focus, I began searching for anything that appeared to have value. I found a large black duffle bag. I looked inside and saw some money so I started shoving in anything else I could fit in the bag, including a bunch of guns. I grabbed the bag and headed back upstairs.

I started to jet out of the house with the two bags slung over my shoulder. The keys to Theory's truck were hanging by the front door and I grabbed them on my way out. I hurried to his truck and fumbled to open the driver's-side door. Then, without hesitation, I threw everything across to the passenger seat, climbed in, and started the truck. I reversed out of the driveway like a madman, not giving a fuck about the neighbors. I was leaving town and it would be quite some time before I returned.

7 | TRIGGER

Soulless

I had been out all day, engaged in our normal routine with AP—getting high and fucking with ho's. When I pulled into my driveway, I didn't see Theory's truck parked there, so I figured he wasn't home. I had only been at our house for a brief second after the fellas and I put down the robbery. I had only been home to drop off my share of the money before leaving with AP.

My cell phone rang as I was getting out of the car.

"Hello?"

"Soulless, where's Calvin?" Tammy asked on the other end

"I don't know. Do I look like I walk around with your bitch in my pocket?"

"Why are you always talkin' shit, Soulless?"

"Can I get some head?"

"Boy, stop playing. Where's my baby daddy?"

"Bitch, I told you that I don't know where the fuck that nigga is. Ask me about that nigga again, and watch I bust yo' mothafuckin' head. Think it's a game."

"Anywayz, boy."

"Bitch, it's too many real ones out here to be playin' games with yo' average ass. Can I slide through later or not? Don't start acting like a punk bitch now that that nigga came home."

"Naw, Soulless. I been told you we can't do that no more."

"Fuck you, you punk-ass bitch. Lose my number."

"Soulless, stop pla—"

I hung up the phone in Tammy's face. *Fuck that bitch,* I thought. *The bitch wants to act sheisty with the pussy because that nigga is out of jail. Fuck her. If he only knew when he's kissin' her that I been nuttin' all in her mouth for the last six years.*

When I made it to the front door, I realized it was cracked open. Initially, I cursed my brother for being so reckless, whether he was inside the house or not. After I made my way inside, I began to get a strange feeling. The comfort of home was definitely not striking me as I moved within its walls.

I then noticed that the door leading down to my room in the basement was open. I rushed down and started looking around. The first thing I did was check for my duffle bag with the money from the night before. It wasn't where I had left it. It was nowhere to be found. I tore the room apart, hoping that Theory had come in and stashed it somewhere.

I pulled out my phone to call Theory. After I dialed, I heard his phone ringing somewhere in the house. I followed the tone back out into the living room. Theory's phone was sitting on the living room table. I started to think something was terribly wrong. Theory never left home without his phone. Maybe he was just upstairs in his room with a female. Maybe he had let somebody use his truck while he stayed behind with his bitch. As I walked upstairs and down the hall, I saw that the door to Theory's room had been left open a little bit as well. I wondered what the fuck was going on.

I pushed the door open and could never have been prepared for the scene I found inside.

"NAW, NAW, NAW—NOT MY BROTHER," I cried out as I rushed to Theory's side, only to find that he no longer played a position in this world. My brother was dead. There was blood everywhere. Theory had been shot twice in the chest and once in the forehead. I bent down over his body and attempted to perform CPR. I was hoping that through some miracle he would regain consciousness. But he was gone. Tears were rolling down my face uncontrollably as I dragged Theory's body into my arms, causing the gun he was holding to fall from his grip. It must have been a robbery gone sour. Someone must have been trying to rob him when he made a move for his pistol.

I'm not sure how long I sat there on the floor holding him.

Somebody had to pay. I didn't know who, but somebody had to pay. I couldn't believe what was happening. I gently lowered his body back down onto the floor before checking the house for any drugs and guns. Whoever had been inside the house with Theory had taken everything but a few guns. As much as I didn't want to, I knew that I had to call the police. I grabbed the gun that my brother had died with and went to lock it away in my car.

When I got back into the house, I took a seat on the living room couch and dialed 911.

"9-1-1, what's your emergency?"

"My emergency is that my brother has been shot. Now, get somebody over here. And don't be taking all mothafuckin' day."

"What's your location, sir?"

"As if you don't know. My brother has been shot and I need an ambulance. Now."

I hung up the phone and just sat inside of my thoughts. As I sat there wondering who in the world could have been responsible for my brother's death, his cell phone rang. I looked at the number on his caller ID, but I didn't recognize it.

I answered the phone. "Who the fuck is this?"

"Nigga, that's no way to answer a phone. What's wrong with you?"

"Who the fuck is this?"

"It's Kim."

"Kim from Alverno College, that Kim?"

"Yeah, who is this?"

"This Soulless. Where you at?"

"Soulless, where is Theory?"

"Theory? You should know where my brother is—you set him up."

"Soulless, what are you talking about?"

"Bitch, don't play dumb. You sent some niggas over here to rob my brother."

"Soulless what's wrong? What the fuck are you talking about? I'm in my dorm room. I just got off the phone with Theory a little while ago. He told me to call him back because he had to take care of something with Calico."

"Calico? Calico was here with my brother?"

"Yeah, Theory sent me a picture of him and everything."

"Calico? Calico killed my brother?"

"Killed?! What the fuck are you talking about?"

"Theory's dead, bitch." I hung up the phone.

It was all starting to make sense. All the things that were missing in the house were things that we had taken during the robbery. Calico was the only person who had knowledge of what was taken and what each individual had.

There was a knock at the front door.

"Who is it?" I asked.

"Milwaukee Police Department. We received a call about a shooting at this location."

I opened the door and let the police inside of the house.

PART II:

A Change in Perspective

8 | RUNNING

North Memphis—one mile ahead. The sign on the side of the road seemed to be calling out to Calico and welcoming him personally. He had been behind the wheel since he left Milwaukee ten hours ago, stopping only for food, gas, and bathroom breaks. It was late morning and, although people were bustling around with their day already in full swing, he was desperate to get off the road and into a motel bed. The driving had begun to fatigue him and he was realizing that, since his release from prison, nothing about his lifestyle had been healthy. It was all taking its toll on him.

He was also still trying to understand how it was that Theory managed to come across Tammy's phone number. The thought of her cheating with his homeboy had crossed his mind on more than one occasion. While he couldn't put anything past Theory, he was sure that Tammy didn't have it in her to stoop so low. Besides, she had a real dislike for Theory and it was no secret to anyone. These days, Calico was sure that he ranked pretty high on Tammy's shit list as well. Hell, he had even managed to get his own father to dislike him.

Life was crazy and, as far as Calico was concerned, he was now a fugitive on the run. He could not pinpoint who to blame for his situation and, through the course of his drive, he had been playing everything out in his head. The last thing he wanted to do was play the victim, but he could not for the life of him come up with a valid alternative for how he could have avoided everything that had happened to him. He had done everything he was supposed to do. Issues had quite literally been forced upon him.

He scoffed to himself at the idea of trying to explain all of this to a judge. The fact of the matter was that he was a grown-ass man, but he also knew Satan was hard at work on him. Though he had a difficult time accepting that he was susceptible to the power of evil, he was starting to have no choice but to believe it. After all, he had seen firsthand what it looked like.

He continued to aimlessly cruise the streets of Memphis, wondering why he had chosen to stop here of all places. He didn't know a soul but he was also sure that no one knew him and he quickly realized that this made it the perfect destination. He had a couple bags full of money and pretty much nothing to lose. What he planned to do was yet to be determined. One thing he knew was that he needed to blend. This meant he needed to find himself a ghetto to fall into.

After a few blocks, he began to notice that the landscape was turning more and more gritty. Though he liked to believe he was a man of the Quran, there were still quite a few gangsta proclivities lingering within him. He was going to need as much game consciousness as he could muster right now.

He pulled into a small, cruddy-looking gas station with a mini mart and began to see that the locals were real sketchy. He could tell from the way they occupied the gangways and parking lot of the small one-stop-shop that this was a routine practice for them. As much as he wanted to keep pushing through, he needed gas. He also wanted guidance from the locals on where he could find a decent motel.

He pulled up to a gas pump and tucked his 9-millimeter into his waistband. *Twenty-one minus five is sixteen,* he thought to himself. *I still got sixteen shots.*

"Say, mane! I got dat fiye-ass weed fa ya," a young man said to Calico as he and his two hood cronies peeped his attire. It was clear to them from the fresh white Nike Air Max 360 running shoes, white Ralph Lauren Polo shirt, and Robin jeans that this dude was not from around the way. "Mane, 'dem Nikes fresh 'den a muddafucka! Where 'bout you get them from?"

Calico looked to the young man as if he were speaking French. It was official. He was a long way from home. The lingo, the accent, the dialect, and the tone were all something that he had not experienced before. He knew that he had been complimented, but he didn't know how to reply without coming off as disrespectful. He decided to simply nod his head and keep moving.

When he entered the mini mart, there was a big, black, Idris Elba-looking fella standing behind the counter. The air inside the store was hot and sticky, causing the clerk's sweaty, white beater to stick to his body. He eyed Calico suspiciously.

Calico made his way to the cooler to grab a soda before heading back towards the register to pay for some gas.

"Let me get fifty on pump three and a box of blunts," he said as he placed the soda and a hundred-dollar bill on the counter.

While waiting for his change, he glanced behind him and saw the thickest set of thighs that he had seen in a long while. He needed to make conversation.

"Aye, you know where I can find a motel for the night?" he asked her.

Simone eyed the handsome, caramel-complexioned man who stood before her emitting an aura that she was certain was not Memphis-bred. The measure of his voice alone was enough to make it clear that he was a foreigner.

"Dat's tacky. You don't look like somebody I would see comin' out a motel."

Calico eyed the girl up and down, completely amazed by her physique. She was a healthy girl, but there was a grace to her curves, which were accentuated by her small waistline. Her hair was in long, golden cornrows that fell to the middle of the arch in her back and complemented her mocha-colored skin tone. She was rocking a pair of tight, beige leggings and an ivory tank top that was rolled up at the hem, exposing her slightly protruding midsection and a tattoo of the initials NS. She seemed to have appeared out of nowhere, but he was beginning to sense opportunity in her presence.

"I'm Calico."

"Calico? I guess… Anyway, I'm Simone and this my son, Marcus."

"So if I don't look like the type to stay in a motel, Miss Simone, then what *do* I look like?" he asked with a charming tone and a playful smile. He noticed that her son appeared to be quite skeptical of him.

Simone couldn't help but blush and smile a little, revealing two extended gold fangs that sat distinctly apart from the rest of her pearly whites.

"Look at you, thinkin' you all cute," she said.

"Nothin' like that," he laughed. "I'm really just looking for somewhere to stretch out. I just got off the road and I'm tired and need a shower. So, would you mind showing me to a nice spot that ain't too hot?"

"Yeah, if you want me to, and as long as you drivin'. You can't walk there from here."

Calico turned his attention back to the clerk and grabbed his change. While Simone was paying for her things, he grabbed a bag of chips from the rack and dropped another dollar on the counter. He had noticed her son eyeballing the chips while they were talking and saw this as the best way to get in good with the mother—through her son. The boy also reminded Calico of his own son back in Milwaukee.

I gotta get some money to Tammy and li'l Cal ASAP, he thought to himself.

Outside, Simone's expression lit up when she saw the Tahoe sitting on 26-inch chrome Lexani rims, giving the truck a look of prominence. Though she was no stranger to heavily dressed vehicles, she had not been expecting such a conspicuous whip from an out-of-towner. Not wanting to come off as a car freak, she collectedly asked, "Is that yo' truck?"

Calico had been feeling bad about killing his boy, but the guilt was not enough to keep him from laying claim in that moment.

"Yes, ma'am," he said as he walked toward the back of truck to start pumping his gas.

"Wait for me right here when you done," she said, then pointed her finger in the direction of a house that sat in the middle of the block across the street. "Let me take these groceries into the house and get my brother to watch my son and then I'll be right back."

"You know where I can get some weed from?"

"What you tryna get," she asked, knowing that she would be able to get a play from her brother. "My brother got it."

Calico dug into his pocket and peeled off three hundred and fifty dollars.

"Let me get an ounce of that shit," he said, handing her the money.

Simone quickly counted the cash before handing him back fifty dollars.

"I can get him to give it to me for three. Just wait in the truck until I get back."

Calico finished pumping his gas, then climbed back into the truck and put on some music while waiting for Simone. He pulled out the 9-millimeter, checked it, and slid it back into his waistband. At the end of the day, he was sitting idle with a rather hefty amount of money in his possession. As far as he was concerned, niggas in Memphis were no different than the niggas he was accustomed to back in the Mil. Simone was a cutie, with a fat ass, but she could have been trained to set niggas like him up for all he knew. Through Theory, he had seen all the tricks in the book when it came to robbery. Bitches were the quickest way to a man's heart and his wallet. As Theory would put it, *Never trust a bitch, Cal. That's one of the original rules.*

He reached across to the passenger seat, grabbed the duffle bags he had taken from Theory and Soulless, and threw them in the back seat on the floor. Nearly eight minutes passed and he had been studying his rearview the entire time. Finally, he saw Simone exit the house and begin walking back his way. As she approached the passenger-side door, he made sure his shirt was pulled over his pistol before reaching across to pop the door open for her.

Simone climbed into the truck and noticed that the interior was heavily customized with LED touch-screen monitors and soft leather seats. There was a new car smell and she could feel the gentle reverberation of sub woofers against her butt. Whoever this dude was, he had spent some cash to get his whip together. In the south, a man's ride was one of his most important tools.

"Did your brother say he would watch your son?"

"Yep, he got him."

"So, I guess you kickin' it wit' me then today, huh?"

Simone was not sure of Calico's plans and she did not want him to confuse her hospitality with anything other than southern character, but she could not help but feel something about him, something that she could not quite put into words. As long as her intuition remained positive, she was down.

"I don't got nothin' else to do," she said.

He handed Simone a twenty-dollar bill and asked her to run back inside the store for more blunts. As she was walking into the store, he jumped out of the truck, walked around, and got back in on the passenger's side. Not being familiar with the area, he knew his hesitant driving could attract attention and he was not in a hurry to make police contact. He had no idea if she could drive, but he hoped that she would have no problem being his chauffer for a while—at least until he found his way.

Simone emerged from the store minutes later and immediately recognized the change in plans when she got closer to the truck. Not wanting to assume anything, she stepped to the open driver's-side window and smiled.

"What you doin' over there?"

"You drivin' to the motel," he told her.

"Okay, first of all, you ain't goin' to no motel. Second of all, I'm not tryna drive this big ol' truck."

"Can you drive?"

She looked at him, folded her arms, and shifted her weight to her right leg. "Yeah, I can drive."

Calico relaxed deeper into the passenger's seat and began rolling up. "Let me know when we get there."

Simone would have been lying if she said she didn't want to be seen around town pushing a ride that fresh on the scene. She reached for the door and struggled to climb inside.

"Whateva, boy. I hope you ain't one of dem back-seat drivas."

9 | AFTERMATH

Soulless stood outside of the seventh district precinct, waiting on AP to pick him up. The police had brought him in for questioning about his brother's murder and had interrogated him for the past three and a half hours. He saw the entire ordeal as a waste of time because he already had plans for the nigga who was responsible.

AP's older-model Infiniti Q-45 pulled up in front of the station and Soulless climbed into the passenger's seat.

"Man, it's some bullshit what happened to Theory, bro," AP said. "I just want you to know that I'm wit' whatever you wit'. Niggas can breathe on the whole city until we find out who did the shit, you feel me?"

"No need," Soulless responded. "I know who did it. It was that bitch-ass nigga, Calico. Take me to get my pistol."

AP was stunned silent. He couldn't believe it was Calico who was responsible for Theory's murder. He also knew it happened like this all the time, though. Niggas were often taken out the game by the one closest to them.

"We goin' to yo' house?" he eventually asked Soulless, who appeared more furious than saddened by the loss of his brother.

Soulless looked to AP, realizing that his chest was burning far too much to waste time. He needed to conduct a manhunt immediately.

"You got yo' pistol on you?"

"Yeah, it's in the trunk," AP confirmed.

"Just head straight to that bitch Tammy's house then."

When they made it onto Tammy's block, AP already knew, without a word being said, to park his car around the corner so it wouldn't be seen. He popped his trunk then got out of the car to grab his pistol. Soulless remained in the passenger's seat, waiting for him to get back into the car with it.

Instead, AP knocked on the trunk of the car and, when Soulless looked back at him, motioned for him to get out.

"Come on, my nigga," AP yelled.

Soulless climbed out of the car, followed AP through a gangway, and came out in the alley behind Tammy's house.

"Here," AP said, handing him the pistol. "Act how you feel. I'm with you."

He grabbed the gun from AP's hand and made his way through Tammy's yard. AP followed him. They stood on the side of the house and listened closely to see if they could hear voices coming from inside, but all they could hear was some kids playing somewhere down the street. They continued to stand on the side of Tammy's house for several minutes to see if anyone came or left the house, but no one did.

"Come on," AP said. "Let's go get the car and pull it around the corner so we can watch the house from there. I don't want to be standing out here all day."

Soulless didn't make a move or say a word at first.

"Stay here," he finally instructed AP after a long pause then walked off toward the front of the house.

AP had no weapon to defend himself so Soulless saw no reason for him to follow. As far as Soulless was concerned, it was either kill or be killed. Either way, he was coming for Calico and he was determined to find out if the nigga was in the house.

Soulless rounded the front of the house, walked up on the porch, and rang the doorbell.

He knew Calico wasn't as much of a killer as the rest of them, but he also knew that he wasn't a ho' nigga either. Calico wouldn't hesitate to pull the trigger.

Tammy's voice came from inside. "Who is it?"

"It's me—Soulless."

Tammy opened the door. "What's up? What you doing here?" she asked.

"Where your baby daddy?"

"I don't know. I haven't seen that nigga since early yesterday," she said.

"Bitch, you lyin'. Get the fuck out my way."

Soulless pushed her as hard as he could and she fell to the floor with a big thud. He rushed past her into the house.

"Soulless, what is you doing?" Tammy yelled. She quickly picked herself up off the floor and followed right behind him as he walked through the house.

"Where he at?" Soulless demanded to know.

"I told you, I don't know where he at."

Tammy's young son was lying on the couch in the living room. "Go upstairs into my bedroom and lock the door," she directed him.

"Li'l nigga, you bet' not move," Soulless commanded.

Li'l Cal was petrified as his fragile mind tried to work through all that was happening. He was familiar with Soulless from coming to see his mother on the regular, but the man had never even spoken two words to him. Seeing the look of terror in his mother's eyes, his small heart began to grow. He needed to protect her from whatever it was that had her scared. He looked to the mean man in his living room and tried his damnedest to roar his command.

"Don't yell at my momma!"

"Shut yo' li'l pussy ass up and tell me where the fuck yo' daddy at," Soulless said before snatching Li'l Cal by his shirt and placing his gun to his head. He then turned his attention to Tammy. "Bitch, you got five seconds to tell me where that nigga at before I pop this li'l nigga head open."

Li'l Calvin began screaming and crying. Tammy eyed Soulless, unable to completely process what had just happened. The sight of a gun to her son's head was so horrific that her mind went numb. "Soulless, what the fuck is wrong with you?"

"FIVE, FOUR, THREE..."

Tammy made a break for her son but was quickly knocked back down to the floor by a swift backhand from Soulless. Her lip was split open, but she didn't feel a lick of pain as she tried to think of a way to get her son out of his grasp.

"Soulless, I don't know where the fuck Calvin is. If I knew, I would tell you. Maybe he's at his father's house."

"Open yo' mouth," Soulless ordered Li'l Calvin before shoving the barrel of his gun into the boy's mouth. He then turned his attention to Tammy again. "Bitch, you think I'm playin'? I will kill this li'l bitch."

"Get that gun the fuck away from my son," she cried as she struggled to make her way to her child.

This time Soulless snatched her by her hair and slammed her to the floor yet again.

When Tammy saw that she had no win, she decided to pull the only card that she had left.

"Soulless, you gon' shoot yo' own flesh and blood? Huh? Huh? You gon' kill our baby?"

Soulless paused before looking at her. He was sure he had heard her wrong. Maybe she was too out of her mind at this point to make any sense.

"Bitch, what? What the fuck you mean my own flesh and blood? What you mean *our* baby?"

"He's your son, Soulless. Calvin Jr. is your son. I lied when the DNA test came back because I really wanted Calvin to be his father. You didn't care enough to ask to see the paperwork for yourself when I first told you, but you're his real father."

"Bitch, you're crazy," Soulless said. "Let me see the papers."

Hopeful that this was a chance to save her son, Tammy jumped to her feet and headed off towards the basement.

Soulless now had his gun aimed at the middle of Calvin Jr.'s chest. He stared into the little boy's terrified eyes wondering if this were some sort of game the bitch was playing to save her son's life. What if she were for real? What if the boy was his? It would in effect mean that Calico had stolen his opportunity to be a father.

Tammy returned to the living room with a small lockbox before opening it and reaching inside. She pulled out a sheet of white paper before handing it to him.

Solstice Smith 99.9%, the paper read.

Soulless began to laugh uncontrollably as he folded the paper and put it in his pocket. "Bitch, you had that nigga breathing on my child? You had my child thinking that *that* nigga was his father? Fuck this li'l nigga. He's not my son."

Soulless squeezed the trigger, sending little Calvin flying back into the couch.

"NOOOO!!" Tammy screamed as she instinctively ran over to try to save her baby. She scooped his lifeless body into her arms, but she quickly realized there was nothing she could do to save him.

"Nigga, you shot my fuckin' son!" Tammy continued to scream as she released her son and lunged at Soulless. She started swinging at him as hard as she could but suddenly stood frozen when the roar of the pistol shot out a second time. A split second later, she looked down at her stomach as she realized she too had been shot.

"Stupid bitch," Soulless said before firing a second shot in her head that ended all her hopes of living. A piece of her skull flew off and landed on the coffee table.

"Come on. Let's get the fuck up outta here," AP said, standing in the doorway. This was nothing like what he had expected, but what was done was done and he had too much reverence for Soulless to disagree with his actions.

"How long you been standing there?"

"Fuck all that," AP said. "Let's roll!"

"Hold on, hold on—let me do something right quick."

Soulless walked over to where little Calvin was lying dead on the couch.

"Give me this shirt, li'l bitch-ass nigga," he said as he ripped the shirt from the boy's tiny torso.

With the shirt in his hand, he walked over to where Tammy was lying on the floor. He kneeled down and pushed the shirt into the missing part of her head, soaking it in her blood. He then walked over to the living room wall and wrote, "FUCK YO LIFE" in big, bold, red letters.

"Okay, now we can leave."

10 | NO SLEEP

Simone pulled into the parking lot of the Hilton and parked the truck at the far end. Calico reached into the back seat and grabbed the two duffle bags before exiting the truck with Simone.

The hotel was crowded. People and their families were gift shopping, window shopping, and heading for the swimming area. Behind the front desk was the blackest, fattest, woman that Calico had seen in all of his life. The woman looked as though she had spent her entire life baking under the sun.

He slipped two hundred dollars into Simone's hand. "Go get a room."

To his surprise, Simone showed her first sign as a down-ass woman. Without any questions or feedback, she did what he asked her.

After she got them checked in, they headed up to room 216. When they got inside the room, Calico handed Simone the bag of weed he had purchased from her brother. Simone sat down on the king-sized bed, cut on the TV, and began rolling blunts. He walked into the bathroom, setting both duffle bags down next to the tub. He was thinking of a way to get Simone out of the room for a while. He wanted to kick it with her no doubt, but he also needed to handle some business. He dug into his pants pocket and counted out eight hundred dollars. He walked back out into the room, where Simone had already begun to smoke.

"What's happening, li'l buddy? You kickin' it with me today?" Calico asked.

"That's up to you, but if I do, let's get one thing straight—I'm not a ho'. Don't think that because we kickin' it and smokin' weed that you gon' get some pussy."

"Wow, calm down," he responded. "I'm no ho' either. I only asked so I know how to plan the day. I don't know much about Memphis and I was hoping you could show me the happening spots in town."

Simone passed him the blunt. "I'm sorry," she said, "I just didn't want you to think that I was that kind of female."

"No sweat, sweetheart. Don't worry about it," he said.

He inhaled the blunt deeply and almost choked.

"This shit is some flame. You said you got this from yo' brother?"

"Yeah."

He smoked some more of the blunt and passed it back to her.

"Simone, can I ask you to do something for me?"

"Yeah, what's up?" she answered.

"Let me pay you to run to the mall and get me something to wear."

"What do you want me to get you?"

"I don't know. What's the dress code down here? Shop for me like you would shop for someone you had feelings for. Grab me two outfits, a pair of shoes and a cell phone."

He handed Simone the eight hundred dollars.

"Oh yeah, and get your son an outfit or two and keep the change," he said.

He watched as she unfolded the money to count the bills.

"It's eight hundred dollars here," she said.

"I know what it is. Keep the change. You can buy me a fifth of Hennessey if you want to. Do what you want. The change is yours."

Simone got up from the bed to leave.

"Is that all? Do you want anything to eat?" she asked. "You know you gon' have the munchies after smoking all that weed."

"Ummm, yeah," Calico answered. "But you can just order room service when you get back. Anything you want to order is cool. Except pig. No swine, baby."

"I got you," Simone said before she turned and left the room.

Damn, I thought she would never leave, he thought to himself as he walked over to lock the deadbolt after Simone left. He then went into the bathroom to retrieve the duffle bags. He brought them back out into the room and threw them on the bed. He unzipped each bag, took out all of the money, and put it on the bed. To his surprise, Theory's bag not only contained money, but also the two bricks of heroin and the diamond Rolexes from the robbery.

He spent the next forty minutes counting the money and valuables from the bags. There was a total of $254,700 cash, the two bricks of heroin, and twenty-two Rolexes. He looked at the drugs again and wondered what he was going to do with two kilos of boy. He had never sold heroin in his life.

In the other duffle bag, he discovered that he had scooped up enough armories from Soulless' closet to support a war. He turned the bag upside down, dumping all of its contents onto the bed. What caught his attention immediately was a double holster and its pistols. He pulled one of the pistols from its side of the holster to read the inscription: .357 Automatic Sig Sauer. The guns were beautiful.

He loaded all of the guns back into the bag, except for the double-holster .357. He took out the 9-millimeter from his waistband and laid it on the bed next to the bags. He checked the Sig Sauers to see how many bullets were in the clip. Even though they were known to hold ten, these two particular guns held twenty-one each. He decided to throw the 9-millimeter in the bag with the rest of the pistols.

He carefully put the remainder of the contents from Theory's bag back inside it as well. He then sat on the bed trying to think of a good hiding place for the bags. He needed to find a place to stash them before Simone came back from running errands. For all he knew, Simone could have been one of those rat bitches. Sure, he had given her some money, but after what he had been through, he put nothing past anyone. He sat there scanning the room for hiding places when he noticed the vent in the wall.

He immediately jumped up and shoved the bags under the bed. He then rushed downstairs to the front desk to get a second room. He would book it for three nights so he could come back for the bags after he settled into the city a bit.

The same fat, black, manly-looking woman stood behind the front desk. He could sense that she was a miserable person by the way she sweated him for his ID after she had just seen him enter the building with Simone. When he realized she was not buying his sob story about losing his ID, he paid her six hundred dollars toward three nights for the second room and another three hundred for her pocket. He was mad, but the experience only confirmed what he learned long ago—money rules everything. He took the elevator back up and headed to the first room.

"Hey, you got some weed?"

Calico turned to see a short, dark-skinned brother with long, French-braided hair. He was fitted—dressed head to toe in Polo gear. Calico could tell that this dude had some kind of hustle for himself.

"Nah, playa, I don't have any weed like that. I got an ounce. I can give you a couple of blunts if you want to smoke."

"It's some killa?" he asked.

"I'm high."

He followed Calico down the hall to his room, where Calico invited him in. Calico walked over to the table on the side of the bed where Simone had put the weed before she left.

"I see you strapped," the dude said, looking at the double holster on the bed.

"Yeah," Calico said, "but I don't mean you no harm. I just carry them wherever I go."

"I understand, playa. I'm a street nigga too," he said with a smile. "Where are you from anyway?"

"The Midwest."

"I could tell you wasn't from around here. My name Boosey," he said as he extended his hand.

Calico embraced his welcome. "Calico."

"How long you in town, Calico?"

"I don't know. Is this the place to be?" he asked, handing Boosey a little less than a quarter ounce of weed.

"Most def'. Take my number so we can get together before you leave and kick it, Memphis style."

Calico took the number with the promise of getting up with him later, then showed Boosey to the door.

He waited until Boosey disappeared, then grabbed the duffle bags from under the bed and made his way back out of the room. He took the elevator up to the next floor and searched for room 347. Once he found the room, he unlocked the door and let himself inside.

He sat the duffle bags on the floor, walked over to the vent, and examined it to see if it would be large enough to stash the bags. It wasn't. He decided that his best option was to simply put both bags in the closet. After he had them situated in the closet, he left the room. He hung the *Do Not Disturb* sign on the door on his way out, checked to make sure the door locked when he closed it, and headed back downstairs.

By the time Simone made it back, he had already showered and fallen asleep. Like the down woman that she was proving to be, she didn't wake him. She allowed him to get his rest.

He slept all throughout the evening and night and woke up the next morning with Simone asleep next to him. He eased out of bed, careful not to wake her. With her showing him enough respect not to wake him, he figured that the least he could do was return the favor.

He went into the bathroom and handled his bodily functions then performed his salat. He spent a lot of time talking and praying to Allah. He was so deep into his discussion with Allah that he lost track of time. By the time he came up from his prayer, Simone had awakened, showered, and ordered room service. He wondered how much of his conversation with Allah she heard. He had expressed deep thoughts and concerns about his life over the past forty-eight hours, thoughts and concerns that he was not comfortable with her knowing.

"Good morning," Simone said. "You were really tired. You slept like a baby. I ordered you some breakfast—no swine," she said smiling.

"Thank you, Simone. Did you eat yet?"

"Nope, I was waiting until you finished praying."

"I apologize, Simone. I didn't mean to fall asleep on you. We didn't have a chance to kick it. What's this town about? Are there any good places where we can go and enjoy ourselves?"

"Yeah, there are, but you forgot I have a child," Simone responded.

"Well, think of some places where we can include him."

Simone looked at Calico through eyes of shock and approval. She had not been expecting him to respond to her this way. All she could do was smile.

"Where's your baby daddy anyway?" Calico asked. "I'd hate to come into town and have to leave with a body."

The comment made Simone uneasy. "He's dead."

"Oh, I'm sorry," Cal said. He felt bad and wanted to change the subject quickly. "What's for breakfast? It smells good."

"Come sit down and see," she replied, also feeling the need to lighten the mood. She knew that he had only meant it as a joke and she hoped that he knew it would not be held against him.

He walked over to the dining table where Simone was taking the lids off the dishes. Hash browns, French toast, scrambled eggs, and turkey sausage links all sizzled in front of him.

"Don't worry. It's all paid for," Simone said. "I paid with my own money."

"Woman, that's the furthest thing from my mind."

He sat down at the table and immediately began blessing his food.

Simone watched him as he prayed over everything and began to wonder if she had it in her to be a woman of Islam. As attractive as he was, she was sure she would not miss a salat if it meant keeping him around.

"You're very religious," she observed after he finished his prayer.

"Not really. Lately, I've been very off-balance with my obligation. I just don't want Allah to feel that I ever strayed from him."

During their breakfast, the two of them shared a long, deeply religious discussion. She had grown up inside of a Baptist church. Her father also ministered, like Calico's own father. When she was 17, her father threw her out of the house because she got pregnant. As dangerous as it was, she had no choice but to live with her half brother, who moved from drug house to drug house.

She was sharing a lot with Calico and he didn't want her to stop. He knew from experience that people needed an outlet to get certain things off their chest. He did not mind being hers.

After breakfast, he took a shower thinking about his situation, Simone, and her situation. As a Muslim, he was feeling a degree of guilt over what happened with Theory. This was mixing with the compassion he was feeling for Simone. In that moment, he felt obligated to help her. He also needed to correct the sin of murder, and helping the less fortunate was a start.

As he was finishing his shower, he yelled to Simone until she stuck her head in the bathroom door.

"What's up?" she asked.

"Did you buy me some underclothes?"

"Oh yeah," she said, and disappeared from the bathroom. She made her way to the dresser where she began rummaging through the many bags she had acquired the day before. After pulling out a pair of Polo boxers, a tank top, and socks, she grabbed a bottle of cologne along with a toothbrush and toothpaste and headed back to the bathroom. She could only hope that her choice of underwear did not come off as presumptuous.

"They're on the toilet," she said before exiting the bathroom.

He listened for the bathroom door to close before getting out of the shower and drying off. When he looked to the toilet, he smiled to himself. She had good taste.

"I bought you three outfits," she said as he came out of the bathroom. "But, I'm dying to see you in this one." Simone pointed to an orange, white, and brown Polo shirt, brown Polo shorts, and white and brown Polo boating shoes that she had laid out for him.

Calico looked to the bed in shock. He was surprised and didn't know what to make of Simone. She hadn't taken advantage of his money. The average female, when offered the opportunity to keep some change, would have done just that, finding the cheapest thing on the shelf. He was anxious to see what the other outfits and shoes looked like.

—

On the ride back to Simone's crib a short time later, Calico sat in the passenger's seat trying to think of a way to make a blessing for Simone. She did not have to do any of what she had done for him. He was still in awe that she had not asked him for a dime. She was not model material, but on a scale of one to ten, he would have given her a six or six and a half. She had taken her hair down and pulled it back into a long ponytail that revealed her sexy caramel complexion. She wore little stud diamond earrings, a pair of Seven jeans, a T-shirt, and white Air Force Ones.

"After we grab my son, I thought we could hit downtown for *Memphis in May*," she suggested, snapping Calico from his thoughts.

"What's that?" he asked.

"It's like a festival that Memphis throws once a year," she said. "You'll like it."

"Alright, but in the meantime?" he questioned.

"In the meantime, I can show you the dos and don'ts of Memphis."

As long as he had his twin .357 automatics, Calico had no qualms attending such a public venue. He just prayed that Simone was not known by too many niggas.

Simone brought the truck to a halt outside her crib. She removed the key from the ignition and turned to him. "Are you coming inside? Because I have to get my son dressed."

Calico looked to the house before looking to her. "Who all inside?"

"My brother and my two cousins, probably."

"Yeah, I'll go in quick. I need some more weed," he said as he checked his guns to be sure they each had one in the chamber. Now that she knew more about him, he felt he could be more open about the fact that he was carrying.

Simone looked to the guns. She liked that he was edgy, but the guns made her somewhat nervous. "Ain't no need for all that."

"Maybe not, but I'd rather be safe than sorry."

Before they even reached the door to the house, it swung open and there stood a big, country-looking nigga with dreadlocks and the words *No Sleep* tattooed across his throat. Now Calico understood what the initials tattooed on Simone's stomach must have meant. Inside the house, Simone introduced the man as her brother, Vision. Calico shook hands with the man as Simone made her way deeper into the house.

Calico bought some more weed from Vision then took a seat on the couch and engaged in some small talk with him. There was no one else in the house, which meant that Vision had been watching the shorty on his own. He hadn't given Simone any flack for being out all night either. Calico could tell that the man had his apprehensions about him, but it was understandable.

He could tell that Vision had love for his sister so he was not at all mad at the man. In fact, he had a lot of respect for Vision for taking such good care of Simone and her child. There needed to be more men like him.

When they reached an awkward silence, Calico excused himself and asked Vision to let Simone know that he would be waiting out in his truck.

It was as he was sitting in his truck waiting for Simone and her son, that he realized he needed Simone as an outlet into the community. There was no way he was going to lay his head down in her brother's crib, though. It suddenly came to him that he could bless her by copping the girl her very own crib. In turn, he would have somewhere to lay his head and stash his possessions. He needed to act quickly and, while he knew he had made the decision in haste, he hoped his proposal would not scare Simone off.

As he was contemplating his plan, he peeped three individuals walk up on the porch and one began to knock rather loudly. Calico scanned his surroundings, hoping that the house was not under any kind of surveillance.

One of the individuals was tall and lanky and was very animated with his hand gestures and body language as he interacted with the other men. Calico was starting to hope that Simone put a move on whatever she was doing. As he clutched his heat inside the truck, he saw Vision come to the door.

Immediately, the tall, lanky fellow began tapping at Vision's chest as Vision stood there listening intently. From where Calico sat, something was off about this picture. He continued to observe as the other two dudes stood with their arms folded, nodding, and giving input of their own here and there. Calico could not hear what was being said, but the passion with which it was all being delivered was real. At that moment, the tall, lanky cat came from under his hoodie with a rather large semiautomatic weapon. He began tapping Vision's chest again, but this time he was using the gun.

Calico was starting to feel uneasy. He was not down with whatever was about to happen. Just as his instincts kicked in and told him to start the truck, he realized that Simone still had the key. He got out of the truck and began to move on foot as he thought about Simone and her son inside the house. Being the man that he was, he could not bring himself to walk away. He did not know Vision, but he was tight with the man's sister and he knew that, if the shoe was on the other foot, he would have wanted someone to help him. Three-on-one was not at all fair game. He did not know what Vision had gotten himself into, but he took a deep breath and headed for the porch with his twin .357 automatics drawn.

"What the fuck?" asked Déjà Vu before realizing that it was too late for him to up his heat.

By the time Nightmare—the tall, lanky one—realized what was happening, he had the barrel of a .357 automatic practically tickling his nose. He was stuck.

"Drop the pistol, mothafucka!" demanded Calico, tossing Vision one of the twin guns as Simone emerged from the house with her son.

"Uhn-uhn, Calico! What is you doin'?"

Vision, who was lost all the way up until he was thrown a gun, looked from Calico to Nightmare and smiled.

Nightmare saw nothing funny as he, Déjà Vu, and Daydream all stood frozen. "What the fuck is this?" he asked his boy Vision.

"It's cool, Calico. You can stand down," Vision said smiling. He handed Calico his heat back to try to offer assurance that everything was copasetic. "These my hitters, dawg. They on our team, but I appreciate you lookin' out for the god, homie. Real talk."

Calico looked from Vision to Nightmare before looking to Simone, who stood in the doorway holding her son close. He felt like an idiot. He lowered his heat before turning to Nightmare. He wanted to apologize, but it didn't seem as though the man would have accepted. "Oh," was all Calico managed to say.

Nightmare looked to Vision for additional guidance. The better half of him was telling him to drill the foreigner where he stood, but something also told him that Vision would not have approved. Having a weapon drawn on him in such a way was not sitting well with him either way.

"It's cool," Vision assured Nightmare before turning to Daydream and Déjà Vu. "It's good, niggas."

He looked to Calico and smiled as he nodded his approval. He liked the way the man had handled himself. His actions had summed up his entire character and, as far as he was concerned, Simone and his nephew were in good hands. He shook hands with Calico before turning to his sister. "This one's a keeper, sis."

11 | STAINED GLASS WINDOWS

The Pepsi-blue Lexus pulled to a stop just outside the home of Pastor and Mrs. Pointer. It was nearly midnight so the block was silent. Truth be told, it didn't matter either way to Soulless. He had his mind fixed and nothing was going to stop him from completing his mission.

He killed the engine, slid out of his ride, and moved swiftly toward the porch with his gun at his side. When he made it to the door, he peered in through the window and saw the pastor and his wife sitting in twin recliners in the living room—the pastor was reading a newspaper and his wife was watching TV. Soulless knocked twice on the door.

Mrs. Pointer heard the knocking and smiled. They were used to late-night visits from parishioners, but she was hoping it was Calvin. Although her husband had a harsher approach to interacting with their son, Mrs. Pointer still thought of him as her baby and was always delighted to see him. She got up from the chair where she had been watching the nightly news to answer the door.

Her smile quickly dropped off her face when she opened the door and saw perhaps the wickedest grin that she had ever witnessed. Soulless could not believe how easy it was to gain entry as he stepped into the house, grabbing Mrs. Pointer by the shoulder and placing the tip of his heat against her chin. In a quiet voice he asked, "Is Cal home?"

The situation was so bizarre that it took Mrs. Pointer a moment to register what was happening. As she began to process everything, she found herself starting to shake uncontrollably. Her eyes moved from his grin back up to his eyes. She could not find even a hint of life in them.

She responded in an even softer tone. "My son doesn't live here and he is not here. It's just me and Pastor Pointer."

"Well, bitch, I know he comes around. Let's see if we can get li'l Calvin back home."

He pushed her further into the house and walked her into the living room with the gun now to her neck.

"I'm happy I put a trailing stop-loss on that stock because it just declined," Pastor Pointer said, not bothering to look up from his paper. "Who was at the door, beautiful?"

"Someone for Calvin," she responded.

It was not the words, but the terror in her voice that caused him to finally look up. Alarmed by what he saw, he instinctively started to stand up in response, but Soulless pushed Mrs. Pointer toward him while keeping his weapon aimed at her. Soulless retrieved a roll of duct tape from his jacket pocket and threw it on the floor in front of her.

"Bitch, tape him into that chair. Make sure it's nice and tight."

She stood frozen in fear.

"Now, bitch," Soulless said louder as he took a step toward her.

Mrs. Pointer, trembling almost uncontrollably, started to wrap the tape around her husband as he sat in the chair.

Pastor Pointer stared at Soulless with a solemn expression. He could not understand what was happening or why. "What is this about, boy? Ain't yo' name Solstice? Didn't I speak at your mother's funeral?"

Soulless cut right into his questions. "Where the fuck is yo' son?"

"I told you, Calvin's not here," Mrs. Pointer tried reasoning as she continued winding the tape around Pastor Pointer. "We don't even know the next time he might come around."

Soulless was not trying to hear any of it. "Go pick up the phone, bitch. Call him and get him here."

Mrs. Pointer looked to the landline in the kitchen. There was not a chance in hell that she was going to call her son for this monster.

Pastor Pointer could see how shaken his wife was and he made the only attempt he was able to make to try to get some control of the situation. "If he owes you some money, son, we can work it out. Just take my wallet. There's about seven hundred dollars in there."

Mrs. Pointer, now kneeling by her husband, began to cry. She saw no other option and began to pray aloud in a soft voice. "The Lord rebukes you, Satan. Jesus is Lord. Satan, we bind you, in the name of Jesus Christ. We bind every devil, disruptive demon, unclean angel, and evil influence that has anything to do with Calvin and our family."

As she began what seemed like a rant to Soulless, he looked to Pastor Pointer and shook his head. It was amusing to see how confident she was that ol' Blue Eyes would help them now. "Give me the number," he commanded Pastor Pointer.

"No," Pastor Pointer spoke in a matter-of-fact tone. "I'm not allowing you to call my son over here. Just take the money in my wallet."

"I didn't come here for no money, *pastor*. I came here for blood."

Suddenly, Mrs. Pointer felt a rush of passion and began praying louder. "In the name of Jesus, the blood of the lamb, and the word of God, I rebuke you, you foul, evil spirit." Her prayers grew bolder. "You have no place, no power, and no influence over us." Her voice then became even stronger as a fire began to burn behind her irises. She stood to her feet and faced the demon before her. By now, there was no longer a trace of fear in her body. "I rebuke your lies!"

Soulless kept his eyes on her as he addressed Pastor Pointer. "Give me his number right now because, if you don't get him over here, Blue Eyes is not going to be able to save you two. I'm going to kill her first and let you watch. Then, I'm going to take my time killing you," he said in a calm tone.

Pastor Pointer could see that he was serious. Desperate to get him out of his home and away from his wife, he tried again to reason with him. "Please, son, go in the back of the house and look in my office. There's an envelope on my desk with the church's tithes and offerings. It's twelve hundred dollars in it. Take it. Just don't hurt my wife. What if she was your mother, son?"

Mrs. Pointer, still praying, started moving toward Soulless. She was now yelling, no longer at the host of the demon, but at the demon itself. "I command you in Jesus' name to go back home, you devil! Leave this child, I command! Go back to the eternal flames of hell and burn, you evil demon. Leave this child!"

She appeared to be in a daze as she prayed. As Soulless watched her, he slowly moved his gun from his right hand to his left and into his left pocket. He then eased his right hand to his waistline, reached under the hem of his Gucci T-shirt, and grabbed the bloodied hatchet he had tucked in his beltline. As he pulled it out, Pastor Pointer noticed it.

"Boy, is that my hatch—"

His words trailed off as he noticed his wife getting too close to the demon. She was reaching out, trying to lay her hand on the boy's forehead.

When she was a foot away from making contact with him, Soulless wondered if she was actually going to go through with it. His question was answered as she continued to advance toward him. Just as she was about to touch him, he went into a frenzy and swung the hatchet, clubbing her in the side of the head with the broad side of the blade.

In a flash, the hard blow came and she felt as if she had been struck by a sledgehammer. She could hear her husband crying out to her in faint echoes. She started to stumble to the floor and reached out for anything that would stop her from falling. Her hand found Soulless' left wrist. She tried to continue praying as she clung to him, but her brain was rattled. Soulless already had his right hand raised toward the moon, holding the hatchet in a tight-fisted grip.

"I told you not to ever touch me again, Teresa!" As he swung the hatchet down, its heavy blade slammed into Mrs. Pointer's left arm, inches above her elbow.

Mrs. Pointer let out a piercing scream of pain. She was aware of everything. She felt the chill of the blade hitting bone as Soulless struck her arm again. She heard the snap of her forearm being completely severed from the rest of her body as he struck a third time.

"Don't ever touch me, Teresa. You fuckin' bitch!" he yelled.

Who is Teresa? she thought as she looked up at her attacker, feeling as if she still had a firm grip on his wrist, but noticing that she was falling to the floor. The sight of her arm still clinging to his wrist sent a horrifying wave of shock and panic through her veins, replacing the scarlet-colored blood that pumped out of her wound.

Soulless looked down and saw her bodiless forearm still gripping his wrist. He discarded the bloody hatchet and the blunt end of the blade hit her in the chest. He then snatched the severed limb off his wrist and tossed it away from him. He reached back down for the hatchet before grabbing her other arm. With two firm whacks, he detached her right arm inches from the shoulder. Blood began to spurt from her body. "Fuck you, Teresa!"

He looked at her but saw an image of Teresa, lying there on the floor in a crimson pool, before Mrs. Pointer's face began to resurface. He turned to Pastor Pointer then walked towards him with the hatchet in his hand and blood covering his arms and face.

Pastor Pointer sat there in shock with his eyes wide open, staring at the demon before him. He began to hallucinate as he stared into Soulless' dead eyes. They seemed to be pitch black with a haze of smoke escaping from them.

Soulless kneeled down in front of the pastor and asked him in a calm voice, "Are you familiar with David saying in Psalms that God is omniscient, omnipresent, and omnipotent—meaning He is all-knowing, everywhere, and all-powerful? That means that God *knew* what Calico was going to do when he did it and did nothing to stop it. And God was *right here* when I came to your door, but He did nothing to stop me."

Soulless reached up and scratched his cheek, smearing more blood on his face as he continued. "Look around you. Where is your God now? He's never around when you really need Him, is He? Do me a favor when you see Him. Ask Him where was He at when I was four years old? When I was seven, nine…."

As Soulless spoke, he rose from his knees, jumped slightly from his feet, and, with all his might, he slammed the hatchet down and wedged it in the middle of Pastor Pointer's head. The pastor's face never changed; his head just slowly fell to the side.

"…Eleven?" he finished saying as he stood back and stared at the sight before him. There was blood everywhere. He looked down at the tan carpet and saw the results of his savagery.

While it somewhat resembled retribution in his mind, Soulless still found himself frustrated. By destroying every connection to Calico that he knew of, he had left himself with no real way of tracking the nigga down. Then it hit him. Calico had a slew of funerals to attend. There was no way the nigga would miss the chance to see his precious mother one last time.

Soulless headed upstairs and found the bathroom so he could clean himself up. He grabbed a towel—careful not to remove his gloves—and washed his arms and face with warm water until he was satisfied that he had done the best he could. Then he left the house.

When he got back to his car, he removed his blood-soaked shirt and tossed it in the back seat. He replaced it with his Pelle Pelle varsity jacket, which he took his time putting on and zipping up. Then he drove off.

—

A short time later, Soulless pulled his Lexus into a gas station and came to a stop at a pump. He put the car in park and rolled himself a blunt. As people came and went, he fired up the blunt and took a few deep pulls before placing it in the ashtray. He then climbed out of the car and made his way into the store where he bought himself a two-gallon gas container, a box of blunts, an Everfresh, and pre-paid for two gallons of gas.

When Soulless got back out to the pump and was filling the gas container, a matte black Range Rover on 28-inch rims pulled up behind his Lexus.

Mister ended his call before climbing out of his truck and heading into the store. It had been a full day of trapping for him and all he wanted to do was catch up with the chick he had met in Foot Locker the day before. She was a thick snow bunny, who seemed to be infatuated with dope boys and foreign whips. Being Puerto Rican and white, with long braids and a gang of tattoos, he fit the dope boy bill. He knew it would be nothing for him to fuck. He had travelled all the way from Racine to get the pussy.

When Mister returned to his ride and climbed back inside, he noticed the Pepsi-blue LS 450 sitting on what appeared to be a set of expensive chrome rims. He looked to the driver and saw that he was filling a gas container. Curious about the ride, he could not help but climb back out and approach the stranger. "Say, man, what kind of rims are these?"

Soulless looked at the man as if he was out of his mind. He had never seen this nigga before and it was clear that the nigga had no idea who he was approaching.

Off the top, Mister took the man's silence as a form of hostility. The last thing he wanted was to cause a situation to jump off out of nothing. "Look, man," he said, surrendering his hands to the air. "I ain't on no bullshit. I was just lookin' at the car. I'm in the market for somethin' to play with this summer and I like this mafucka."

When he saw that the man was not at all accepting of his presence, Mister decided to appeal to his pockets. "Check it out, homie. You look like the type of nigga who get money out here. I ain't from here, but I know a real one when I see one." Mister went into the pocket of his hoodie and pulled out nearly an ounce of kush before extending it. "This on me, bruh. Just fuck with me. I got whatever you need—and them prices can't be beat. We can talk about the whip some other time. Just take my number and get up with me whenever. I'm just a hop, skip, and a jump away from the Mil. You feel me?"

Oh, this nigga just out here advertising his product, Soulless thought to himself as he marveled at the meal that had just walked right up to him. It was niggas like this who made it possible for niggas like him to feast. He had no clue who Soulless was, but the mere fact that Soulless stood next to a Lexus dressed in a few designer brands had caused him to make unsafe assumptions. He had assumed that they were birds of a feather when in reality Soulless was a wolf and he was just what he was.

Since he was currently preoccupied with other things, Soulless decided to take the man's number. Without saying a word, he went into his pocket and pulled out his phone. He entered the number into his phone then climbed into his whip without so much as a word of departure.

He placed the gas container on the floor of the passenger's side and smashed out of the gas station lot, headed for Pastor and Mrs. Pointer's church.

—～—

He pulled up in front of the church and grabbed his blunt from the ashtray along with the gas container before hopping out of his car and making his way through the churchyard to the back of the church. He tried kicking the door in, only to realize that the wood was much thicker than he had antici- pated. The thought that some *higher power* was trying to deny him entrance was enough to build his strength. After three more kicks, he noticed that the door was beginning to give. By the fourth and fifth, he was able to place his shoulder into the frame and remove it from what was left of the hinges.

Soulless moved about the back of the church until he found himself inside Pastor Pointer's office. On the desk, he spotted a framed picture of the pastor with his wife and their precious Calvin. Soulless grabbed the picture and slammed it to the floor. He kneeled down and plucked the photo from the shattered glass and rolled it up tightly. He then began dousing the office with gasoline. "Omnipotent, my ass," he said to himself.

After dumping part of the flammable liquid onto the desk, he pulled the blunt from behind his ear and sparked it. He took a few deep pulls before lighting the photo and tossing it onto the desk. As the flames began to spread, he stood there in anticipation of a small light show. He found himself becoming hypnotized by the flames. It was not until he was fully immersed that a wave of heat rushed his skin, snapping him out of his daze.

As he made his way towards the front of the church, he thought back to the last time he was here. It was when his mother died. He could remember the many weeping faces as clearly as if they were in front of him at that very moment. He had only attended her funeral to confirm that the bitch was really dead. It was funny how Pastor Pointer managed to deliver such a highly characterized eulogy of Teresa as if she were some sort of patron saint. The conviction with which he spoke to her grace as a mother was all the proof that Soulless needed to know that the pastor was no better than a false prophet. Not once had he mentioned the fact that she always spared the rod when it came to Theory but was never satisfied with a punishment for Soulless that fell short of her own fists. The entire funeral was one big joke.

With the church now empty, Soulless stood at the podium and looked out into the pews, trying to imagine how powerful the pastor must have felt leading his unknowing flock. Soulless laughed to himself. It amazed him how eager people were to please this god who placed them through trial after trial, yet claimed to be the most glorious in His love for them.

As the smoke began to billow in from the back of the church, he turned around and stared up at the crucifix above his left shoulder. He began to throw gasoline on it as well. He doused the choir's section and the pulpit then set the stage ablaze.

"Don't nobody wanna go to yo' blood-stained paradise," he said aloud as he began to pace in front of the stage. "All-powerful? You couldn't even stop a war before it happened in yo' precious paradise. You kicked yo' truly faithful servant out of heaven, for what? Exposing you? How can you truly hate evil, yet allow him to continue to exist? And you all-powerful? You could have simply destroyed him or never allowed him to exist. You needed him to do what you couldn't do. That's a coward in my book."

He took a seat in the front row and eyed the crucifix as he began to wonder if all of this was a part of some grand scheme that God had constructed. As if the crucifix was God himself, Soulless began to speak to it. "Were the people in this congregation so evil that you had to kill my brother just so I could burn this bitch down? I know you omniscient, so you knew how this was gon' play out. So, are you all-knowing and powerless to stop me, or are you all-powerful and ignorant to the havoc I can cause? When you let Cal kill my brother, that decision alone gave me the permission to kill them mothafuckas the same way you gave Satan permission to torment Job. And I ain't gon' stop. Nah. You gon' have to kill me to stop me, but I know you can't. I know you ain't... I'm starting to feel like you enjoy this shit. If that's the case, you ain't no better than me. We one and the same."

Soulless stood to his feet and started making his way toward the burning alter. "You had these mothafuckas fooled in here, thinking that you were so grand and powerful, but people who actually met you face-to-face and looked you in yo' eyes, they didn't think so. Like Lucifer and the angels who followed him out of heaven—obviously heaven ain't all that heavenly. And what about Adam and Eve, who you physically walked with through the Garden of Eden? They didn't even respect yo' power. Man, you really got the churches fooled," he said with disgust.

"But you can never fool me. I know you're the true architect of evil," he continued. "Fuck it. If this is what you want, when I catch that nigga, I'm killing him first, then I'ma kill everyone around him. Better yet, I'ma gut him, then I'ma cut him in half, in yo' name."

When the heat from the flames began to singe him, Soulless found himself taking a step back. He slammed the gas container to the floor before turning to walk towards the front doors. He puffed on his blunt as the flames began to race along the walls and down the shoulder isles on either side of him. When he made it to the door, he stopped and looked back at the burning cross. "I know what they don't know. Without them, you would die."

Soulless walked back out to his car, climbed in, and reclined his seat as he stared at the thick cloud of smoke that was beginning to swell into the night sky. He could hear sirens in the distance as he continued to pump the marijuana gas into his lungs. The stained glass windows began to burst from the red-hot, blazing fury that was engulfing the church.

As the sirens grew louder in their approach, he noticed that neighbors were beginning to gather in awe of the exhibition. Some even seemed disturbed by what was happening. He stared on, unable to comprehend their displeasure, but this did not stop him from reveling in the moment. He believed they were fools to be so mournful of a mere structure, a petty representation of a power that subjected them all to misery and pain. In his eyes, they were all like battered wives, making allowances for the many transgressions of their oppressor. They referred to him as a loving father, even when beaten by his own hand. The shit was sickening.

As the first squad car arrived, followed by EMTs and the fire department, Soulless lowered the window, inhaled the fragrance of disorder, and vibed with the melodic bars of confusion. As firemen and officers scrambled to restore balance, Soulless wondered if this was how God felt when He destroyed cities and wiped out nations. He felt intoxicated from the sight of what he had caused. His decisions had compelled others to react in accordance with his will. He had single-handedly engineered this condition. Power was the ultimate narcotic.

—◆—

Mrs. Pointer was still alive, barely, despite her amputations lying on her own floor, sopped in a pool of her own blood. She tried to be still. She could hear her attacker coming down the stairs and if there was any hope of her surviving, she knew she would have to play dead. It was more than a relief to see him go straight out the front door without coming back to make certain that she was dead.

As a testament to her own strength and determination, she summoned the last of her energy to brace herself against the couch. As she sat there to catch a breath, blood rushed from her wounds.

Don't go to sleep, she thought to herself. *This is not the end for you.* She continued to press herself against the couch as she struggled to push herself to her feet. When she finally got to her feet, she looked down at where her arms used to be. Bloody pulp and fatty tissue spilled from what remained as her muscles seized and palpitated in uncontained suspension. She rose what was left of her limbs over her head to keep from bleeding out.

That demon has to be stopped. Lord, give me the strength to stop him. I can't let him hurt anybody else.

She stumbled and staggered her way into the kitchen where the phone was mounted on the wall. The entire way over, she could feel the blood draining from her brain as she came in and out of semi-consciousness. When she finally made it to the phone, she knocked it from its base with her chin and it fell to the floor. Things were beginning to go dark....

When she came back to awareness, she noticed that she was leaning against the wall, sliding down. The mind-numbing pain, coupled with the blood loss, had her continuing to drift in and out of consciousness... She started to fade once more but she pushed through the darkness taking over her mind, stood herself back up, and tried to dial 911, only to remember that she had no hands. She tried to dial with her nose, but could not press each button without also pressing others... She drifted off again and came back around to the sound of the dial tone... She looked into the distance and saw that her left arm had been discarded near the back door, between the stove and the wall where she stored the broom and dustpan. She could tell that it was her left arm from the diamond ring that sat on her ring finger, which now shined brighter than she had ever seen it shine. This brought her to thoughts of her loyal, faithful husband of 34 years. As she drifted into thoughts of him, she released her grip on the last bit of life she was clinging to and slowly slipped away into infinite darkness.

12 | THE PAINTING

"One thousand eight hundred thirty-two dollars and fifty-four cents," the clerk at the arts and crafts store informed Soulless.

He dropped nineteen hundred dollars onto the counter, grabbed his supplies, and headed out of the store without bothering to wait for his change. It had been two full days since his encounter with Cal's parents. Their murder and the burning down of the church had been all over the news. He placed the five-foot by seven-foot canvas board, 26 pints of paint, and the easel he bought in the cargo space of the Tahoe he rented before climbing into the driver's seat and smashing out of the parking lot.

When he got home, he took all of his new supplies to his bedroom in the basement. He snatched all of his old paintings off the walls, broke them into pieces, and tossed them out back in the trash.

He then returned to the basement and set up his new easel. He proceeded to open all 26 pints of fresh paint one-by-one before grabbing his brother's urn. He opened the urn and poured a little bit of Theory's ashes into each pint then prepared a tray with a variety of the colors. Now he was ready. He sat down on a stool in front of the board with a paintbrush in one hand and a blunt in the other. As he dipped his brush into the paint and began to stroke the blank canvas, he thought about how much he missed his brother. Theory never judged him, only loved him...

Theory pulled into the parking lot of the liquor store with Soulless in the passenger seat. "What you wanna drink, li'l nigga?"

"I'm drinkin' whatever you drinkin'," Soulless answered, not bothering to look up from the book he was reading on his iPad. He hated reading from tablets and preferred the feel of an actual book in his hands. The experience of turning the pages gave him far more enjoyment. Theory had bought him the tablet, though, so he made a point of using it around him to be sure that Theory knew he appreciated the gift.

Theory could do nothing but smile as he stared at his little brother. As he climbed out of the car, he heard Soulless call out, "It's a Dark Night, so make it right."

Theory laughed at the notion of Soulless being a street nigga and turned back toward him. "Li'l nigga, you turned sixteen two days ago. What the fuck you know about a Dark Night?"

The moment Theory entered the store, a black Suburban pulled up two cars down from where Soulless sat. The occupants climbed out and were headed toward the door of the store when the passenger looked toward Theory's ride and spotted Soulless. "That's the one who robbed me for the loud right there."

The driver looked to the whip and thought it looked familiar. "Ain't this Theory's shit?"

The passenger was beyond words as he pulled out a chrome .380 and charged up to Soulless' window. "Nigga, get the fuck up out the car."

Soulless considered the gun he had under the seat and thought to himself, Damn, I should go for this mafucka. This nigga Freddie a ho' anyway. If he shoot me, he better kill me.

Soulless grinned as he exited the ride and leaned against the frame.

"Oh, you think this a fuckin' game?" Freddie asked.

"Calm down," the driver ordered his young hitter before turning to address Soulless. "You know that half pound you took was mines, right?" he asked in a cordial tone.

"I should kill yo' li'l bitch ass for hitting me with that pistol," said Freddie, ready to put on for his mentor. "I had to get twelve stitches, nigga."

Before the driver could speak again, Theory walked up and stood next to the duo. He saw the gun in the younger man's hands. He had already pulled his AP-9 from his waistband and used the brown paper bag he was carrying to shield it near his chest. He looked to the driver. "What's goin' on, BW?"

"Your li'l mans right here robbed my li'l mans for a half pound."

Theory chuckled. "That's it? We goin' to gunplay over that light-ass shit? Come to the back of the car."

He yelled for Soulless to pop the trunk as he lowered the paper bag. He could tell that the two men were thrown when they finally saw the gun in his hand. He opened the trunk, lifted the spare tire and revealed four pounds of vacuum-sealed loud. He grabbed one and tossed it to Big Wood. "We good, right?"

"Fa' sho'," Big Wood replied, pleased with the compensation.

Theory then turned his attention to the young shooter and addressed him.

"If you ever pull a gun on my li'l brother again, the stars and the sky gon' fall all around you."

While Soulless was pissed that Theory had compromised with the niggas, he admired the way his brother had his back. Theory was always there.

A few nights later...

After sitting on BW and his workers for a number of days, Soulless finally found the right time to strike. He had been anticipating this moment so much that he was practically salivating. Not only had they had the nerve to confront him, but they had also embarrassed him in front of his brother.

Soulless watched BW and Freddie step out of BW's whip then checked his Millennium once more before crouching low on the side of the house. As he prepared to make his move, two men wearing ski masks emerged from a van parked in front of the house next door and ran up on BW and Freddie. One held a large, chrome pistol-grip pump, while the other brandished a 9-millimeter

Berretta handgun. BW nervously opened the front door at gunpoint, then the masked men hurried everyone inside. The door closed and Soulless heard the deadbolt lock.

He tried to look in through a window to see what was going on inside, but all he could see were distorted figures through the large fish tank that sat in front of the window. He could see that the figures were moving towards the back of the house and he moved towards the back as well. He approached the kitchen window and looked inside. No one was in the kitchen. He kept moving until he found another window and peered through. It was a bedroom and he could see that one of the masked gunmen had placed BW on his knees in the room.

"Man, ain't nothin' in here," Soulless heard BW say as the man stood over him. "I got like five g's on me. You can have this shit. Just don't shoot me, bro."

The man pulled the mask up just enough to reveal his face as he continued aiming at BW's head.

"Oh, shit!" Soulless said to himself as he continued watching. "Bro?"

While he was excited to see Theory demonstrating, he was curious to know just how far his brother was willing to take the situation. Soulless decided to remain in the shadows—for now.

"Come on, man! I ain't know that was yo' brother," BW pleaded as Theory held the Berretta to his face.

"But you knew it was my car, bitch-ass nigga."

"Yeah, but my li'l nigga jumped the gun on that one. I told him about it when we got in the car."

As the second gunman appeared in the room with Freddie at gunpoint, Soulless now knew that it had to be Five-Seven behind the mask. Five-Seven entered the room and shoved BW's young gunner face-down on the floor next to him.

"You got it?" asked Theory.

"Yeah," Five-Seven responded. "I got a li'l more."

"Hold on," Theory said as he went into BW's pockets, retrieved the five g's, and tossed it to Five-Seven. "Take it all to the car and give me two minutes. I'm right behind you."

As Five-Seven made his exit, Theory forced Freddie off his face and onto his knees.

"Man, yo' li'l man was bogus," BW said. "We was just tryna get back what was taken from us. You know how the streets is."

"His name ain't 'li'l man', it's Solstice, and I don't give a fuck what he did. Now, say his name. Say Solstice, both you bitches."

"My fault," spoke BW, hands surrendered. "Solstice, man. Solstice."

BW's young hitter could not stand to see his big homie trying to reason with Theory. The last thing he was going to do was beg. "Man, eat a dick. I ain't sayin' shit. Fuck yo' brother. That nigga shouldn't—"

Soulless watched as the bullet travelled through the young man's head before exploding out of the back and coming through the exterior of the house, just a couple feet away from his own head.

BW simply closed his eyes before being shot in the head as well. His body instantly collapsed the rest of the way to the floor.

Theory started to walk out of the room but turned back and addressed the young worker one last time. "I told you the stars would fall, li'l nigga," he said, walking back up to him and snatching the solid gold Byzantine chain from around his neck. He placed two more rounds into each of the men before leaving the room and walking out the front door of the house.

Soulless exited the back yard and made his way down the alley before disappearing into the night.

Soulless was lying in his bed with his eyes closed and his music turned down low when Theory came running down into his bedroom and tossed a pound of loud at his head.

"Wake up, li'l nigga."

"I ain't sleep." Before Soulless could say another word, Theory dug into his pocket, produced a wad of money and the Byzantine chain, and threw them at his little brother.

"What's this for?" Soulless asked.

"Shut up," Theory ordered only half jokingly. "You let some lames get the ups on you a few nights ago," he said, ignoring his little brother's question. "It's a cold world out there. You don't ever keep yo' heat under the seat. You keep that shit in yo' hands or on yo' hip. Remember that. See what happens when you don't follow the original rules? You'a find ya'self hemmed up against a car."

Theory turned and noticed a painting on Soulless' easel. "Damn, this mafucka look like a photograph. When you finish?"

"It ain't finished," Soulless quickly told him before Theory had the chance to reach out and touch it. "It's an oil painting. It'll take months to completely dry."

"It look dry to me," he said, taking a blunt from behind his ear and tossing it to Soulless. "Now roll up, li'l brother." Theory then grabbed the painting and headed for the stairs. "I'll let it dry in my room."

Six days later, Soulless sparked a blunt as he sat looking at the newly finished mural of his late brother. Theory stood on the bridge in front of the Milwaukee Art Museum with the wings of the Brise Soleil sprouting from his back. Soulless saw no wrong whatsoever in his brother and the image was consistent with his view, portraying Theory as an angelic presence towering over life. The sun in the painting added a lustrous gleam to Theory's image that made his essence pop from the page. It looked incredibly lifelike. Soulless checked his watch. It was time for him to go.

He checked his Draco to make sure it was ready to go. It had fifty in the clip and he had two extra clips. He then tucked his 40-caliber Millennium into his waistline. He grabbed the ounce of loud that he had on the table and quickly headed for the door. He wanted to be the first person to arrive at the viewing for Calico's parents.

⸺

Soulless sat in the parking lot of the funeral home for hours watching every person arrive—from first to last, and the continuous stream of people coming and going in between. No Calico. He looked on as they loaded the bodies into the hearses and drove off leading the procession. No Calico. He jumped into traffic behind the procession, not letting anyone out of his sight as he continued to search for Calico.

He parked his car far enough away from the burial site not to be seen, but close enough to see everyone. Still, Calico was nowhere to be found.

Just like a bitch-ass nigga, not showing up to his own parents' funeral, he thought to himself as he watched them place the caskets into the ground. He rolled a blunt, lit it, and took a pull as he stroked the Draco that had been on his lap for hours.

He sat in the car and continued to scan the crowd, looking everywhere in sight for Calico, coming up with nothing as the crowd slowly dispersed. After everybody left, he remained in disbelief that he had miscalculated Calico's actions. He unconsciously pulled out his lighter and ran the flames slowly up and down his forearm as he thought to himself. *This is exactly why I had Theory cremated immediately. I would never let a bunch of fake-ass mafuckas act like they gave a fuck about him and be cryin' all over his casket like this.*

"Shit!" he said aloud, realizing that he allowed the flame to sit in one spot for too long. Then he grabbed his blunt out of the ashtray. *My brother was all I had,* he continued thinking as he rested his head against the headrest and began to completely zone out. He went so far into his own head that he was no longer aware of his environment.

13 | FROM SOLSTICE TO SOULLESS

" " *Then I saw a great white throne and him who sat upon it, from whose presence earth and heaven fled away, and no place was found for them. And I saw the dead, the great and the small, standing before the throne and books were opened; and another book was opened, which is the book of life; and the dead were judged from the things that were written in the books, according to their deeds. And the sea gave up the dead which were in it, and death and Hades gave up the dead which were in them; and they were judged, every one of them according to their deeds. Then death and Hades were thrown into the lake of fire. This is the second death, the lake of fire. And, if anyone's name was not found written in the book of life, he was thrown into the fire.'"*

"Mothafucka, you ain't finished," Teresa said as she sat back in a chair at the kitchen table while staring at the back of young Solstice's head. A Crown Royal bottle sat on the table as she cradled a half-empty glass in one hand and a cigarette in the other.

"Revelations, chapter twenty, verses eleven through fifteen," Solstice finished.

"Now, read Job."

Without looking, Solstice flipped through a few pages pretending to find the book of Job before beginning to cite scripture from mere memory

"'There was a man in the land of Uz and his name was Job, and that man was blameless...'"

If God was so smart, *Solstice began to think to himself while still absent-mindedly reciting the story of Job,* how did he let Satan finesse him into doing everything that he wanted to do to Job? *At just 11 years old, he had already learned this entire story and others, front to back, without even having to look at a Bible and his mind had begun to work through certain inconsistencies and contradictions that were not always apparent on the surface. With everyone around him seeming to be completely pacified to sleep by the "Good Book"—except Theory, who was not compelled to read the Bible at all—he had to rely on his own judgment.*

Solstice's blood was beginning to boil at the anger and humiliation he felt at that moment. The bag of rice he was kneeling on had started to dig into his flesh, causing grooves to break into abrasions. After countless times being subjected to this practice, he was surprised that the calluses on his knees had not formed to the point of numbness. He had been caught for the umpteenth time searing his own flesh with a lighter and Teresa had immediately ordered him into the kitchen where she placed the rice bag in a corner and commanded him to assume the position.

He continued to think, If God knew everything, he knew that it would be pointless to try to prove anything to the devil. He had given the devil permission to destroy everything positive in Job's life, to rid the world of everything that gave him joy. He even let him kill his kids, something that could never be replaced.

Just then, Theory walked into the house from a night out with his home-boys. As he entered the kitchen, it took a minute for him to register what was going on. He looked from his little brother kneeling in the corner to his drunken mother then immediately jumped into action.

"What the fuck?" He rushed over to his little brother and snatched him up by the arm. "Get yo' ass up off that floor!"

Teresa stared at her eldest son as if she had been caught with her hand in the cookie jar yet again. She knew how he felt about her doing these sorts of things, which was why she always tried to make sure he was out of the house before she began to purge Satan.

"Ma, what I tell you about doin' this shit? You hurtin' him." Theory walked over to the table and grabbed the liquor bottle before slamming it into the wall, causing glass to fly everywhere. "You gotta leave that shit alone."

"What, baby? I'm just tryna make him clean, make him whole, like you. And I don't want nobody to see those burns on his arm and think I'm the one doing it to him."

Theory shook his head, sick and tired of having to go through the back and forth. He knew that it was pointless to try to reason with her. She was drunk, and no matter what he said in that moment, she would not be moved to have mercy on her own flesh and blood. "Ma, just go up to your room. I gotta clean this glass up."

Solstice looked at Teresa as if she were less than the scum underneath his shoes. Who was she to make anyone whole when he had watched her diminish into less than a fraction of the woman she once was. She was the last person who should be talking about making someone whole.

"Man, Solstice, take yo' ass in your room and lay down. I'a be down there in a minute."

Solstice did as he was told, grateful that, yet again, his brother had come to the rescue. He always came to the rescue. He turned around and watched as his older brother grabbed the broom. "You want some help?"

Theory looked at his little brother standing in the threshold that separated the basement from the kitchen and forced a smile. "Nah, li'l bro. I got it. Just give me a minute."

After getting the kitchen back in order, Theory went up to Teresa's room to apologize to her, but she was passed out on her bed with her shoes still on. He removed her shoes before placing the cover over her and kissing her forehead. She was a mess, but he loved her no less.

He went into his room and grabbed a shoebox from under his bed. He sat on his bed with the box and stared off in a daze. He had no clue what he was going to do about the situation between his mother and his little brother, but he was scared that one day he would not get there in time and it would end up costing him more heartache than he was willing to live with.

He headed down to the basement and found his brother sitting on the bed staring at the cuts in his knees while Lucky, their eight-month old Rottweiler, sat at his feet. Theory knew that the shit had to hurt. He sat next to Solstice and handed him the shoebox.

Solstice looked to his brother before opening the box. When he saw the fresh pair of kicks, he looked to his brother's feet. Theory was rocking the same pair. Truthfully, Solstice never really cared about sneakers, but the idea of dressing like Theory made him feel proud and the gratitude he felt toward Theory at that moment was indescribable.

"I hate her," Solstice said.

"That's still yo' momma, Solstice. She just strugglin' right now. You just gotta try to understand that."

No matter what Theory said, it would not change the fact that he hated Teresa with all of his being and there were often times when he thought about just leaving the house for good. He knew that was what she wanted and he was not above it himself. But, Theory made everything worth staying.

One week later...

"This stuff is easy, Lucky," Solstice said as he mounted the roof of the garage, preparing to do what he had just watched a few of the neighborhood kids do. Lucky stood on the ground staring up at Solstice as he positioned himself on the roof. Although Solstice was not much for hanging out with other kids, he would often sit in the background and watch how they interacted with one another. Through studying their conversations and mannerisms, he gained his own understanding of what was appropriate and what was not.

As he eased his way to the corner of the roof and looked over, he thought about how many times it would take him to master the technique. He was betting on three. He stood on the edge of the roof, then pivoted so he was facing forward. He didn't even have to think about it. He jumped into the air and tried to maneuver his body, but he couldn't get himself to complete the flip for some reason.

Before he knew it, he was lying on the pavement in pain as he stared at his ankle. He couldn't move it. His leg was also cut and bleeding. When he tried to stand, he fell back down. The pain was nothing. He was more upset at the fact that he could not make it home on his own. He lay there, bleeding and frustrated as he searched up and down the alley for someone to notice him. He looked to the left of him and saw that the same group of kids who had been flipping was now standing there laughing at him. He knew that one of the boys lived in the house just next door to him, yet he did not even attempt to go for help. Theory will come looking for me, he thought to himself. He always comes.

Two weeks later...

"Solstice!" Theory yelled, storming down the steps to the basement like a madman as he summoned his brother. "Where you at?"

"I'm right here," Solstice yelled back as Theory made his way into the bedroom. He was still on bed rest after jumping off the roof. Luckily for him, the owner of the vacant house needed to do some electrical work to the garage and found him passed out on the side of the structure. After he was taken to the hospital and treated, he was released to Teresa, who made it clear that she wished he had broken his neck.

"I got something for you," Theory said as he plopped onto the bed where his brother lay. "Remember that nigga Basquiat that we saw on TV the other day?"

"Yeah," said Solstice, staring at the large wooden suitcase in his brother's hands. "What about him?"

"Well, I remember you saying that you could do the shit he was doing. I found something for you."

The truth was that Theory had been trying to move a quarter of an ounce of crack that he had gone half on with his best friend, Calico. Although the paint set had cost them a twenty-dollar rock, he didn't mind taking it out of his cut. Solstice had been through hell. He needed some way to escape. "I wanna see if you can really do that shit. If you can, we can sell yo' work and get paid. If not, I'ma clown you."

Solstice was more than up for the challenge. There was nothing he didn't think he could do. "Let me see it. I got this."

Theory laughed as his brother snatched the art set out of his hands. He loved his little brother and it was times like these that he cherished the most.

"Boy, get up here and eat!" Teresa screamed from the top of the stairs. "This food is getting cold."

"Aight!" Theory yelled back. "Fix Solstice a plate so I can come grab it right fast."

"No," Teresa yelled back. "Just you. I'll feed his ass later."

Theory looked to Solstice, who was too busy trying to get a feel for the different sized paintbrushes to pay any attention to what Teresa was saying. The fact that he had become so desensitized to his own mother treating him like a dog was pitiful. Either way, she knew damn well that Theory was not going to eat without Solstice.

"I'm not hungry," Solstice said as he opened the fresh pad of painting canvases. It was nearly three-o'clock in the afternoon and he had not eaten since the night before, but he was prepared to starve to death before he asked her for anything. His only plans at the moment were to get lost in his new project. "Go ahead and eat. I'll be down here."

"Hell, nah," Theory said as he stood to his feet. "I'ma go get both of us a plate. If she ain't got one for you, I'm takin' hers. We gon' sit down here, eat, talk shit, and paint a masterpiece, just you and me."

Solstice looked to his brother in disbelief. "You for real? No Calico either?"

Theory waved him off. "Man, later for Calico. I'm kickin' it wit' you right now."

One month later...

Solstice had barely healed, yet he found himself playing inside of a garage with their dog, Lucky. He and Lucky were engaged in what he considered to be a pretty intense wrestling match, in which he had already gotten a hold of Lucky twice, choking the dog until it nearly lost consciousness.

During the third round, Solstice found himself so excited by the power he was wielding that he forgot to let go. When he finally did, Lucky's body fell limp, leaving Solstice confused as to what had just happened. He kicked the puppy twice to try to revive him, but nothing happened.

Knowing that Theory had given the dog to Teresa, he understood what it would mean if he showed back up at home without him. As he tried to think of a way to hide the body, he pulled the lighter from his pocket and subconsciously began to run the flame along his forearm. The second he felt the sting of his flesh being charred, it came to him. He needed to burn the entire garage down.

Unsure of where to begin, young Solstice grabbed an old two-by-four and held the lighter to it until it finally started to smolder. The gradual burn was slow and, for a while, he became tired of watching it. Then, it began to smell good. In minutes, the entire back wall of the garage was in flames. Young Solstice began to dance in complete excitement as he cheered for the flames to reach the roof. Smoke was beginning to fill his lungs, but none of this stopped him. He was determined to see this through to the end. With Teresa constantly telling him that he was born to go to hell, he needed to see what it would feel like.

Before long, he found himself in rapture. He had no idea what made everyone else so afraid of fire. He had forgotten all about Lucky lying dead on the floor. Only when he heard the sirens did he start looking for a way out. The door was in flames, but it was his only way out. He rushed over and tried twisting the knob with his hands. The pain was enough to send him stumbling back six feet before falling to the floor. The challenge was one he welcomed.

He calmly stood to his feet in the center of the madness and walked back over to the door. He took a deep breath, inhaling all of the smoke and toxins before reaching for the knob once more. The pain was otherworldly, but he was determined to get through it. He managed to turn the knob, and as soon as he opened the door a burst of fire came rushing out behind him, cooking his shirt and nearly burning the flesh on his back. Young Solstice stepped into the alley and stared at the sight. It was magic. He felt like a god. He was the god of fire. Something that everyone else feared, he had managed to conquer and control. He looked down at his hand as it began to blister and ooze, nearly to the point of irreparability. The grin that spread across his face in that moment made it clear that he was satisfied with his newfound love. He had just found his weapon of choice.

Three weeks later...

Theory found himself being awakened by Solstice as smoke began to fill his lungs. "What the fuck is goin' on?"

"Come on," *Solstice said, grinning at the fact that he had just got even with the kid next door for leaving him hanging the day that he hurt his leg. He had set fire to the neighbors' house but miscalculated his timing. Part of the problem was that watching the fire had sent him into a world of his own and he lost track of time. When he saw that it was spreading to Teresa's house as well, he got an idea. First, he had to save his brother.*

Theory jumped out of bed and began putting on his shoes. "Ma!"

"Naw," *Solstice said, grabbing Theory by the arms in an attempt to pull him towards the exit.* "Just you. Leave her here. Ain't no time."

"Hell, no!" *Theory said, snatching away from Solstice. When he realized that the boy was truly trying to force him out of the house, he gave him a slight two piece which forced him to step back.* "Get yo' ass outside while I go get Momma."

⌒

The following morning, Theory went down to Solstice's room and found him still asleep. Theory sat down on the bed and the movement caused Solstice to wake up, but he didn't open his eyes.

"Little nigga, you ain't sleep," Theory said, not caring if he was asleep or not. Solstice then opened his eyes and looked at him without saying a word. "So, it's been yo' li'l ass setting those fires around the neighborhood."

Solstice continued to be silent and just looked at Theory.

"I know it was you. So, you been sneakin' yo' ass out this house in the middle of the night when everybody sleep, setting shit on fire?"

Solstice remained silent.

"You know three people died in that yellow and brown duplex that you set on fire. So, what the fuck you got to say about that?" he asked him in a serious tone.

Solstice just lay there not knowing what to say or do. Theory looked to him with a serious expression on his face for a full minute before a big-ass Kool-Aid smile appeared. "I see you following the original rules—speak no evil," he laughed. "I love it," he continued, giving him a little shove as he got up. "I love your little bad ass."

He took two steps to leave the room then turned around and said, "Fuck them mothafuckas in that duplex and next door, but if your actions woulda caused my shit to go up in flames, I woulda killed your little ass and then brought you back to life before beating your ass back to death."

As he turned back towards the door, Solstice spoke for the first time. "Can I go with you? I don't wanna stay here with Teresa."

Without looking back, Theory said, "Get dressed, pyro man. We out this bitch. Where you want to eat?"

Two summers later…

"What in God's name—" Teresa came completely down the stairs as she tried to figure out what had possessed the boy to make such a mess with his paint. She had been looking for a reason to put him on the rice bag and he had just given it to her. Theory had been telling her how talented the boy had become with his painting and she had seen a few of his works. She was shocked at his skills, but not impressed because even Satan's children possess talents.

She was fed up with how ungrateful the boy was as well. *After finally convincing the insurance company to pay for the damage caused by the fire two years ago, she bought the boy a new bed set. Had Child Protective Services not been all over her, however, she would have left him in the same bed he had been in for years. It was the bed that her mother soiled the night she died in it, but, as far as Teresa was concerned, it was too good of a bed to go to waste.*

"Goddammit, what the fuck you think you doin' gettin' paint all over this basement flo'?" she questioned.

It was then that she noticed what was in Solstice's hand as he stood there, staring at her wide-eyed. She was both terrified and angry at the same time and her reflexes prompted her to cock back and swing her closed fist with all of her might, connecting with the boy's eye. The blow knocked him unconscious for a moment, but he managed to come back around when he hit the floor. She was screaming at him and sobbing as she removed her house shoe and commenced kicking him in his mouth with her bare heel, causing his head to smack the floor with every devastating blow.

"You mothafuckin' evil-ass li'l bitch!" she screamed.

Solstice had long since dropped the decapitated head of Plush, Teresa's cat that Theory had rescued and gifted to her after she cried about Lucky being missing.

Teresa then spotted the Blue-ray player that used to belong to Theory before she bought him a new one and went over to it.

"I told his ass not to give you this mothafucka!"

She raised the Blue-ray player above her head. "Son of the living God, give me the strength to deliver the world from this evil!"

Solstice didn't even bother to brace himself as the Blue-ray player came down on his head. It was not enough to knock him out, but it split the back of his head on impact. There was a horrible cracking sound as it crashed into his skull. Dense blood began to flow from his nostrils.

He wished it had killed him. He wanted to die. It was in this moment, though, that he made a vow to himself. The day would come soon enough when he would make sure that she had put her hands on him for the last time.

Teresa snapped him out of his thoughts as she grabbed him by his bare feet and began dragging him up the stairs. His head bumped and scraped along every step. When she made it halfway up the stairs, she flung him back down, causing his body to tumble then smack against the concrete floor at the bottom of the stairs. She followed him down, grabbed him again, and started dragging him back up the stairs.

"You look just like yo' damn daddy. He would still be here if yo' wicked ass would never have been born. You fuckin' demon."

When she got him to the top of the steps, she bent down and slapped him in his face with all the force she could muster, causing the blood from his nose and mouth to spray out. It was loud enough to echo throughout the house. She then continued dragging him to the back door.

"I can't wait until you burn in hell for this, you fuckin' demon. Get the fuck out my house," she screamed as she threw him out of the house and slammed the door.

She watched him through the window in the door for a few seconds and saw him trying to get up. She opened the door back up, ran out, and kicked him in his ribs so hard that his body did a semi-summersault.

"And I know you had something to do with Lucky disappearing too. I hate yo' ass," she said before dragging him to the garage and locking him in.

Solstice lay in there hurting. He wanted to leave, but he knew that if he used the door she would see him. He tried to lift the door that the car goes through, but it wouldn't budge.

━━

A couple hours later that night, Theory drove into their alley in a stolen car and parked it a few garages down. As he was making his way through their back yard, he heard a rustling sound coming from inside of the garage. Initially, he thought it was just a raccoon or some other animal and was going to ignore it, but then he remembered that he and Calico had stashed their pack in the garage. He pulled out a .25 automatic that Five-Seven had given him and made his way to the door.

He took out his key and quietly slid it into the lock, prepared to catch whoever was inside red-handed. He slowly opened the door and was ready to fire—until he saw that it was his brother. "What the fuck is you doin' in here?" he asked as Solstice turned to face him.

As he looked closer, he noticed that his brother appeared disheveled. Then he realized that his brother was badly beaten.

"Who the fuck—" he started to ask.

It did not take Theory long to figure out that this was the work of their own mother. Without thinking, his feet moved toward the house, the gun still in his hand.

"I should kill this bitch."

Solstice stared on, hoping that his big brother went through with it. He would be more than happy to take the gun and do it himself.

Catching himself before he did anything that he would regret, Theory went back, grabbed his little brother by the stretched collar of his shirt, and left the garage. "Come on, man. You comin' with me."

As the two of them stepped out of the garage, Solstice was the first to see that Teresa was making her way out of the house.

"Wait a minute, baby," she tried pleading with Theory. "Do you know what this evil mothafucka did? He cut the head off the beautiful cat you gave me."

Theory looked from his mother to Solstice's beaten face, finding no just cause for her to have done what she did to him.

"What the fuck did you do to him? Look at his face, ma!"

"Baby, I would never do that to you," she said as she noticed Theory moving swiftly to get his younger brother away from her. He helped Solstice to the car and then they drove off.

During the drive, Theory found it hard to even look at his little brother.

"What the fuck happened, Solstice? What was she talking about with the cat?"

"Man, I cut the cat open. I just wanted to see what was inside."

"What the fuck you mean, you cut the cat open?"

"Well, I cut the head off, and she walked in when I was trying to look down his neck."

"Why?" asked Theory.

"I wanted to see what his voice box looked like."

While the thought of it all was kind of disturbing to young Theory, he paid it no mind. The fact of the matter was that Solstice was a child and their mother had no business beating him the way that she had.

"Man, fuck that cat," Theory said, placing a hand on Solstice's shoulder in an attempt to console him. The two of them said nothing the rest of the way.

Five-Seven answered the door and immediately noticed that young Solstice was a mess. "What the fuck happened to this li'l nigga?"

Theory walked into the house practically dragging his brother behind him. "We gotta stay here for the night."

"Who did that to yo' li'l brother?" asked Calico, who was sitting on the couch in shock.

"This li'l mafucka done cut the head off the cat and she got mad."

"Get the fuck outta here," Five-Seven said, finding the statement both humorous and disturbing. "Why the fuck would you do that? Don't you know that's one of God's creatures?"

"I just wanted to see what was inside," Solstice replied.

"Let me go get this li'l nigga a towel," said Five-Seven. "I got a li'l CNA bitch on line too. I'ma call her and have her come through to tend to all this blood."

After Five-Seven grabbed the towel and came back to hand it to Solstice, he stared at the boy for a moment. The look in the boy's eyes reminded him of his uncle after he came back from the war. When his uncle made it back home, he had no sign of life in his eyes.

"I had a uncle just like you that got fucked up over there in Iraq. He ain't never been right since. It's like he came back without a soul, like he lost it in that war... Solstice, you aight, li'l bro? Nah, you ain't Solstice no mo'. Yo' name Soulless now, li'l nigga."

Theory did not like the sound of it. "Don't tell him no bullshit like that, nigga."

Five-Seven could see that it was not sitting right with Theory, which told him that it was no secret about something being off with his little brother.

"Yeah," Calico agreed. "Don't say no shit like that."

Calico removed his throwaway T-shirt—the one he wore on top in case they were ever chased by the police and needed to change up his description—and handed it to Solstice.

Solstice grabbed the shirt and looked at it with disgust before tossing it to the ground. "Man, fuck you."

Calico just stared at him before turning to address Theory. "Let me holla at you for a minute."

Calico led Theory to a back room and pulled the door closed before speaking his mind. "Man, you gotta stop this. She gon' really kill dude one day. What's her problem?"

"Man, you already know she takin' the fact that pops left out on little dude. And the fact that he died in Detroit and ain't never comin' back and will never be around to help out. She really thinks that he woulda came back and would still be alive if Solstice was never born. I just gotta try my hardest to never leave them two alone for very long. She don't want to admit that pops *was in the streets. He was a playa, he gambled, he fucked with bitches—all that shit. He tried to square up for her, but it didn't work out. She brought that shit on herself. She shoulda knew better than to think she could change him. She was tryna drag a street nigga to church and shit. The pussy wasn't good enough to stop a rolling stone. It is what it is tho' and she can't keep takin' it out on my li'l brother."*

"Man, that's fucked up. For some reason, your li'l bro don't like me, but if you ever need me to check on him from time to time, just let me know," Calico offered as they exited the room.

Theory looked to his little brother and saw that he was still in disarray. When he noticed that Calico's shirt was still on the floor, it was clear that he would not accept anything from anyone but him.

"Aye, Solstice. I'm finna go and grab you some shoes and T-shirt real quick."

"Don't call me that no more," Solstice told his brother. "My name Soulless now."

Theory looked to Five-Seven as if he wanted to strangle him. "See what the fuck you did?"

"Man, shit," Five-Seven tossed his hands up. "I was just stating the facts. I ain't expect the li'l nigga to run with it."

"Yo' name is Solstice," Theory told him.

"I don't want no name that that bitch gave me," Solstice countered firmly. "Fuck Teresa and fuck her name. My name Soulless."

Not wanting to argue it any further, Theory decided it was simply something he would have to accept. "Aight," Theory surrendered. "But, don't expect me to call you that shit. Stay here. I'a be back. I'm finna go grab you some shoes and shit."

One year later...

Soulless walked into the back door of their house and found Teresa sitting at the kitchen table waiting for him. Theory had warned her last year about putting her hands on him and, although she still treated him like less than a dog, she had eased up a little on her physical punishments.

He got the feeling as he looked at her sitting at the table, however, that she was done trying to be on her best behavior. She stood up as he entered the house and approached him.

"Mothafucka, you ain't been to school in two weeks and now you got these mothafuckas callin' here. Why the fuck you ain't been goin?"

Soulless, now as tall as her, looked her straight in the eyes. "Listen, Teresa. That school and their lazy-ass teachers are a joke. Everything they try to teach me I already learned a long time ago through my own reading. So why waste my time? Plus, I thought about going back but you made it clear that I'm goin' to hell anyway, so what's the point?"

Teresa cocked her arm back and slapped him in the face as hard as she could. The moment she connected, she realized that she had done it for the last time. The boy stood there with a grin on his face that caused the hairs on the back of her neck to stand.

Without even thinking, Solstice snatched up a knife from the kitchen counter. When Teresa saw the knife in his hand, she grabbed a chair to protect herself. Solstice came at her immediately and she swung the chair at him, barely missing his head. He side-stepped and went in with the blade as the chair went flying. He had aimed for her face, but she dodged him and the knife penetrated her shoulder.

"JESUS!" she screamed, as she started stumbling backwards, trying to get away from him. Soulless stayed right with her, though. His hand was still gripping the knife lodged in her shoulder when her back slammed against the doorframe. The impact caused them to tumble to the floor together and Teresa landed on top of him. With his hand still gripping the knife, he used it as leverage to roll her off of him and then mounted her in one fluid move.

"Solstice, no!" she yelled as he snatched the knife out of her shoulder and brought it back down. She tried to block it with her hand but the knife

went right through it. He continued to push towards her neck realizing just how strong he had become.

"Solstice, please!" she pleaded, knowing that she no longer stood a chance with him physically. "You gon' go to hell for this."

She could do nothing but stare helplessly at him as the last six inches of the knife slowly slid into her esophagus.

"Die, bitch! Die!" he screamed, enjoying every moment as he watched the light leave her eyes. He experienced a state of euphoria unlike anything he had ever felt before.

When Soulless heard the loud sound of Teresa's bedroom door slam and immediately lock, he snapped out of his daydream. He looked down at his hand and noticed that, although he had not actually killed her, he was indeed gripping a knife.

He also noticed a wet feeling in his pants and thought he had urinated on himself, but quickly realized that the release he felt while he "killed" his mother had made him ejaculate. He was confused by it at first, but his confusion quickly transformed into anger when he realized that it had happened completely outside of his control. He didn't want to think about it anymore, just clean himself up.

When he tried to put the knife down to grab the towel by the kitchen sink, he found that the muscles in his hand were locked in a state of paralysis. His hand was wrapped so tightly around the knife that it took a couple minutes for him to relax the muscles enough for him to open his hand and release the knife. When his hand finally opened, he tossed the knife in the sink, grabbed the towel, and headed to his room in the basement.

As he cleaned himself up, he thought about what had happened upstairs with Teresa. There was no need to kill her. He knew that something had been communicated between them that made it clear she would not be placing her hands on him ever again. He was confident that she would not be a threat to him any longer.

Feeling a new sense of control over his mother, he went over to his bed to relax. He pulled out his Bible and his notes—not because Teresa told him to, but because he wanted to finish reading 1 Samuel 28:14. There was something about the scripture that he couldn't wrap his mind around.

One year later...

"I got that loud on deck, Soulless."

"Let me see what it look like," Soulless said, as he stood posted outside of his brother's ride pumping gas.

Freddie walked up to Soulless, brandishing the weed as if it was legal.

Soulless grabbed the small baggie before looking at it. It was certainly some of the best-looking weed he had seen in a while. It smelled good, too. His birthday was coming up in twelve days and he figured this weed would be a nice gift to himself. He looked at Freddie and wondered if there was more where this came from. He knew Freddie worked for BW and, although BW was cool with Theory, robbing Freddie had nothing to do with their relationship in the streets.

When Freddie went into his jacket and pulled out nearly a half pound of the same grade, it was a no-brainer for Soulless. "Good lookin' out, bruh. This me," he said, snatching it out of Freddie's hand and putting it in his own pocket.

"Yeah, okay," Freddie laughed, as if it was some kind of joke.

Soulless finished pumping the gas. When he was done, he hung up the nozzle and turned to Freddie. "What you still standing here for, nigga? Scram."

"You got me fucked up," Freddie said before seeing the chrome and black .45 coming from Soulless' waist. Before he could react, the barrel of the pistol cracked him in his forehead and blood was trickling down his nose.

"Get yo' bitch ass on," said Soulless. "I told you to charge this shit. Now, move the fuck around before I stretch yo' ass out right here."

Freddie took off down the street just as Theory was making his way out of the gas station.

"Did you get the gas?" he asked as he climbed into the car.

"Yeah," Soulless said settling into the passenger's seat before pulling the weed from his coat. "Look what I just caught."

"Li'l bro, where the fuck you get that shit from?"

"Don't even trip," smiled Soulless. "It's better than that shit we been smoking lately."

"Let me see that shit," Theory said as he grabbed the weed from his brother. He smelled it. His little brother was right, it was some good smoke. He had no idea how he had come up on so much of it in such a small window of time, but he had an idea. He checked their surroundings before pulling into traffic.

"Roll up one, li'l bro. You feel like grabbin' some burgers from Chicago Subs up the street?"

"It's whatever," said Soulless, getting to it.

"Hold up," Theory said, slowing down and forcing his brother to lower the blunt as they passed a cop on a motorcycle who had a driver pulled over. "That's Officer Thompson's bitch ass. He always tryna sweat me for petty shit. I should throw on the dreadlocks and blindside that bitch—with the whole clip."

As they passed, Soulless got a good look at the officer before sitting back in the seat. By the time they made it to the sub shop, he had an idea. He waited until his brother went in before reaching into the back seat where Theory kept a dreadlock wig along with a hooded sweatshirt and sunglasses. He hopped out of the car and hit a few yards before disguising himself. He then pulled the same .45 from his waist and made his way towards the block where Officer Thompson was conducting his traffic stop.

Theory heard six shots ring out as he stepped out of the sub shop. He also saw that his brother was missing and, in his mind, he knew what had just gone down. Part of him regretted even making the comment about Officer Thompson, but he would have been lying if he said he didn't know what his brother was capable of doing after receiving the information. He climbed into his car and stabbed out in the direction of the shots. He just hoped that Solstice had not gotten himself hurt.

After putting six shots in the police officer's torso from behind some bushes near the traffic stop, Soulless slipped back through a gangway before dropping his disguise. He then walked out onto a residential block, where he spotted a young lady walking with a backpack and he jogged to catch up with her. When he reached her, he swiftly unzipped her bag and dropped his gun inside before coming out with a book, all in one smooth motion.

She looked up to see that a stranger had placed his arm around her. She knew that he had done something with her bag, but she was so confused by everything that she had no time to truly react. "Boy, what is you doin'? I'm finna scream."

"Man, yo' ass bet' not scream," *he said with his arm still around her. He looked to the book in his hand and saw that it was one of his favorites.* "What you know about To Kill a Mockingbird? I bet you didn't even read this. You probably just watched the movie."

"I did both," *she said.*

"I bet I can tell you what your favorite part is from the movie—it wasn't in the book—the part where Atticus was sitting on the porch listening to Scout asking her brother about their dead momma."

Damn, *she thought to herself.* How could he know that?

"Boy, get the fuck up off me. I don't even know you."

Soulless saw the swarm of squad cars hitting the block they were on, and just as he was preparing to bail, a marked cruiser screeched to a halt in front of them. The officer lowered the window to address them.

"Where are you two coming from? Have you seen anybody running this way?"

The questions came so rapidly that she did not know which to answer first. What she did know was that the stranger next to her was exactly who the police were looking for. What he had done, she did not know, but, for some reason, she wanted to protect him. "We comin' from school. Nobody came this way that I saw. Sorry."

The officer whispered something to his partner before the car smashed out. Soulless looked to the girl and smiled.

"I don't know what you smiling for. I still want you to get away from me. You probably just killed somebody."

"Man, be quiet," said Soulless. "Ain't nobody dead. I just hate them bitches," Soulless said as he watched the squad car move down the street.

"Anyway," Soulless continued, "one of the things that I liked about the book was the alliteration that Harper Lee used to describe Maycomb... What's your name anyway, little girl?"

"Tammy. And I ain't no little girl. Why?"

"Well, Tammy, let me break this book down for you right fast."

One year later...

Soulless called Tammy's phone from the front porch. When she answered, he said, "Bitch, I'm at the door. Hurry up. I ain't got all day."

Within seconds, she was at the door. As soon as she opened it, Soulless pushed his way in and walked straight to her bedroom, a path that he had taken on many occasions. She didn't try to stop him. She just followed behind him saying that he couldn't stay because Calico was on his way to pick her up for a house party and she had to get dressed. There was something about this bitch that he could not bring himself to walk away from. She was sexy, but so were all of the other bitches that he fucked with. He was beginning to think that it had to do with the fact that he could not tame her.

As they entered her bedroom, she didn't even look at him. She turned to the mirror above her dresser and started to fix her ponytail. There was no way that she would be able to face him. As good as he was looking, she could only hope that she had the power to resist him.

Soulless stood there admiring the shape of her body through her thin, pink summer dress. There was just something about her that he could not get enough of. She turned around and looked him straight in the eyes and said, "Soulless, you gotta leave before Calico gets here. Last night was the last time.

I can't be fucking two niggas at the same time. I ain't gon' get pregnant and not know who my baby daddy is."

Soulless cut right in, "Bitch, you ain't no nun. And fuck that nigga."

"Well, I don't care how you feel about him or how you feel about me. You can't be poppin' up at my house. It's been fun, but I can't be fuckin' with you like that anymore."

"What?" Soulless said nearly laughing.

"I'm really feeling Calico and he's a stand-up guy. The streets be talking and that shit you be on gon' get you killed and I ain't got time to be goin' to no funeral."

Soulless waved her off and said, "Man, shut the fuck up. Like I said, fuck that nigga."

"Soulless, get the fuck out my house," Tammy said before turning back to the mirror.

Soulless walked up behind her. She could feel his hardness against her ass.

He stood there a moment and took her silence as a go ahead. He began running his hands along her curves.

She spoke in a less determined tone, "Soulless, leave."

No longer listening to her, he brought his lips to her ear and whispered, "Bitch, you belong to me." His hand drifted until his fingertips were playing with the hem of her dress.

"I don't belong to nobody," she said. "That's yo' problem. You think that you can just pop up and fuck me whenever you feel like it."

As his hands moved along her thighs, her tone softened into a whisper. "No, Soulless. Calico is on his way. We can't do this anymore."

Soulless whispered back, "This my pussy and you belong to me."

He moved his fingers up her thigh until he felt her panties. Her wetness had soaked through the material and he could feel her soft, fat pussy through the cotton. He slid his fingers across the material to where her clit poked out and rubbed it through the material. Tammy's mouth opened but no words *came out. With his middle finger, he moved her panties to the side. Tammy's body went into auto drive as she placed her hands on the dresser in front of her for support. Without even thinking, her legs moved apart. Her movements gave him better access to her body as she stood up on her toes. He pushed his finger into her wetness. Her pussy soaked his finger as he moved it in and out of her. He pushed another finger in and she whispered his name. She started pushing her pussy on his fingers to bring them in deeper.*

She opened her eyes and looked in the mirror, locking eyes with Soulless' reflection as she started to ride his fingers. She knew damn well that she was out of order for everything she was doing in that moment. The shit was downright trifling. She started to think about the conversation she had just had with her girlfriends the day before. One of their homegirls ended up pregnant with no real way of knowing who the baby's father was and this made Tammy begin to understand that she needed to quit Soulless. The sex was so damn good, though. On top of that, he had an edge to him that she was in love with and, although she knew she should feel disrespected when he called her "bitch," she kind of liked it.

DING DONG

"Aw, fuck! That's Calico. You gotta get the fuck outta here. Go out through the window, Soulless, please," she almost yelled as she turned around and pushed him away from her. She quickly slipped off her wet panties from under her dress, grabbed some fresh ones from out of her dresser drawer, and pulled them on.

Soulless went over and sat on her bed. "Fuck that nigga. Come over here. You ain't gotta answer the door. You want me to answer the door and tell him you ain't goin'?"

"No! Please, Soulless, can you just go out the window. You gon' fuck everything up. I really like him."

As she walked over to the window to open it for Soulless to climb out, he looked at her with disgust. "Bitch, you got me fucked up, and if you say something about me going out the window one more time, I'ma slap the fuck out yo' ass."

The doorbell rang again.

Soulless continued, "I don't give a fuck if Melchizedek was at the door. I'm leaving this bitch the way I came in."

Tammy, confused for a second, asked, "Who the fuck is Mel—? Will you at least go out the back door?"

Soulless climbed further onto her bed, kicked back, and pulled out his phone. "I gotta call my brother, so you got five minutes to get rid of that nigga before I walk out that front door."

DING DONG...DING DONG

Soulless gave a grin and said, "You better quit playing before I be the only one in this house capable of walking out the front door." He pulled out his gun and put it down on the bed beside him as he continued to scroll through his phone.

Tammy's cell phone started ringing. "Fuck! That's him calling!"

"Time is ticking," Soulless said before turning all of his attention to his phone. "What's up, big bro? Where the ho's at?" he asked his brother in a loud voice.

Tammy knew it was hopeless. "Fuck you, Soulless," she said as she stormed out of the room, slamming the door hard as she left.

She checked her dress one last time before heading for the front door then yelled at the top of her lungs, "Stop ringing my momma doorbell before you break it!"

She opened the door with a smile on her face.

"I thought your momma was at work," Calico said as he tried to step into the house.

"She is at work," Tammy said as she blocked him, pushing him back onto the front porch.

"What took you so long to answer the door, baby?"

"I was in the bathroom trying to get ready for yo' fine ass."

Calico wrapped his arms around her and kissed her neck. "Let's go to your room first. I got something I wanna show you."

"Nigga, we ain't goin' in there, so you can stop kissing my neck. I wanna get to King Lew's party before the haters get there and start some shit, but we can go back to your house after the party and do whatever you wanna do."

Tammy then grabbed his dick and gave him a smile. "Right now, I'm ready to dance." She turned around, put her ass on his dick and popped. As she danced against him, she looked through the window in the front door and could see the light from Soulless' phone coming down the hallway toward them. With a panic in her chest, she turned around fast, grabbed Calico by the dick and squeezed as hard as she could, causing Calico to clench his fist. She quickly ran off the porch, down the steps, and down the sidewalk.

As Soulless reached for the handle on the front door, Calico was running down the porch steps, chasing after Tammy and yelling out to her, laughing, "I'm fucking you up when I catch you."

Soulless stood on the edge of the porch wishing the nigga would glance back just once. Instead, he saw Calico catch up to Tammy in the middle of the block and put his arms around her. Soulless shook his head and muttered, "You fuckin' lame."

He slowly walked down the steps and followed the concrete path into the night.

14 | BACK TO THE MIL

"Vu, come through and shoot some of that money," said Snake, a local who could barely even be trusted by his own family.

"Nah," said Déjà Vu from the passenger seat of Calico's Maxima. "I ain't fuckin' around unless y'all shootin' twenty or better," he said before turning to Calico. "I ain't fuckin' with these niggas, bro. Pull off. They'a have a nigga out here all day for crumbs."

Five weeks after leaving Milwaukee, Calico was quickly settling into Memphis. He and Simone got a house in a nicer part of the city and, after copping the low-key Maxima from Déjà Vu, he burnt Theory's truck. He had also gotten himself an old school Camaro Z28 and stripped the interior and wheels, turning it into nothing but a shell. Although he had been telling everyone that he was putting it together for the summer, he was really using the trunk of it to stash the quarter mil and heroin that he had stolen from Theory and Soulless.

He had become cool with all of the *No Sleep* niggas and was especially tight with Déjà Vu. Déjà Vu's real name was Darius, but Calico told him his name should be "Friv," because it was frivolous to talk to him about anything besides money or how to get more money. Déjà Vu was from Chicago—off a set called Killa Ward—and had followed some money to Memphis. He stood at a slim 6'6", was baldheaded, dark-skinned, and kept a nice pair of Carti's on his face. Of all the *No Sleep* niggas, he was the only one with an exit plan out the game. The only thing holding him back was that he was trying to bring everybody else up with him.

As Calico drove through traffic, Déjà Vu broke down his views on life to him.

"It's about the chickens and the eagles," Déjà Vu said as he passed Calico the blunt they were smoking. "These little boys is chickens. They eat off the ground, they kick it in flocks, and they eyes is constantly lookin' down, so all they see is crumbs. I'm a mafuckin' eagle. What I look like standing on the ground next to a bunch of chickens? Man bro, fuck them. Right now I'm suffering a hustler's greatest dilemma."

"What's that?" asked Calico.

"Fuckin' recession," said Déjà Vu. "These boys out here goin' crazy with the prices—$3,150 for a zip, $12,500 for a hunnit grits. Shit is crazy out here."

Calico could not understand why people put themselves through so much unnecessary stress. He and Theory had tried their hands at a lot of things as shorties, but the dope boy shit was not in him. He didn't have the patience for it. "What you gon' do, sell dope all ya life?"

Déjà Vu looked up at him as if he was out of his mind. He hit the blunt and let the smoke out slowly. "Bro, I'm a eagle for real. I got a family to take care of. My brother dead and left me with nieces and nephews to take care of. As soon as I get my money right, I'm opening up a car lot—For Eagles Only, baby. This shit I'm on now is just temporary."

Calico could see the vision as he pulled up to Déjà Vu's house to drop him off. If there was one thing he respected, it was a man who knew how to chase something bigger than the ghetto. He was certain that he could be of a lot of help to Déjà Vu.

———

The next day, Calico hit up Déjà Vu and told him to come through. With Simone frying eggs and turkey bacon, he had no plans of leaving the crib. The way he saw it, he needed Déjà Vu just as much as Déjà Vu needed him. He was about to see if the nigga was really about what he was talking about.

An hour and a half later, Déjà Vu pulled up to the house before hitting up Calico's phone.

"I'm outside," he told Calico when he answered.

"Come on."

Déjà Vu got out and headed to the door, where Calico greeted him.

"Follow me," Calico said and led Déjà Vu into the basement. Calico was never one for too much small talk so he got right down to it, pulling two ounces of heroin from his pocket and tossing it to Déjà Vu.

Déjà Vu caught the work and stared at it. Knowing what it was, he looked to Calico. "What's this about?"

"I was thinking about yo' exit plan," Calico said. "I know you be gettin' it. Let's see how serious you are about gettin' out of this shit."

Déjà Vu looked to the package once more before looking back at Calico. He had no clue where the nigga had gotten the shit from, but there was no doubt that it had come right on time for him. Calico was a real nigga.

"Give me seventy-two hours," Déjà Vu said before turning and heading straight for the door.

Calico smiled as he watched Déjà Vu leave to get right to work. He grabbed his phone and dialed Tammy, but it went straight to voicemail. He knew that she was probably upset about him leaving so abruptly, but he knew she would have never understood if he tried to explain it to her.

He left her a message. "Man, it's goin' on six weeks and you still playin' these games? I just want to hear my son's voice, so I would appreciate it if you would answer the phone or just let him answer it. I'm trying to get some money to you too so quick playing games. Tell my son I love him."

Calico ended the call frustrated and mad. Had he not been on the run, he would have made his way back to the Mil to check her ass.

"Hello?"

"I'm outside."

It had not even been forty-eight hours and already Déjà Vu was pulling back up in front of Calico's house in his LS 400 Lexus.

Calico came out and climbed into the car. "What's to it?"

Déjà Vu said nothing as he handed him twenty-six bands.

Calico looked at the cash, not even sure if it was correct or not. "Man, you like a day early."

Déjà Vu simply laughed and fired up a blunt as they sat in the car.

Calico looked at him and smiled as he opened the glove compartment. "This is for the vision," he said, and tossed the four rubber-banded stacks of money inside. He then opened the center console. "And this is for your nieces and nephews." He began pulling ounces from his hoodie pockets and stuffing them into the console.

Déjà Vu, who was counting the ounces as they dropped into the console, did the math quickly in his head. *One, two, three, four,* he thought to himself as the zips continued to fall. *Ten, eleven, twelve, thirteen, fourteen.* His eyes remained locked in the distance as the sound of the ounces falling was all that he could hear. *Seventeen, eighteen...* He knew right then that Calico had just given him half a brick. He was going to take the eighteen, re-rock it, and turn it into damn near a full brick by the time he was done. He knew he would have close to a quarter of a million dollars when he got done with it. He had to giggle a bit to himself.

As Calico closed the console, Déjà Vu looked to him and smiled. He loved it when he met real ones. Déjà Vu wondered if anyone else in the crew knew just how loaded Calico was. As far as he was concerned, it was none of their business.

"No less than thirty days," Déjà Vu said as they shook hands.

"For Eagles Only," Calico replied.

Just then, Simone's son burst out through the front door of the house and ran up to the car with a super soaker in his hands. He trained the plastic weapon on the car where Calico was sitting. "My momma said get out of the car right now. The food is done."

"This li'l mafucka bet' not—"

Before Déjà Vu had the chance to finish what he was saying, Simone's son was spraying the car.

Both men hopped out and got on his ass, but he was able to make it back to the safety of his mother before either of them could catch him.

"You might as well stay and eat," Calico said.

"No," said Simone. "Déjà Vu can eat at home, or whatever bitch he finna go fuck can feed him."

Déjà Vu looked to Simone and laughed. She knew that he still had a crush on her, but he was far too cool with Calico to even look at her in such a way these days. "Just for that slick-ass remark, I'm staying. And, I want a big-ass plate."

After they ate, Déjà Vu left and Calico helped Simone with the dishes before she left to take her son to visit Vision. Being home alone, he found it the perfect opportunity to try Tammy again. Again, he got no answer. Just as he hung up the phone, Li'l Larry from next door popped into his head. He quickly dialed the number and got an answer after a few rings.

"If it ain't about money, I'm finna hang up!"

"Listen, li'l homie, it's Calico. I need you to do me a favor."

"Calico?" asked Li'l Larry staring at his phone. "Like, Calico, Calico?"

"Yeah, man. How many Calicos you know? Check this out, li'l dog. I need you to run next door and give the phone to Tammy. I need to holla at her right fast."

Li'l Larry was stone silent as he searched for the words. Was Calico really this far out of the loop?

"Hello? Larry?" Calico looked at his phone, thinking maybe it had disconnected, but then Li'l Larry spoke again.

"Man, bro…man, bro. Where you been at? You ain't heard?"

"Heard what? Spit it out," demanded Calico. "What you gotta say, man? Go take her the phone."

"Man, listen. She gone."

"What you mean she gone? Where she go?"

"Man, bro, I'm just gon' have to be honest with you."

Irritated by the delay in conversation, Calico began to raise his voice. "Look man, I ain't got time for no bullshit—talk to me."

"Man, that shit was all over the news. The police was all over the hood. Everybody was looking for you, man. Mafucka went in there and shot her and li'l Calvin up."

Calico's mouth dropped open. He could not believe what he was hearing.

"And that ain't even the half of it," Li'l Larry continued. "That same night, somebody stopped by yo' OG crib and chopped them up with a axe."

As tears filled his eyes, only one word could escape his lips: "Who?"

"Look, man. I fuck with you, so I'm gon' tell you what it is. Word on the streets is that it was that nigga without a soul."

It was all Calico needed to hear and he ended the call abruptly. He stormed into his bedroom and grabbed his pistol and the two extra clips then snatched the three g's that he had on the dresser before storming out of the house, not even bothering to close the door behind him. He jumped into the Maxima and stabbed out, leaving his phone in the house. He was on his way back to Milwaukee. He was going to find Soulless. As he drove, he knew that his actions were going to put him back in prison for life. *Waupun. Damn. Waupun.*

They stole the language of my ancestors
From me and my people
Still, I rose out of the fire
The wings of my inner phoenix
Scorched from the heat of the fiery pit
Where black bodies lay, on top of black bodies
Devils, with their white supremacy, never settling
Dark clouds of pure hate, so thick it's binding
But I survived the fires of blasphemy and bigotry
Like Shadrach, Meshach, and Abednego
Calvin, Black man
Blessed with the spirit of Shaka The Great
Soul of a warrior
Locks like Samson
Never to be severed
This fight will never be settled
I will forever stand up for me and mine
As long as these soulless bodies
Continue to bring me and mine down
Calvin, African man
Blessed with the spirit of his ancestors
Watching over him
Unbreakable—men
Zulu—men
Won't bend—men
Men—fashioned in the image of the Creator
By the Creator
Out of beautiful, majestic, southern African soil
The Mother Land
Where men of my caliber are built, not broken
Brought up, not brought down
Still, they slash at me
I feel them

These blue-eyed, soulless serpents
Ripping at my very being
Trying to hold down the king in me
Still, I ascend
Out of this furnace of affliction and distress
Destroy my dream
I'll create a grander one
Tear a limb from my body
I'll grow back a stronger one
I will always come back whole
A king, with no cut
Walking down an unnamed, loose soil road
With an ebony cloth draped over his solid shoulders
That was unmatched, untamed , and unscorched
And that ebony cloth came out of
The Lost Tribe of Shabazz

"Aye, what you think about this title—Majestic Soil?" Calico asked his cellie as he walked into the room.

Asad had an obvious look of discontent on his face.

"What's wrong, Asad?" Calico asked.

Asad looked to Calvin, who was sitting against the bunk with his pen and notepad in hand. It was clear that he had been working on one of his latest poems. Asad had met the young man three years ago when he first came through the joint. The two of them had been in the same cell since. He liked the fact that Calvin, unlike most of the other youngsters, had a head on his shoulders. It had taken some time to convince the young man to take his Shahada, but Calvin finally got down and submitted to the will of Allah. From that day forward, he had been like a sponge, soaking up every jewel that Shamir had for him.

"Man, that young brother who killed my son just got here."

Calico needed to hear no more. He'd had this conversation many times with Asad. Because it had always been a hypothetical, Asad never committed to what he expected to do upon seeing the young man. Now that the moment had arrived, Calico could tell that there was a lot of anger coming from the man.

Asad was a stocky fellow with seven thick locks that went past his lower back like Samson. He was from the east cost and was only in Wisconsin for four months when he caught his case. Calico had gotten all of his understanding of Islam from Asad and he was still learning. He had a feeling that in this moment it was for him to be the voice of reason, however.

"What you plan on doing?"

"I'm killing him," Asad stated simply.

"Hold it, Asad. A Muslim only has the right to defend himself with the same amount of force being used on him. There is no threat in this situation. This can only be an act of vengeance. That's not just, my brother. Killing is prohibited. We did not come from killing. If you have the power to preserve life, do so, because you will be accountable for everything that you have killed in the last day, even a small insect."

"It's easier said when your son's killer isn't a few hundred feet from you. I will never intentionally disobey the will of Allah by committing the act of murder, but I see this as a kill or be killed situation. I feel that this young man poses a threat to me, so I am dealing with him the way that I see fit. If I am wrong, I will get on my face to the east and ask that Allah forgive me. There is no way for me to step away from Islam while I do this, so my only option is to deal with the consequences. I could never say that I am no longer a Muslim because of what I am about to do, even though I am not a Muslim for the moment."

Asad knew that Calvin would be looking for a more in-depth explanation and the truth was that he had no way of making it simpler. The fact of the matter was that, even if he could, he did not have the time to sit down and spell it out for him. As he turned to leave, Calvin spoke once more.

"Talk to him first, Asad. See if he is remorseful for what he did. At the end of the day, he is a kid, and if you can seek forgiveness from the Merciful Allah, who are you to rob him of that right?"

Had it not made sense, Asad was certain that he and Calvin would have been fighting. He was acting as if he had no regard for the feelings that he was experiencing. At the same time, he knew Calvin was only speaking truth.

"Okay, young man. I'll give him a chance to speak. But, if I don't like what I hear, I'm sending him to Allah leaking."

As the tiers were called for chow, Asad spotted the boy going into the chow hall with a different tier. Though they were dining with the tier, he needed to make certain that he was able to get a seat at the same table. He waited patiently for the boy to grab a tray before he skipped everyone in the line and made his way over. There were some in the chow hall who knew what he was on, and he knew that they were waiting for it to go down. Today, he was not at all fucked up about putting on a show.

"Whattup?" the young man asked as he carefully eyed the stranger sitting across from him. With this being his first time in prison, he had no idea what to expect from anyone. He had gotten a few pointers from some of the cats that he had been bunked with in intake, but there was still apprehension in his spirit. He just hoped that it wasn't showing to everyone else.

Asad eyed the young man, trying his damnedest to keep a promise. "How's it going, young brother? This ya first time locked up?"

The young man stared for a moment before responding. "Yeah man, I fucked around and got jammed up in this weak-ass system."

Asad laughed to himself as he listened to the young man speak about what he barely knew about. "If you don't mind my asking, how long they give you?"

"I lost at trial and got life. Why, you good with that law shit?"

"I'm the best," said Asad. "Though you lost at trial, you may still have some grounds to get back on. What was the situation with your case?"

"I popped this nigga who owed me some cash."

Asad began to breathe slowly as he stared over at Calvin and a few other brothers in the distance. "What made you do something like that?"

"Well, he was my nigga, but I let him hold a dime of some loud one night and he acted like he ain't wanna pay me the next day. So I got on his ass."

Asad already knew the entire story from a friend of his son. The kid gave his son the weed as a gift for his birthday. The next day, he came back demanding payment and Asad's son refused. That was when he was shot. The shit was senseless.

"Why would he not want to pay you?" Asad continued to question.

"His bitch ass gon' say somethin' like I gave him the shit. But I don't never give my shit away."

"Is it possible that you were drunk and don't remember?"

"I mean, I was turnt up, but I don't just be givin' away money and shit. Either way it go, that bitch-ass nigga knew how I get down. He should've paid me."

Asad chuckled as it became evident that the young man did not seem to feel a shred of remorse for what he had done. However, he continued to look for any sign of hope in the boy. "That's real messed up," Asad continued. "Don't you feel bad for doin' him like that? What about his family?"

"Shit, fuck his family. What about me? I'm the one in this mothafucka with life."

This was all that Asad could stand. It was going to happen. Asad knew exactly what he needed to do to get it done. First, he had to pack all of his property. He was certain they would ship him off to supermax after this one and it would be awhile before he made it out.

"I feel you, young brother. Well, they call me Asad. If you need anything, I'm around. Just watch who you deal with in here. A lot of these men will try to get over on you. As a matter of fact, do you smoke?"

"Why? You got some loud?" asked the young man, anxious to distract himself from reality.

"Yeah. I got some loud."

"Is it some loud, loud though?" he smiled as he forced an expression of disbelief. "'Cause you know all I smoke is loud. The shit I had left niggas paralyzed."

As the wiggling and giggling continued, Asad found himself desperately needing to move around. "Check it out—meet me on the rec field at one thirty, and we gon' burn one, aight?"

The young man nodded his head eagerly. "Aight, aight. Don't be bullshittin' though, Skool. I'ma be out there, man."

"I got you."

Asad made his way back to the cell hall and headed for his tier. When he got there, he crept a few cells past his own to talk to a killer named Sandman, one of the heads of a major gang in the prison. They were tight so he knew that this was his best source.

"Let me see the scissors," Asad requested.

"Which ones?" asked Sandman, already knowing the situation.

"The ones you need the screwdriver for," Asad confirmed. It was clear that he was going to break them down and make a shank with them.

"Let me do it," offered Sandman. "I already got some other business to handle anyway. I can knock that out on the way to doing what I gotta do."

Asad just stood and looked at Sandman. It was the look in Asad's eyes that told him that Asad had to do this one himself. Sandman passed the scissors to him.

"Get rid of it when you done, homie. It's been real. I might be up there in Boscobel with you in a minute if these niggas act like they wanna push on us."

One thirty could not have come quickly enough for Asad as he made his way out onto the rec field. Like clockwork, the young man was standing there waiting to get high.

"You got it?" he asked as Asad walked up.

"Yeah, yeah," Asad said looking around. "Let's go to the far end of the rec field, though. I don't like all these dudes in my business."

As they began to walk, Asad pulled out a joint and a lighter from his coat pocket. When they got to a good spot, he handed them to the young man and said, "We good now. Fire that shit up."

The young man did as he was told before immediately choking from the smoke. "Damn!" he said, quickly passing the joint as he tried to contain the slobber coming out of his mouth. "That some mothafuckin' gas. Where you get that shit from?"

Asad laughed. "You can't handle it, young man? I thought you only smoked the best."

"Yeah, but I been locked up fighting this ho'-ass case for the last year and a half. I ain't been able to get my hands on no shit like that."

Asad kept walking, leading the young man as far away from everyone else as possible. Though they were right under the tower, he knew that it would still take forever for first responders to get to them.

"Speaking of your case, I think I discovered some new evidence for you."

"Already?" asked the young man as Asad took a number of deep pulls from the joint and passed it back to him.

The fact that he had passed it in clear view of the tower did not settle well with the young man. When he saw that the guard was not looking, however, he accepted the joint and continued smoking. He still wondered why Skool had been so reckless.

"What kind of new evidence you got?"

"Well, it might not get you back in court, but I think it's important for you to know before you get where you goin'."

"What? What the fuck you talkin' 'bout, Skool?"

"That was my son that you killed, young man."

In an instant, the young man saw the resemblance and stepped back. He dropped the joint, took another step back, and pulled a sharpened pencil from his waistband. Before he could make another move, Asad was all over him.

The first right hook cracked his eye socket, leaving him dazed and completely blind in that eye as blood spilled from it like a faucet. From there, Asad grabbed him by the collar of his coat and his pant leg before flipping him off his feet and driving him into the earth with a force strong enough to crack his ribcage. The alarm bell was already ringing and Asad could see the officers running toward them in the distance. He knew he didn't have much more time.

He snatched the boy up by the collar of his coat and began smashing punches into his face as he thought of his only son lying cold in the ground. As the officers got closer, he pulled the broken half of the scissors from his coat pocket and delivered punctures to the boy's neck as deeply and rapidly as he could manage. The feeling of warm blood greeting his hand with every stroke was satisfying. The sound of the boy's gurgling gasps for help was music to his ears.

He got the weapon into the boy's neck and esophagus close to thirty times before a female officer tackled him with all that she had. She was surely a rookie, as the veterans knew to let it play out before they intervened. For her, it was a rookie mistake that could have ended her life that day. It was clear that he could have easily killed her as well, but he surrendered instead. He had done what he came to do.

—◆—

After seeing his mentor escorted off the rec field in handcuffs, Calvin knew it would be the last time he ever saw Asad. The man was a lifer and he was sure that he would never be going where Asad was headed.

He made it back to the room and saw all of Asad's things neatly packed up in a box by the door. Calvin threw his favorite book on top then sat down *at the desk to write a letter. The situation was fucked up and he needed to share it with Tammy. He picked up the pen and—*

AAAAAARrrrrrhhhhh!!!!!

—⬤—

Calico snapped out of his thoughts and quickly realized that he was drifting into the wrong side of the highway. He had zoned out remembering the important conversation he had with Asad about murder and Islam. Now, he was able to understand Asad's plight. While he knew his mind was made up about what he intended to do to Soulless, he also knew that there would be no way for him to temporarily step away from his beliefs. He had no idea how he was going to reconcile his transgressions, but he knew one thing for sure—Soulless was about to die slow.

15 | FINESSE

The day was sunny and beautiful in Milwaukee. The gas station was jam-packed as an all-white Lincoln Navigator with 24-inch stock rims pulled into the Citgo. Five-Seven jumped out of the driver's seat and swiped his card at the pump.

As he stood there pumping his gas, he watched the traffic go by. A slick-ass blood-red Maserati Quattroporte sedan caught his eye as it skated by on some 24-inch Forgiatos.

Damn, he killin' the city, he thought. *The way that machine is purrin', I know it's clutchin' a twin-turbo V8 under the hood.*

The Maserati slowed as if the driver sitting behind the tint had missed his turn into the Citgo. Five-Seven continued watching as the car busted a smooth U-turn, pulled into the gas station, and parked at the pump right across from him. With an uneasy feeling in his gut, he reached for his snub-nosed .357 Blackhawk. He kept it close to his side, prepared to shoot. Hyper-focused on the tinted window as it lowered, he locked eyes on the driver. It took a second to recognize him because he had cut his dreads and now had a low cut. It was Maserati with a big smile on his face.

"Five-Seven, the streets told me that you went out and copped this year's model. That same day, I was sitting in my closet going through shoe-boxes looking for the right color of Gucci loafers when I came across a li'l money I had misplaced in one of the boxes. So, I took the li'l Gucci box into the Maserati dealership and copped this ol' thang."

Five-Seven could not believe this nigga. He looked at Maserati with a stone-cold stare and liquid nitrogen running through his veins. Had it not been broad daylight with witnesses all around, he would have shot him in the face right then and there. All he saw was red as he walked over to the car with his pistol still in his hand and close to his side. Seeing this, Maserati laughed and raised both hands up in the air playfully.

"Hands are up. Don't shoot, my nigga. Jump in for a minute."

Five-Seven, curious about what this bitch could want, made his way around to the passenger-side door and jumped in.

"Roll up the window," he ordered Maserati. He still felt the need to pop him and, if he did, he at least wanted it to be behind tint.

Maserati complied and closed the window. "Man, look. I'm here to atone for all of my transgressions, baby."

"It's been over seven weeks, Maserati. What makes you think it was okay to pull that shit on me? What gave you the impression that I was a lick?" Five-Seven asked out of genuine curiosity.

"Look, Five-Seven, someone pulled it on me and I'm not talkin' about a light-ass nine zips. But, it's a new day and I got something new for you, baby. Look in the glove compartment."

Five-Seven opened it and found nine zips of dope inside a zip-lock bag. As he reached in and removed it, Maserati continued talking.

"Look, I'm giving you that, even though I already know you got that nine zips off. Because it was dope, just stepped on a few times too many. But I'm back like the second coming of the Messiah—with straight drop and I really walked on water this time to get it. The real question is, are you gon' straighten out all your people?"

Five-Seven looked down at the zip-lock. "This don't straighten out shit with me. I'm still feelin' some kinda way."

His grip tightened around the Blackhawk. He knew that this would be the perfect opportunity to lace Maserati because he had never seen him by himself.

Maserati saw that Five-Seven was on the edge and close to pulling something. "Easy, Chi-town. I got you like Burger King."

He picked his phone up out of his lap and turned the screen so that Five-Seven could see it clearly. His fingers hit the letters quickly—*let me get four whoppers*. He then hit send. In less than five seconds, there were two knocks on Maserati's window. He let his window down.

It took Five-Seven by surprise. He watched Maserati's top shooter, Tango, pass a Burger King bag inside the car to him. Maserati then passed it to Five-Seven and rolled up the window. With a smile on his face, he watched Five-Seven as Five-Seven watched Tango jump back into the tinted, black Explorer that had been parked behind them the whole time. He picked up a joint of sour diesel out of his ashtray and lit it.

"See, Seven, I coulda let my young wolves loose because they always ready to eat. Shit, they instantly started salivating at the sound of your name. But, I stopped to bless you and you come walkin' towards me with a six-shot in your hand. You lucky I pushed on the brake pedal to stop them because those young boys got some shit in their hands that people only see in the movies—shit that would take down the Predator."

He gave a little laugh.

"It's no less than three hundred and fifty shots in that truck right now, along with four wolves who are trained to go, ready to kill and die for me."

For the very first time, Maserati lost his smile as he looked Five-Seven directly in the eyes.

"Out of respect for your fallen comrade—Theory—I ain't on no gangsta shit. So do yourself a favor and loosen up your grip on that iron and put it in your little pocket before I take my foot off the brake pedal and things end badly for you."

Five-Seven then understood that the brake light was the signal and the only thing holding Maserati's men back. He realized that he had underestimated Maserati and knew he wasn't lying. Tango's body count was enhancing weekly. According to Soulless, Tango's sadistic pleasure wasn't about the affliction of pain or killing alone. It was more about his assertion of power and his lust to dominate, to reduce other men into submission and see the fear in their eyes—especially OGs. Soulless told him to watch out for the young soldier, who was only 19, but not a fool and not to be taken lightly.

Five-Seven did not move as he weighed his options. He was outmanned and outgunned.

Damn, he thought.

Living for moments like this, the smile reappeared on Maserati's face. "Anyways, there's four more zips in that bag for you, baby. You can add that to the other nine."

Smile now and beg for your life later, Five-Seven thought as he slid the Blackhawk in his pocket. He opened up the Burger King bag and dropped the other nine zips in it.

"Until next time," Five-Seven said as he opened the car door and climbed out of the sedan. As he headed toward his Navigator, he locked eyes with Tango in the truck. With a mug on his face, Tango waved *bye bye* to Five-Seven with a fully automatic Glock 10 in his hand with the 100-round monkey nuts fastened to it.

"Well played," Five-Seven said under his breath.

He jumped back into his Navigator, pushed start, and pulled off into traffic.

"Well played, indeed."

"Man, look," spoke Five-Seven from his couch where he sat as Glock and AP listened intently. "I know this nigga got a load, just on the strength that he in a position to straighten all the niggas he finessed."

"Didn't he unload nine zips of wham on you, too?" asked AP, recalling the beginning of the summer when Maserati flooded the city with shit stepped on so heavy, it may as well have been bricks, halves, and quarter slabs of straight baking soda.

"Yeah," Five-Seven lamented through gritted teeth, "but his bitch ass damn near tripped over hisself tryna straighten me when I caught him in traffic. He dropped four on top of a fresh nine, right there on the spot. This new shit is straight fish scale too."

Five-Seven thought about how he must have sounded to his homies in that moment. He didn't want any confusion as to where he stood on the subject of Maserati. "I don't give a fuck if he had a whole brick for me. I'm killin' his bitch ass for tryin' me, like my name ain't velvet in the streets. He think them *Screw Tape* niggas from Miami gon' keep him safe. I don't care who his new plug is."

"He really get his muscle from Tango," Glock clarified. "It's gon' be hard for us to catch up wit' him anyway. He moves like a ghost through the streets."

"Tango bet' not jump his young ass in my business," Five-Seven declared, knowing that Tango's reputation preceded him. He popped a Perk 30 in his mouth and chased it with a bottle of orange juice. "I fucked around and found a flaw in Maserati's armor. His main vibe, Syretta, likes the taste of pussy, on the low. My li'l cousin from Atlanta got her in her emotions, and they only been knowing each other for a few weeks."

Glock sat upright knowing that Five-Seven only had one little cousin from Atlanta. "Megan's li'l thick ass is bisexual?! I knew she was a li'l freak!"

Megan was 5'5" with the body of a stripper. She had an hourglass figure with wide hips and a near exact one-inch gap between her thighs. Glock never hid his infatuation with her. "She still in the Mil?"

"Yeah," Five-Seven smirked, recalling a conversation he had with Megan concerning Glock. "She made a quick run back to the A today to knock out some business. She'll be back in a few days, but her li'l stankin' ass don't like bitches. She just loves attention. I guess Syretta really wanna crack her li'l ass because li'l cuz be all through the city in Syretta's truck and rockin' designer like the shit is free."

Five-Seven looked to Glock. "Megan said she's too thirsty, like yo' ass." Before Glock could protest, Five-Seven continued, "She said that they was ridin' and shit one night and she started to doze off the lean. Syretta damn near tried to rape her because when she woke up they were pulled to the side of the road and her dress was pushed up, her panties were down around her ankles, and Syretta's head was between her legs."

"Damn!" Glock salivated. "She don't know that's yo' cousin?"

"Nah, cuz ain't giving out that kind of info. Anyway, cuz ain't got no feelings for the bitch. She just see a bag. She said for five racks, she'll get the bitch alone for me."

"So, what's good?" AP asked.

"We snatch the bitch, make her tell us where Maserati lays his head, we bring him back here, and get him to answer the million-dollar question— where the cash at? Then we make 'em disappear," Five-Seven explained.

"Make 'em disappear?" Glock questioned as he stood to his feet and put on his jacket. "I ain't dealin' with no more body parts. I'm leavin' them mafuckas wherever they die. Y'all can do whatever you want after that."

"Man, look, you betta stop playin'. We gon' do whatever we got to do to pull this off right," Five-Seven argued. "We walked away last time with damn near a half mil, so if it's not broke, don't try to fix it."

When he saw that Glock was still on the fence, he continued. "Man, look, I already talked to Soulless and he wit' it. We worked out what we'll need to make 'em vanish. So, as soon as li'l cuz touch back down, it's a go. I already went out and bought all the shit we need, so just play ya position."

"Man, fuck what Glock talkin' 'bout," AP said. "Run that shit by me again, Five-Seven."

"We gon' snatch the bitch up first and then force her to tell us where he live, who be in the house, and the layout to it. When we get him, we get the money."

"Like I said, I'm leaving the bodies where they fall," Glock reiterated. "I ain't got time to be dealing with all that blood again."

"*I ain't got time to be dealing with all that blood again,*" AP mocked Glock in a whiny voice before turning to Five-Seven. "Man, what we gon' do with these mafuckas?"

"You know that big pipe in the basement? Well, after we get all the information we need from them, we gon' hang 'em up by their feet over the drain in the floor, cut their throats, and let the bodies bleed out in it. After we got 'em in pieces, we gon' use the wire cutters I got to slice off they fingertips to throw off identification. We gon' use the pliers to take out they teeth. I got some concrete down there and some empty paint buckets, so we can weigh down the buckets with the concrete after we put they heads in them. Then, we gon' throw the rest of they pieces into thirty-three gallon trash bags I bought and dump they asses in different locations. Oh yeah, and I got some boric acid down there to scrub down the basement and everything afterwards," Five-Seven explained as he went to put on his jacket.

Glock continued to complain, "I'm tellin' you—I ain't fuckin' with all that blood, Seven."

"Nigga, I'm telling *you*–dead bodies don't bleed after you drain the blood from them. That's why Soulless said we should let them bleed out down in the basement for eight to ten hours before we touch them again. Listen, I just saw something about it on forensic files, too, man."

"Man, I'm with you, Seven" said AP

"Fuck it—by any means," Glock added as they made their way to the door.

"By any means, then. Next time, put some bass behind it," Five-Seven said as he reached for the doorknob."

Just as Five-Seven opened the door to leave his crib with Glock and AP, they found themselves at gunpoint. "Whoa, Calico! What's good, baby?"

Calico stood on the other side of the door with his pistol trained on the three men coming out of the house. He scanned the hallway, prepared to empty every shell at the first sight of Soulless. "Where that bitch-ass nigga at?"

AP, who had been standing behind Glock and Five-Seven, immediately pulled his heat and aimed at Calico. "Hold up, nigga. You got us fucked up."

"Drop it," demanded Calico, "before I put all of you down!"

"Wait a minute, wait a minute," said Five-Seven, trying his best to get both men to relax. He turned to Calico first and lifted his own shirt. "Look, Calico. We all got heats, but why take it there if we can figure this shit out like men. Come on now, baby. We been fuckin' with each other for too long for this."

"Where that savage at?" Calico asked again, completely disregarding AP.

It was clear to Five-Seven who he was talking about. "Shit, Soulless ain't been fuckin' with us since he went off the rails, G. He ain't been the same since his brother got killed. For some reason, he thinks you had something to do with it. We told him that you and Theory had been best friends since the playground, but you know how that li'l nigga get when his mind made up. Ain't no reasoning with him."

Calico lowered his weapon a little and Five-Seven instructed AP to do the same.

"Look, Five-Seven, that shit wasn't supposed to go down like that," Calico began to explain.

"Well, come in the house before the neighbors fuck around and call the police. I know you fucked up about that foul shit Soulless pulled with ya people, but you at home when you here, dawg. You know that."

As they all stepped back into the house, Five-Seven continued to rap to the boy. "Yeah, that shit was fucked up, Cal. Everybody been looking for you. The police ran up in here saying that they was looking for you for questioning. They think you snapped and killed ya people but me and Glock was just talking about that shit. We all know who it really was. I mean, I don't know if you men could ever sit down and talk about the shit because too many loved ones are involved but I'm gon' try to text the nigga and let him know that you wanna meet with him. Y'all handle it how y'all handle it, you feel me?"

Five-Seven pulled out his phone and quickly texted: GET THE BASEMENT READY AND CALL SOULLESS.

As Five-Seven went back to finessing Calico to distract him, Glock felt his phone vibrate. He checked it and realized that he had gotten the text from Five-Seven. As Calico, AP, and Five-Seven headed into the living room, Glock pretended to head for the bathroom before dipping down the stairs into the basement. When he got downstairs, he called Soulless' cell as he pulled out a box containing the items Five-Seven purchased, starting with the gallon of boric acid.

"Talk to me," Soulless answered.

"We at Five-Seven's and that nigga upstairs right now," said Glock as he laid everything in the middle of the floor before rolling out the plastic.

Glock thought he heard someone yelling for help in the background on Soulless' end of the line, giving him pause.

"Shut the fuck up!" Glock heard Soulless demand. Then he heard a loud crash in the background.

"Where the fuck you at? What you doin'?" asked Glock, beginning to cut the plastic into sheets before taping it to the walls and floor of the basement.

"Shit, in the middle of nowhere, busting a move. Anyways, who upstairs?"

"That ho'-ass nigga, Calico," Glock said, as he began to cover the basement floor and walls in plastic.

"What?!"

Glock heard a series of gunshots on the other end of the phone. "What the fuck was that?" he asked Soulless. "What's goin' on?"

"Keep that nigga there," Soulless commanded, "I'm on my way. Y'all bet' not let that nigga leave the house. I'm about twenty-five minutes out."

Back upstairs, Calico found himself sitting on Five-Seven's couch explaining what had gone down between him and Theory the night that Theory died. Although Five-Seven was hearing him out, AP seemed to be emitting an awful lot of heat from where he sat and Calico was starting to question whether the nigga believed what he was telling them.

After about twenty minutes of talking, Calico finished with, "So, that's how the shit went down. Bro got upset because I got the best of him and he pulled a pistol on me."

"Yeah, but why the fuck you rob him?" asked AP.

Calico looked to him. "To keep it real, I wasn't thinking. All I knew was that I was on the run for so much shit and I had nothing. In hindsight, I was bogus for that, but me and Soulless coulda straightened it all out. He didn't have to murder my mothafuckin' kid and my momma."

"How the fuck was y'all gon' straighten him having to bury his brother, nigga? That shit foul."

Five-Seven could see that AP was starting to rock his emotions on his sleeve. He needed to regain control of the dialogue if he wanted Calico to remain still. When Calico first sat down, he had set his heat down on the coffee table, so Five-Seven was sure that they would be able to get the ups on him if needed.

"Look, Calico. I know how Theory could get at times," Five-Seven assured him. "He had pride issues, just like all of us. It's fucked up what happened, but I'd hate to see you and Soulless kill each other over this shit."

"I'ma keep it real with you," Calico said as he looked Five-Seven in his eyes. "One of us gotta die. It gotta happen. That nigga took everything I love."

"Nigga, you took everything he loved, too," AP reminded him, nearly on the edge of his seat.

Calico looked at AP in shock before seeing that Five-Seven was signaling for him to calm down. Something was not right about this picture. He was beginning to wonder if he was a sitting duck. He looked to Five-Seven, who stared back at him. Then they both looked to the gun that Calico had set down on the table. Calico realized that this was potentially a fatal mistake. He should have known better than to think he would be able to reason with any of these niggas. He slowly made a move to stand before speaking.

"Look, man I need to get up out of here and visit my momma's grave."

Five-Seven saw that the boy was going for his gun and upped his. "Hol' up, Cal. You know I can't let you do that."

Calico looked to AP, who had also pulled his heat. "What the fuck is this?"

"You know what the fuck it is, nigga." AP was now on his feet as he aimed his gun at Calico. "You killed Theory and robbed him like he was a nobody. Now, you finna get it."

Calico looked around, wondering if they had alerted Soulless that he had shown up. Under these circumstances, he knew that if Soulless walked through the door, his life was over. As Five-Seven swiped his gun from the table, Calico made up his mind that he would much rather risk being gunned down by them than be subjected to the psychopathic mind of Soulless.

"Nigga, Theory wasn't no mothafuckin' angel. Y'all know how he got down," Calico said.

"Nigga, yo' bitch wasn't no angel either. I saw the ho' come out the basement with the DN—"

Before AP could finish his sentence, Glock walked into the room, triggering all three men to divert their attention to him. Calico saw the moment as a sliver of opportunity and knew it would be the largest window of escape that he would get. It was now or never. Immediately, he made a run for it and dove for the big bay window, hurling himself through as shards of glass found refuge in his flesh. His adrenaline was pumping so hard that he felt nothing. He had barely touched the ground before he was up on his feet and running through the front yard. The moment he sprang from the curb, he was nearly smacked by the hood of a car. He leapt up and slid across the hood as the shots rang out.

PART III:

Looking Down on Reality

16 | CUJO

"**M**an, I know this ain't that nigga, Ready Red," Cujo said to himself as he pulled into Johnny's Chicken Shack.

"This nigga got me fucked up," he continued muttering to himself as he watched Ready Red step out of the driver's seat of his whip. "And he went and copped that new Audi A-8 on me, while I'm riding in this punk-ass bubble Chevy?" Cujo growled with pure hatred in his eyes.

Ready Red only took a few steps before going back to his car as if he forgot something. He leaned down and spoke through the open driver's side window to his girl, Tina.

"Damn, bae, I'm high as fuck. What you say you want to eat again?"

"Hmpphh, that's why you should stop smoking that shit," Tina stated in a frustrated tone. "I said I want a Italian beef, double-dipped, baby."

As he watched Ready Red leaning in the window, Cujo noticed a fat-ass gold rope with a diamond Jesus-head medallion dangling from around his neck.

"This nigga got money like that, that he goin' and buyin' me shit? 'Cause I know he bought that for me," Cujo mumbled to himself, convincing himself that the chain was his.

Cujo stepped from his car. "This gon' be like taking candy from a baby," he told himself as he quickly approached Ready Red.

As Cujo started to reach out to grab a hold of Ready Red's chain, Tina noticed him. She reached across the driver's seat, tapped Ready Red on his hand, and pointed in Cujo's direction.

At the same time, Ready Red felt someone grabbing his chain. He quickly stood up and pushed Cujo back with one hand as he grabbed his .45 automatic with the other, keeping the pistol at his waist and pointed downward.

"Aye, hold on, fam. What you on?" Ready Red asked as he took a few steps back. He knew Cujo was an animal and could lash out quickly.

"What? This shit wild! Niggas putting guns in my face now," Cujo stated, looking at Ready Red but talking to himself.

"Cujo, I ain't point no gun in yo' face. You trippin', man. You know it ain't even like that. You just came out of nowhere and reached for my jewels. I'm just being cautious," Ready Red explained.

"Naw, naw, naw, you a big boy," Cujo replied with fire in his eyes and nitrogen in his voice. "You know what you doin'. You upped a gun in my face and threatened to kill me," Cujo stated seriously.

"Man, you on one, fam," replied Ready Red as he opened the driver's door to get in. "I don't want no smoke and I ain't threatened to kill nobody." Ready Red got in the car and pulled off, expecting Cujo to show the killer side he was known for.

Three days later...

Cujo was riding down North Avenue coming from his li'l thot Trish's house. It was a good day. He had not only just gotten the best head of his life, but he also got seventeen hundred dollars out the bitch. He was on his way to cop some loud from his mans, Blunt, when he thought he saw Ready Red driving in the opposite direction.

"Hold on," he said to himself, "I know that ain't that bitch-ass nigga Ready Red," he muttered as he did a hard U-turn in the middle of rush hour.

"Is that a Audi truck on fo's?" he asked himself with a look of disgust on his face. "Man, where the fuck this dude gettin' these cars from?"

He took his window of opportunity as the light turned red, and as he inched up just close enough to see inside the truck, he was able to confirm that it was Ready Red. Cujo dropped back and followed him when the light changed.

Ready Red was too busy on his phone to notice that he had a tagalong. When he arrived at his sister's house, he jumped out of his truck and went to the driver's side back door. As he opened it, Cujo began slowly riding up on the truck.

Keeping his eyes on Ready Red, Cujo could see he was taking out a car seat. As Ready Red then put a baby bag over his shoulder, Cujo rolled up closer—window down—and fired three shots into Ready Red's chest. The impact of the bullets slammed him against the truck and then he slowly slid down the best paint job Cujo had ever seen. As Ready Red took his last breath, his son began to scream at the top of his lungs from the car seat.

Even though he had just murdered a man in broad daylight, Cujo was still preoccupied with something else, which poured out with hate as he put it into words. "And this bitch-ass nigga riding in a Audi truck!" he yelled as he beat the steering wheel like a madman before pulling off.

━━━

A short time later, Cujo pulled up on 32nd and Keefe where all the young hustlers posted up. As he put his vehicle in park and killed the engine, 19-year-old Ra-Ra walked towards him from a group of rowdy li'l niggas shooting craps.

"What it do, Cujo?" Ra-Ra asked as he extended his fist through Cujo's open window to show him some love.

Cujo dapped him back. The Glock 19 with the stick on it that he had just killed Ready Red with was on the passenger seat and Cujo casually picked it up.

"Shit, ridin' down on my li'l niggas and peepin' the landscape," Cujo replied as he began twirling the Glock on his pointer finger in Ra-Ra's view.

"What y'all fools over there on?" he asked rhetorically, clearly seeing a craps game in progress.

"Shit, gettin' the paper as usual," Ra-Ra said, then continued, "Oh, yeah, I heard that fuck-boy shit Easy pullin' on you. So, is he really asking you for fifteen g's *and* your whip?" Ra-Ra asked. "I know you ain't finna give this whip up."

"Man, fuck this piece of shit. I'm tryna sit in somethin' foreign anyways," Cujo responded.

"Piece of shit?! Man, you must be crazy. This mafucka hot," Ra-Ra commented. "This boy *still* sittin' up high, this mafucka *still* cocaine white with a sparkling shine finish, and the peanut butter leather guts *still* smooth as fuck. And hit that system for me, fam."

Cujo reluctantly turned on the sound system and boosted the volume as Future blared through the six twelves and four tweeters, causing the ground to tremble and bass to overtake the ghetto.

"See, fam. That's what it do," Ra-Ra smiled as he glorified the exceptional car.

"Yeah, man. I know," Cujo stated.

"Man, it's fucked up that Easy bitch ass didn't die. If you had bodied that fool, he wouldn't be coming at you like this," Ra-Ra responded.

"Man, what? I hit that nigga twice in the head, twice in his chest, in his arms, in his legs, up and down his back, in his neck, and in his ass," Cujo stated frustrated. "That pusy-ass chump must got like nine lives," he said as he continued twirling his gun in circles trying to entice the young hustler with it.

"But, fuck all that. Why you keep lookin' at this?" Cujo asked, holding up his Glock. "What you got out here?"

"I got this," Ra-Ra replied as he pulled a snubnosed .38 from his pocket.

"Man, quit playin'," Cujo laughed as he looked at the .38. "What you gon' do when them li'l young niggas come down here draggin' them clips? Man, what you got in yo' pockets?"

"What?" asked Ra-Ra, uneasy and unsure of what Cujo was on.

"Calm down, young shooter. I'm tryna help you by getting you something with more shots," Cujo reassured him.

"Aw, man—I just got hit so I only got like two-fifty on me," Ra-Ra replied.

"Aight, that's all you need. Plus, I need that little pop gun you got so we'll call it even," Cujo negotiated.

Ra-Ra dug into his pockets and handed Cujo the two hundred fifty dollars and his .38 through the window. Cujo then traded him the Glock.

Cujo counted out the money and said, "Fuck it—since I fuck with you, here go a hundred back. Shit, I'm finna break the gamble anyways."

"Good lookin', fam. That's one hunnit right there," Ra-Ra said, not realizing he had just tucked a gun that Cujo killed somebody with less than twenty minutes ago.

Cujo climbed out of the car and he and Ra-Ra started making their way over to the gamble.

"I got that defense, miley cyrus, loud, and a few Dracos with the nuts and a hunnit shots," Cujo informed Ra-Ra. "Everything must go. I gotta get that fifteen g's up for Easy bitch ass."

Ra-Ra studied him. "Nigga, you should *have* fifteen g's."

Cujo stopped walking, looked right at Ra-Ra, and said, "Li'l nigga, stay in your lane and just call me if you know anyone lookin'."

When they reached the gamble, everybody greeted Cujo as he knelt down and placed a bet.

"Aight, it's my turn on the dice," Cujo stated as he picked up the dice between someone's roll.

"Who gon' bet me?" Cujo taunted the crowd. "Y'all must be some broke-ass li'l niggas," he ribbed as he shook the dice.

"Man, you got me fucked up," three of the young men said in unison, not wanting to look like pussies in front of Ra-Ra.

"Aight, that's what I'm talkin' 'bout. Put y'all money where y'all mouths at," Cujo stated.

Nearly twelve hundred dollars hit the ground as they all started to get amped up and competitive, placing side bets.

"Aye, watch this nigga crap out ASAP," one of the braver ones barked.

Cujo released the dice from his hand with a spin and shouted, "Eleven," as the dice hit eleven. "Give me my money, you chumps," he demanded as he snatched the cash.

"Bet back," Cujo continued as he dropped his entire pile of cash at Ra-Ra's little brother's feet. He noticed the little nigga had on J-Bones with the snakeskin on them. *What the fuck?* Cujo thought to himself. *This li'l nigga out here wit' four-hundred dollar sneakers on? A nigga like me supposed to be rockin' those.*

Shaking the thought away, he rolled the dice and, just as he was crapping out, his phone rang. He drove his hand over the dice as he said, "Hold on, let me get this call."

"Speak," he said to the caller.

"I told you I'd call, so check it out. I got a move that's gon' benefit both of us," Soulless stated through the receiver.

"Aight, what you talkin' 'bout?"

"I got a move on somethin' heavy."

As Cujo heard *heavy* come from Soulless' mouth, he smiled, knowing that he meant weight.

"Who all know about this?" Cujo asked.

"Shit, me, myself, and I. And now you," Soulless replied.

"Aw, bet. You gon' come to me, or I'ma come to you?"

"You come to me," replied Soulless. "Meet me at the gas station by the Kitty Korner."

Cujo ended the call then looked around before picking up the dice and putting them in his pocket.

"Aye, what's good, fam?" a few men barked.

Scooping the eighteen hundred dollars into his hand, Cujo mugged Ra-Ra and said, "Shit, I'm gone. Plus I was finna win eventually anyways."

He stood to leave as the crowd looked to Ra-Ra for direction.

"Man, you got us fucked up. You crapped out, fool," Ra-Ra's little brother complained, looking to Ra-Ra for support as Cujo walked away.

Not being on his usual shit, Ra-Ra chose to let it go as he waved his hand toward Cujo's back and told his little brother, "Man, fuck that li'l chump change."

This caused a domino effect as the group began to murmur in the background.

Ra-Ra, feeling some type of way, thought, *Man, I should rock this fuck nigga to sleep.*

He thought twice, however, remembering that Cujo didn't have any sense whatsoever and his brothers were just as dangerous as him.

Cujo jumped into his car and mugged the group before pulling off to go meet up with Soulless.

17 | SPEAKERPHONE

Cujo pulled up to the gas station and looked around for Soulless' car.

"Man, where the fuck this fool at?" Cujo asked himself as he pulled out his phone to dial Soulless' number.

Before he could dial, someone tapped on his passenger-side window, making Cujo jump and reach for his Glock before remembering that he only had Ra-Ra's pop gun. It was Soulless.

Soulless walked away without saying a word but waved his hand for Cujo to follow him.

He got out of the car and followed Soulless as they walked around the corner to Soulless' car. *I see why I couldn't find this nigga whip,* he thought to himself.

Cujo opened the passenger door to get into Soulless' car and saw a book on the seat. He picked it up and tried to read the title.

"Basic Writings of N...Nitz—?"

Soulless reached over and snatched the book out of his hand. "It's Nietzsche, you plebeian. Get in."

Cujo eyed him, wondering if he should feel insulted by the comment. *This nigga really got me fucked up,* he thought to himself. *When we get back, I'ma push his shit back and take everything from this bitch—even his bitch-ass book.*

After jumping into the Lexus, Cujo relaxed in the body-hugging seat and thought, *Damn,* everybody *ridin' better than me around this bitch.*

"Aight, give me the script to this move," Cujo said.

"This cat got weight and he ready to buy the Lex ball with cash or boy. So, you already know how to play ya position out." Soulless replied.

"Yep, I got you—say less."

They got on the freeway and rode in silence as they passed a blunt back and forth.

"Man, you ain't got no Jeezy in this mafucka?" Cujo asked as he began fumbling with Soulless' very expensive sound system. Feeling as if someone was watching him, he looked up to see Soulless with an eerie grin on his face.

Soulless firmly pushed Cujo's hand away from the system's controls and warned, "Don't touch my shit. We ain't listening to no Jeezy."

Soulless then searched for C-Murder on the system.

Cujo, feeling disrespected, sat back and thought, *Man, fuck this old-ass music. And fuck this bitch-ass sound system and fuck him... Man, I can't wait to kill his ass when we get back to Milwaukee. Then I'm gon' take this punk-ass sound system out and put it in my whip.*

They finished the rest of the ride listening to the C-Murder album before reaching their destination, Racine County.

As they got out of the car, Soulless tossed Cujo a roll of duct tape and said, "Let's make this shit fast."

Cujo stuffed the tape in his jacket pocket as they approached a well-kept house.

When they made it to the door, to Cujo's surprise, some light-skinned pretty boy with long hair answered the door.

"What up, Soulless? Let's talk some business," the pretty boy said as he motioned for them to come in.

Before he would step in, Soulless asked, "Man, who all in this bitch?"

"Shit, nobody but my guy, Hands, and my cousin, BD. And they glued to that damn PS5. I got that new Madden."

Soulless then stepped into the house and made introductions as Cujo followed.

"Mister, this Cujo. Cujo, Mister."

The three men walked into the living room where Hands and BD were sitting on opposite ends of the couch playing Madden. They were so focused on their game that they didn't even look up when the men entered the room.

"Aight then—let's get to it," Soulless said as he took a couple steps towards a hall that led to the kitchen.

Mister stopped him.

"Hold up. From this point on, it's just gon' be you and me. Tell ya dog to wait here."

Soulless turned to Cujo. "Aye, fool, wait here while we go take care of this business," he said and gave him a nod.

Cujo, knowing what the nod meant, nodded back and went over to take a seat on the couch between Hands and BD. As he sat, he brandished the little .38 revolver.

He watched the two of them play the game for a few moments then scooted to the edge of the couch with excitement.

"Ooh, my team playin," he said. "Which one of you bitch-ass niggas got the Packers?"

"Me," BD said nervously as he looked to Cujo's gun, wondering what he was on.

"Aight, pussy. You bet' not lose," Cujo warned as he reached over and pointed his finger in the man's nose.

He continued to watch them play for a few moments then jumped up suddenly and said, "You know what?" and started checking both of their waistlines.

Looking confused, the two men were speechless at the audacity Cujo had to come into their spot, pull a gun, and act this way.

After Cujo finished searching them, he noticed that Hands had a gold and diamond chain tucked in his shirt. As Cujo reached towards him, Hands recoiled, not knowing what Cujo was reaching for.

"Whoa, be easy, fam," Cujo instructed, pointing the gun at Hands before reaching back out and taking hold of his chain.

"Yeah, that's a nice piece, li'l dog. Take it off."

Hands, not wanting any problems, nervously took off his chain and handed it over to Cujo.

After taking the chain, Cujo sat down and growled, "Now play the game, li'l pussy—and don't lose."

The two men resumed playing, but now with nervous intensity, afraid that the madman with the gun would shoot them at any moment if he didn't like how the game was going.

"Maaan, yo' bitch ass bet' not let him get that touchdown," Cujo warned BD.

The opposing team, however, did score a touchdown on the Packers and Cujo gave BD a look of fire.

After leaving Cujo in the living room, Soulless and Mister had stepped into the kitchen, which looked to be under construction.

"What you doin' in this mafucka, man?" Soulless asked.

"Shit, I'm just doing some remodeling. Me and my niggas in the living room been at it all day."

The men talked for quite a while about Mister's plans for the kitchen before Soulless eventually got them back on track.

"Let's get to this business," Soulless said.

"Aight—what you want for the whip?" Mister asked.

"Shit, give me forty."

"Come on, man. That's outrageous. I'll give you six zips of boy."

"Naw, man. I ain't feeling that right there."

"Fuck it. I'll give you eight g's too."

Before Soulless could respond to Mister's last offer, they heard a loud crash come from the living room and both ran in to check it out.

Cujo, upset about the touchdown against the Packers, had stood up, grabbed BD, and threw him into the 74" flat-screen TV.

When Soulless and Mister arrived on the scene, Cujo was standing over BD with his gun in his face while also yelling and pointing at Hands. "You move nigga, I'ma pop you!"

Mister hurried toward them and asked, "Aye, what the fuck is you doin', dawg?"

As he turned to confront Soulless on his guy's actions, he was met with Soulless' gun pointed at his head.

"Aye, be easy," Soulless told Mister with a grin.

Cujo began kicking BD as he lay confused on the broken TV.

The moment Cujo took his attention off BD for a second, however, Hands jumped up and snaked Cujo with a hard left, then a right hook, causing Cujo to stumble off balance and drop his gun.

As Cujo stumbled to catch his footing, Hands approached him and took a fighter's stance before punching Cujo in the rib cage, causing him to double over in pain.

Hands stepped in closer to get in an uppercut, but Cujo, seeing he was about to be taken down, rushed Hands with his 5'10", 190-pound body. Cujo began throwing close punches, hoping to end the fight.

Hands was a true fighter, though. He allowed Cujo to get in a few short jabs as he balanced himself and then gave Cujo a punch to the side of his head with expert precision, causing Cujo to see stars.

Cujo was not going to go down without a fight. He grappled Hands' legs, scooped him in the air, and brought him down with a powerful force that took all the fight out of him.

Cujo steadied himself from the spinning he still felt in his head from the last punch then took Hands' head in his hands and kneed it as if it were a soccer ball. As he turned to check his surroundings, he saw Soulless standing against the wall with a grin on his face.

This bitch-ass nigga gon' watch and not shoot the nigga? Cujo thought. *Aight, let's see if he still has that grin on his face when I off his ass later.*

As Cujo refocused, he lifted Hands to his feet and growled, "You thought you could fight god and win, bitch nigga?"

Enraged, Cujo power-punched Hands with an uppercut so hard that it broke his jaw on contact. The sound of his jaw cracking echoed through the room.

"Good job," Soulless said as he sarcastically applauded Cujo with his hand and gun. "Now, get yo' shit together and wrap these niggas up."

Cujo picked up his gun, aimed it at the brave attacker, and fired it into his ass before he yelled out, "That's for tryna show yo' ass in front of company." He then savagely kicked Hands in the ass.

Hands groaned in agony as Cujo reached into his jacket pocket and pulled out the duct tape Soulless had given him. He ripped a piece off and aggressively slapped it over Hands' mouth as he growled, "Shut yo' bitch ass up."

Cujo then duct taped everyone's wrists and ankles. When he was done, he dragged them into the kitchen one-by-one and shoved them down in the chairs that currently sat table-less in the middle of the construction area. Hands' screams were muffled by the duct tape as Cujo shoved him down on his wounded ass. Hands immediately shifted his body in the chair to try to relieve the pressure and pain.

Soulless proceeded to question Mister about where the drugs were stashed. When Mister wouldn't answer, he tried to beat it out of him, but Mister still wouldn't utter a sound as he accepted the beating Soulless was putting on him.

Cujo became impatient and tried to take matters into his own hands. He shoved the .38 into BD's mouth and threatened, "You got one time to tell me where the shit at or I'ma blow yo' face into a million pieces."

BD looked to his beaten cousin in desperation then confessed in a weak voice, "It's in the pantry...in the cereal boxes."

Cujo, not believing that someone would hide dope in cereal boxes, started pistol-beating BD. Blood began gushing from his pumpkin-sized head.

Cujo then leaned down and whispered to him, "If the shit ain't there, I'm killing you."

Hoping that BD was lying so he could just kill him, Cujo stepped into the walk-in pantry, grabbed a box of cereal off a shelf, and tore into it.

"Man, I bet ain't shit in here."

Cujo began digging in the cereal. He felt something odd in the box and paused as a surprised look came over his face. He grabbed the object and pulled it out of the box, revealing a zip of boy. He then ripped open another box, and another, seeing that there was not only boy in the boxes, but money too.

Cujo yelled out to Soulless in excitement, "Bro, it's in here! It's all in these boxes." He lifted a zip in the air to examine it closer.

Soulless stepped into the pantry behind Cujo. "I'm going to give you one of the Original Rules," he said to the back of Cujo's head.

"What?" Cujo asked, not understanding, or caring, what Soulless was talking about as he kept his focus on inspecting the zip of boy.

"You should be aware if the person you talkin' to got you on speaker-phone or not," Soulless responded.

Mystified by the comment, Cujo finally turned around to look at Soulless but his eyes instead made contact with the pistol Soulless had pointed at his face. *Damn,* was the only thought he had time to form in his head.

Soulless sent a slug straight into Cujo's right eye. His body hit the shelves, knocking cereal boxes down with him as he fell to his knees. He braced himself to try to stand back up and Soulless stared at him in disbelief. As Cujo tried to stand, Soulless slapped him on top of his head with the butt of the gun. Cujo still didn't fall to the floor and, with his head down, tried to stand once more.

Soulless took two steps back, assessed the scene in disbelief, then charged three steps forward and placed the gun point-blank to the top of Cujo's forehead. He squeezed the trigger and Cujo crumbled on the spot. This time, it was clear that he was finally dead. Soulless bent down, grabbed Cujo by the feet, and dragged him out of the pantry. He then went to look for a garbage bag.

After he found a garbage bag in one of the kitchen drawers, Soulless went back into the pantry and started grabbing the cereal boxes, removing their prizes, and dropping the money and dope in the garbage bag. As he worked his way through the boxes, he recalled the night he copped the kush…

Soulless didn't feel like driving so he asked Glock to take him to the store to pick up a new iPhone. He had dropped his and the screen had a small crack in it. It still worked, but the crack was driving him crazy.

They smoked a blunt and listened to music on the way but otherwise rode in silence. Soulless was texting back and forth with a bitch named Porsche who had been trying to get at him for weeks.

The music got cut off as Glock's phone rang through the car's speakers and Glock answered it. Soulless continued texting but was still listening to the conversation. It was Cujo.

"I know you good for it," Cujo said. "You got a move for me?"

Glock frowned at the bold ask. "Man, what you really on?"

"You know I gotta drop this car and fifteen g's off to ol' boy that I hit eleven times or he gon' show up to court on me. I can't believe this mafucka tryna extort me," he said more to himself than to Glock.

"I ain't got no move for you right now, playboy," said Glock. "But, if something comes up, I'ma get at you."

"Tell them niggas anything, man. Tell them I got boy, some Mini .14s, some Dracos—tell them whatever. If a nigga bite on any of that, let me know. All I got for real is some shells, but they don't need to know all that," Cujo laughed.

"Aight, I got you," said Glock.

"Aight, One," said Cujo.

The music cut back on when the call ended. Soulless had heard all he needed to hear, even though most of his attention had been focused on the pussy and ass shots that Porsche had just sent him. She was trying to entice him to come over later.

She succeeded.

———

On his way to Porsche's house later that day, Soulless stopped at Blunt's weed spot. When he stepped into the house there was a nice gamble taking place. He was tempted to jump in, but decided against it as he chopped it up with Blunt and gave him one hundred seventy-five dollars for a half of kush.

When Blunt disappeared into the back, Soulless decided to place two side bets. He dropped a hundred dollars with the shooter just before the point came back. He then dropped the two hundred and the very next roll was his point. As he picked up the cash, Blunt tapped him on the shoulder and passed him the half ounce.

"Aight then, I'm out this bitch," Soulless said.

"Damn, that's how you gon' play it?" asked some dude named Trey. "You just gon' run off with my money?"

"Naw, player," I'a be back tonight to give you a chance to win your money back. This li'l light-ass four hunnit ain't gon' make life stop—at least not mines."

"Preach," Trey said and smiled as Soulless dapped him.

As Soulless made his way out the front door and down the porch steps, he heard the door open back up behind him. He looked back and saw Cujo step out smoking a blunt.

"Let me holla at you, Soulless."

Soulless turned around and made his way back onto the porch. Cujo took another hit from the blunt then offered it to him.

"Man, listen, you already know I shot li'l Easy up and the bitch nigga lived. Now, this pussy want my car and fifteen bands, so I'm letting everything go 'cause I gotta get this money.

"What you lettin' go?" Soulless asked, denying the blunt.

"I know you play with them pistols. I'm lettin' the Dracos go for five a piece. Matter of fact, I got the nuts to go with them. Fuck it, I fuck with you so give your boy fifteen hundred. I'll put a bow around the two Dracos with the nuts and add a Mini .14 with three 50-shot clips for you."

Cujo watched as a grin appeared on Soulless' face.

"I'm good," Soulless said as he turned to walk away. As he headed to the car, all he could think about was that Cujo was willing to do him in over fifteen hundred dollars. Was that all his life was worth to the nigga?

He turned back around just before Cujo made it back into the house.

"Aye, I might have a move for you," Soulless told him. "I'a call you, don't call me."

"Aight, love, my nigga. We all we got."

Soulless got into his car, turned up the music, and was off to Porsche's.

～

Soulless loaded the garbage bag with what looked to be forty thousand dollars, seventeen ounces of boy, and some Fentanyl patches in a small zip-lock sandwich bag. As he walked out of the pantry with the bag, he almost tripped over the cord to a five-inch handheld belt sander Mister had been using for his remodel. Soulless put the garbage bag down and picked up the sander to test it. It came on loud and powerful. He turned it off, set it down, and stepped over to Mister, BD, and Hands. He grabbed the duct tape and taped Mister's and BD's mouths since Cujo had only taped Hands' mouth earlier.

Soulless looked at Mister as he tried to say something through the duct tape but it only came out as a mumble.

"You gotta speak up. I can't understand you," Soulless said. Then, with a grin on his face, he lifted Mister's shirt over his head before picking the sander back up.

Even though it covered his face, the T-shirt was thin enough for Mister to see through it. His eyes followed the belt sander as it moved in Soulless' hands. Mister's eyes widened and started to tear up at the sound of the sander as Soulless turned it on. He could smell remnants of cedar wood on the 80-grit sandpaper as it spun on the belt. He attempted to plead for his life, but all attempts were muffled by the duct tape.

"So look here," Soulless said. "I only have one question for you—"

In one swift motion, Soulless dragged the sander across the full length of Mister's chest. The course sandpaper immediately ripped a quarter centimeter of flesh off his chest, sending it into the air in the form of a white mist and exposing a five-inch thick strip of white meat. Both Hands' and BD's blood turned ice cold with fear as they watched the strip stay white for only a second before it changed from bright white to a deep red that started flowing from the wound down his stomach. Mister's chest felt like it was set ablaze as he screamed helplessly into the duct tape.

Soulless turned off the sander, removed the T-shirt from Mister's head, and bent down until his face was just inches from Mister's face. He looked into Mister's tear-filled eyes in silence for a few seconds, absorbing the moment.

"Is there anything else in this house?" Soulless asked as he started peeling the duct tape back from Mister's mouth. Before he got it completely removed, his phone started ringing. It was Glock. Soulless lightly pressed the tape back on Mister's mouth.

"Talk to me," Soulless said as he answered.

"We at Five-Seven's and that nigga upstairs right now," Glock said from the other end of the line.

Mister yelled out half audibly, "Help!"

"Shut the fuck up!" demanded Soulless as he viciously hit Mister hard across the chest with the sander, knocking him backwards in his chair and causing him to crack his head on the floor.

"Where the fuck you at? What you doin'?" asked Glock.

"Shit, in the middle of nowhere, busting a move. Anyways, who upstairs?"

"That ho'-ass nigga, Calico."

"What?!" Soulless dropped the sander and before it could hit the floor, he had his pistol in his hand. He put two in Mister's head then touched Hands' head with the pistol before letting one go. He then pointed at BD's head and let one go.

"What the fuck was that?" Glock asked. "What's goin' on?"

"Keep that nigga there," Soulless commanded. "I'm on my way. Y'all bet' not let that nigga leave the house. I'm about twenty-five minutes out." Soulless ended the call.

Before leaving Mister's house, Soulless grabbed a bottle of Henny from the table and poured it out over the dead. He then grabbed a cushion from the couch and placed it on the stove before cutting all the burners on. He grabbed the garbage bag with all the merch in it and closed the door behind him as he exited the house.

He jumped in his car, skated off, and was on the highway in minutes—doing 85 in a 65. He was beside himself with jubilation as he cranked the volume on the C-Murder album.

He climbed from 85 miles per hour, to the dash, the entire ride down I-41 as the thought of having Calico began making him salivate. He had so many plans for the nigga. The first thing he planned to do was dismiss the entire crew. He knew that it would be days before he finished with Calico. He also knew that none of them would have the stomach for what he planned to do. He was going to make artwork out of the nigga's blood and bone.

He reached Milwaukee in record time and headed straight for Five-Seven's house. The moment that his Lexus turned the corner, he began to scan the block for any familiar rides and saw AP's ride parked behind Five-Seven's. As he passed their rides and started to pull into a parking spot in front of them, he almost hit someone running toward his car from the right side. As the person leapt up to avoid getting hit, he saw that it was Calico, within arm's reach and sliding off the hood of his car. "What the fuck?"

Before he had a chance to react, he spotted Five-Seven running past in pursuit of Calico—then came Glock, then AP.

Soulless didn't even place the car in park as he hopped out and gave chase. He couldn't believe that these niggas were about to let this shit slip.

He raised his Draco and looked for a clean shot, but with Five-Seven and the rest of them in his way, it was hard for him to lock in on Calico, who was incredibly fast as he weaved in and out of yard after yard.

AP spent his entire clip trying to take off Calico's head.

BLOCKA BLOCKA

—

"You tired?"

"I'm straight," Calico replied, breathing heavily.

"Man, you got to control yo' breathing," Asad advised as the two of them jogged laps around the yard. "Yo' life might depend on this someday… You at a six-minute mile. We gotta get you down to a five-minute mile. Keep this in mind, young brother—if you can do two miles in ten minutes, you can last four minutes in the cell. So, control yo' breathing and keep up. Remember, inhale through yo' nose and breathe it out slowly through your mouth."

—

BLOCKA BLOCKA

Only if Asad knew that those training sessions wouldn't save his life in prison, but at that moment out on the streets. Calico took a deep breath through his nose. When he released it slowly through his mouth, he felt a burst of energy, which allowed him to increase speed and take flight. He was out of there.

BLOCKA...BLOCKA BLOCKA BLOCKA...BLOCKA...BLOCKA

Soulless was seconds away from knocking his own three homeboys off just to create a clear path to Calico.

"Fuck these niggas," he said to himself after a few more gangways. He switched the weapon from semi to full and began to spray in Calico's general direction. The shots flew right above them. Five-Seven heard three fly right by his head, just missing him. AP saw five hit the house in front of him. One hit Glock in the hand, taking off a finger. Everybody had to hit the ground so they didn't get shot, or get shot again in Glock's case. Five-Seven, Glock, and AP looked at Soulless as he got closer. Unfortunately for him, Calico had kept moving.

"What the fuck is you doin'?" asked Glock as Soulless caught up to them. "You shot my fuckin' finger off."

Soulless was in a state of rage as he frantically scanned the area. Calico was nowhere to be found. He could not believe that these niggas had fucked up in such a monumental way. He thought of killing all of them right then and there. He was sure that Calico would get lost for good this time and never be seen again. "Fuck!"

18 | EMMETT

Déjà Vu jumped into the car with Nightmare.

"Man, peep game—you gotta slow ya role. Men like him, those the ones you want on ya team," Déjà Vu reasoned.

Nightmare's heart was still pumping with adrenaline and anger over the stranger who pulled a gun on him on Vision's porch. "I don't give a fuck what you or Vision say—"

Déjà Vu cut right into his sentence. "We done talking about that shit for now. Get back to what you were breaking down to Vision. How many of them bitches they got? How many come in a case?"

"Mafucka, do I look like a sergeant in the army? Maybe twenty or thirty," Nightmare replied.

"How much did you pay for the two you got?"

"The white boy said he wanted twenty-five hundred but he let me slip through the cracks for two bands each. Shit, I basically got three-in-one for each pistol, though. I got the slide to the .357 and the .40, so I can swap it out with the 9-millimeter when it get dirty," Nightmare said, then, still unable to let the altercation on the porch go, muttered, "Damn, that nigga Calico lucky I ain't have no clip in this bitch."

"Nigga, stay focused and get that honky on the phone," Déjà Vu ordered.

"I been tryin' to call him all week," Nightmare explained. "He ain't been answering. I'ma hit you the second he hit me though."

Five weeks later...

"Dog, the white boy gon' be at the club tonight," Nightmare informed Déjà Vu from the other end of the phone.

"Which club?" Déjà Vu asked.

"Bar of Soul, downtown. He gon' be there around eleven."

"Okay," Déjà Vu said and ended the call. He had just left Calico's house and was making a pit stop at the smoke shop to buy some pills and other ingredients he needed to stretch the dog food. He planned to turn the first two ounces of his new supply into four. The only fucked up part was that once he stretched it, he was on the clock.

After he got everything from the smoke shop, he rushed home and went straight to his kitchen, where he pulled out two ounces of the new dog food he got from Calico. He grabbed a glass plate and put it on the table, then pulled out his coffee-bean grinder from under the sink. He took the grinder to the table and plugged it in, then opened the pill bottles and counted out the pills. He was ready to get started.

Break open pills

Turn on grinder

5 minutes to settle

Weigh up cut... 50 grams

Add cut to dog food

Final weight... 100 grams

Re-rock

Five hours later, he hit the door and was back in his Lexus, ready to make it happen. He had just caught a heavy pass from Calico and he was about to capitalize. *Sixteen ounces to go,* he thought to himself.

In no time, he was pulling up to Bar of Soul when his phone rang and cut off the music in the car. It was Nightmare.

"Don't even bother getting out the car," said Nightmare, "I'm bringing him yo' way in about two minutes."

Déjà Vu said nothing as he ended the call and waited.

Like clockwork, Nightmare appeared at his ride two minutes later with the white boy in tow. Nightmare opened the back door for the white boy to get in then climbed in the front and sparked a blunt.

"What's up, bro?" greeted Tommy as he stared into the front seat at Déjà Vu.

Déjà Vu looked to the back seat and could immediately tell that the dude had some kind of habit. "You tell me. My mans say you got them heats on deck. I'm tryna see what the tag look like."

"Well, Haans wants three each, but I'm sure he might come down a couple hundred if you buy five or more."

"Three g's?" Déjà Vu looked to Nightmare, who seemed to be lost as well. "I thought you said it was twenty-five hundred?"

"It is," said Nightmare, turning to the back seat. "You tryna middle-man my guy?"

"Wait a minute. Hol' up," Déjà Vu interjected, "You ain't even the one callin' the play? Where the boss at? I'm tryna spend some money with him, and you finna fuck it up for him."

"Well, I might be able to get him on the phone," Tommy said, "But, you guys gotta show me that you're for real and that this is no bullshit."

Déjà Vu reached over to the glove box and pulled out the four ounces of heroin and some of the cash Calico had allowed him to keep. "I got work, and I got that don't stop. And it don't stop. Now, get ya mans on the phone before he lose out on all this money."

He could tell that the white boy was on the verge of salivating. The money was the furthest thing from his mind after he saw the dope.

"Head north," Tommy instructed. "I'll give you directions from here."

The houses were getting farther and farther apart as Déjà Vu drove. Each property now looked to sit on about ten acres.

"It's the next driveway on the left," Tommy said as they finally arrived at their destination.

Déjà Vu turned into a long driveway that led up to a ranch-style house with an attached two-car garage.

"Park just past those trucks," Tommy directed as he pointed to two Silverado 2600s parked off to the side about halfway up the driveway. Both trucks were covered in mud—which made sense since they sat on 38" mud tires—but Déjà Vu could still tell that they were late-model vehicles. One of the trucks had a nice-ass boat attached to it.

As Déjà Vu pulled into the spot next to the trucks, he scanned the scene. The house looked old and rundown. Much of the paint had worn away over the years and any shutters that were still hanging were crooked. Various clutter and junk was scattered all over the yard. There were two mud-covered four-wheelers parked right in front of the house and a Suzuki motocross dirt bike parked on the side. Next to the garage was a target area with two 3D deer targets and various other stands with bulls eyes.

The garage door on the far side of the house was open, revealing the only thing about the house that looked clean. The inside of the garage appeared spotless. It was home to a '68 Chevy C-10—candy blue.

Déjà Vu shut off his engine.

"Follow me," Tommy said as he got out of the car.

Déjà Vu got out of the car and started to follow Tommy, but paused to talk to Nightmare.

"Play ya position," he instructed Nightmare.

"Whatever you say, boss," Nightmare said as he popped a Percocet in his mouth and washed it down with a swig of Everfresh.

Déjà Vu examined the scene to try to get a sense of what to expect. They were about to walk into a strange house with strange people and they needed to have their guards up.

"I know their kind, man. I met 'em before," he said to Nightmare. "If I ask you what time it is, you know what to do."

The two of them resumed walking to catch up to Tommy, who was about twenty feet ahead of them. As they got closer to the house, they saw the front door swing open and out stepped a big-ass 250-pound Stone-Cold-Steve-Austin-looking white boy. He was wearing a bloodstained apron and held a machete in his right hand and the entire hindquarter of a deer by the hoof in his left hand.

Nightmare stopped walking and immediately pulled his heat. Déjà Vu quickly stepped in front of Nightmare to block sight of the gun. He kept himself and Nightmare at a distance and let Tommy do the talking.

"Who the fuck did you bring around my house?" the man asked Tommy as he looked suspiciously toward the two black men standing in his yard.

Tommy jogged the last several steps to the porch to smooth shit over.

"It's cool, Haans," he said in a hushed voice. "You said you wanted to get that shit off and I brought the money to you. They might just buy everything. The fuckers are loaded."

"I don't give a fuck," Haans said, matching Tommy's quiet tone. "You know better than to bring niggers to my house. They better have money like you say or I'm fucking your ass up."

"I got you," Tommy assured him, then returned to speaking in a normal volume to make his new friends feel more at ease. "These are some cool brothas."

Déjà Vu could see that the man was a backwoods country boy who more than likely hated Black people. If he was going to have any chance of a peaceful transaction, he knew that it was best for him to do the talking himself.

"Look here, buddy. This business," Déjà Vu explained to Haans as he and Nightmare edged closer to the porch. "You got something I like and I'm willing to drop as much cash in yo' hands as you need me to right now. But, I gotta have those weapons."

To make sure that the country boy knew he meant business, Déjà Vu pulled the cash from his pockets. "This should be the only language that matters right now."

"Follow me," Haans said after a long pause, then turned around and entered the house.

They all followed him into the house and into the living room, which was just inside the front door.

"Have a seat here, bro," Déjà Vu instructed Nightmare. "I got it from here."

Déjà Vu left Nightmare in the living room and followed Haans.

Nightmare felt the Percocet beginning to kick in as he looked around the living room. *What the fuck kind of shit is this?* he thought to himself as he stared from the lamps to the end tables. Everything seemed to be made from deer antlers and wood. There were giant bass and catfish mounted next to deer heads on one of the walls. Sprawled on the floor in front of the fireplace was a bearskin rug with the head still attached.

He walked toward a plush chair to have a seat and noticed a confederate flag draped across the back of it. He snatched the flag off and tossed it on the couch before sitting down. *Where the fuck am I at?* he thought, hoping Déjà Vu would ask him for the time soon.

Tommy sat down on the love seat across from Nightmare and instantly reached into his jacket pocket. With trembling hands, he pulled out a small bag of heroin, a spoon, and a lighter and put them on the coffee table in front of him. He also pulled out a small syringe, uncapped it, and put it on the table as well. He then removed his belt and started trying to fasten it around his upper arm.

"Hey, man, you wanna give me a hand?" he asked Nightmare.

"Hell mafuckin' naw," protested Nightmare. "Kill ya'self by ya'self."

Tommy eventually got the belt fastened around his arm, then placed the substance from the bag on the spoon and waved the lighter flame back and forth along the bottom of the spoon. When the heroin turned to liquid, he quickly grabbed the syringe and drew up all of the dope through the needle. He searched his arm for a vein and when he found a decent target he began injecting himself.

That's when Nightmare noticed a gold Rolex on his wrist. "Man, what you want for the watch?" he asked.

"What you got?" Tommy responded as he instantly started to nod off into oblivion.

—

Déjà Vu and Haans walked into the kitchen. Haans stepped through the connecting garage door, tossed the deer leg onto a rack, slammed the machete into the meat, and stepped back into the kitchen.

Déjà Vu stood in the kitchen as he watched the white boy. "Your boy was telling me about those military-issued demos with the interchangeable slides. I'm tryna see what's good with them."

"You got enough for those?" Haans asked.

"What you talking?"

"Twenty-five hundred."

Déjà Vu pulled the four rubber-banded stacks of $6,500 out of his pockets and counted the value for Haans as he placed each stack on the kitchen table, one at a time.

"$6,500… $13,000… $19,500… $26,000… And it won't stop. I just need to see one to see the quality. If I like what I see, then all I need to know is how many you got."

Haans yelled over his shoulder, "Becky, bring me one of those," then muttered, "you fucking slut" under his breath as he turned his head back toward Déjà Vu.

About twenty seconds later, a woman came into the kitchen with a gun in her hand. Haans gave her an irritated look and said, "You fucking cunt, go and get the other two pieces." She turned around and disappeared for a few moments, then returned with everything Haans wanted and set it all down on the table in front of him. Haans picked up the gun, popped the empty clip out, and held it by his face, waving it from side-to-side as he spoke to Déjà Vu.

"This right here is an army-issued M-17 Sig Sauer. A standard magazine holds sixteen rounds. Best firearm in the world. It comes with Uncle Sam's stamp of approval, too." Haans took aim at Déjà Vu's chest. "The beauty of it is that once you kill someone..." he squeezed the trigger, letting the hammer hit home before finishing, "...Pow!"

Then, in four moves, he removed the top half of the gun before replacing it with one of the other slides on the table. "You had a 9-millimeter and now, within a few seconds, you got yourself a 40-caliber."

He tossed the gun to Déjà Vu, who had been peeping his gestures and innuendoes all along. The country boy was most certainly a racist. *The white boys are sweet, though*, Déjà Vu thought to himself.

"Now, you can simply destroy the slide to the 9-millimeter and leave no evidence," Haans explained.

"What's the deal on thirty of them?"

"Seventy-five thousand."

"Come on, quit playing," Déjà Vu said. "I know you can come better than that."

"The lowest I can go is twenty-two hundred a gun, boy. And that's a deal."

Absentmindedly, Haans grabbed the charm on his necklace—an AK-47 mechanical bullet—and twisted it. It clicked twice and produced two hits of heroin, which he brought to his nose and inhaled. "Twenty-two hundred is a good number," he continued, "I know how you boys like to kill each other with handguns and AKs."

Haans stood up and walked over to his pantry. He came out holding up a Smith & Wesson M&P10 for Déjà Vu to see.

"It's not about how many bullets you have in a magazine, it's all about performance. You see this?" Haans asked, pointing to the scope. "This baby has six times variable zoom range, which means I can hit you anywhere on your face I choose from a thousand yards away. On top of that, it has ambidextrous fire controls, twenty-inch match-grade threaded barrel, rifle-length gas system, and fifteen-inch free-float rail with a two-stage match grade trigger."

Damn, thought Déjà Vu as he found himself intrigued by how much this racist mafucka knew. "It just look like a gun to me."

"Well, it ain't just a gun, and that's the problem. You boys like to run around with hundred-round magazines killing everybody except who you came to kill. Shit, I have a thirty-shot magazine to this baby right here, but I ain't never put it in. You see what I got in it," he said as he removed the clip and showed Déjà Vu before popping it back into the rifle, "A standard ten-shot clip. You wanna know why?" he asked, before answering his own question, "because it's one shot, one kill. If I come for you, I don't even need the other nine bullets."

Haans laid the gun down on the kitchen counter, went back into the pantry, and came out with a big smile on his face and a crossbow in his hand.

"This is the perfect weapon for when you're hunting deer or men," Haans said as he held up the crossbow, looking at it as he spoke. "Once I lock eyes on a warm body and pull the trigger, this arrow will fly towards you at 415 feet per second, as quietly as Casper the friendly ghost. You can kill a man from seventy yards with this beauty, but I did it from eighty last year."

Haans stared at Déjà Vu with a serious look on his face.

"Yeah, I see you know ya weaponry," Déjà Vu responded. "Throw that crossbow in and you got a deal."

Haans walked over to Déjà Vu and handed him the crossbow. "I guess we got a deal then. But remember, this ain't a gat, homie."

Déjà Vu took the crossbow from Haans and collected the 9-millimeter along with the interchangeable slides to the .357 and the .40 from the table.

"I'ma take all this with me," Déjà Vu said, then pointed to the cash, "and leave that with you." He knew that the man was a blatant racist, but it was nothing. "I'ma be back in twenty-four hours with the other forty bands. For now though, here's something for your necklace I think you might like." Déjà Vu went into his pocket and pulled out fourteen grams of boy folded up in tin foil and tossed it to him.

Haans laughed and said, "I see you're not like the rest of 'em. You must be one of the good ones."

"I'm not like nobody," Déjà Vu corrected, "I'm a eagle." He then turned and walked out of the kitchen.

As Nightmare saw Déjà Vu walking towards him, he asked, "What the hell is that crossbow for?"

"Let's get the fuck outta here," was Déjà Vu's only response as he walked past Tommy and made his way for the door. Nightmare got up and followed Déjà Vu out.

As they were walking away from the house, Haans came out behind them.

"After tomorrow, don't come unless I send for you. You hear me, Emmett?" Haans yelled.

Déjà Vu looked back and saw the smile on Haans' face as he delivered the message. He simply smiled back and saluted him. "Alright, boss."

"Did he mean Emmett Till?" Nightmare asked. "Man, I'ma go back and kill that racist-ass cracker right now."

"Say less," Déjà Vu said as they continued walking to the car. "Sometimes, you have to let the fish swim. We eagles, we fly high above the waters. We see them and their movements. We can swoop down and snatch them out of the water any time we ready to eat."

They got in the car and Déjà Vu dialed his phone as they pulled off.

"Vision, baby," he said when he got an answer, "What you doin' right now? I might have something for us."

19 | FBI

Déjà Vu pulled up to the front gate of the storage facility and hit the code. The gate crawled open and he slowly pulled his Lexus into the lot. He drove down long rows of units the size of two-car garages until he reached unit 41. He parked the car and he and Nightmare sat in silence.

Twelve minutes later, two more cars pulled up behind them—a Chrysler 300 and a Ford 500 Limited Edition. Daydream jumped out of the 300 and Vision and Black jumped out of the 500. Déjà Vu and Nightmare followed their lead and the five men approached the door of the storage unit.

Vision removed a key from the chain around his neck and unlocked the door. He lifted it open and they all stepped inside. Daydream was the last one in and closed the door behind him. Inside were two vehicles—a dark blue Suburban and a stolen U-Haul truck. To the side of the U-Haul was a floor safe with a stack of bulletproof vests sitting on top of it. The vests all had fake FBI logos on them. In a storage bin next to the safe was an assortment of FBI tactical gear, badges, hats, and equipment belts with holsters attached to them.

"Gear up," Vision instructed.

As they all started to get dressed, Vision looked to Déjà Vu.

"Run it," he told him.

After giving them the rundown, Déjà Vu jumped into the driver's seat of the U-Haul while Vision opened the door for him to back out. Daydream, Nightmare, and Black climbed into the cargo area of the truck and pounded on the wall twice when they were ready to go. Déjà Vu started the engine and pulled out. Vision secured the door when the truck was out then jumped into the passenger seat and Déjà Vu drove off.

———

Thirty minutes later, Déjà Vu pulled the truck up on the grass at Haans' house and came to an abrupt halt right in front of the front door. Immediately, Black tore open the cargo door of the U-Haul and the squad filed out rocking FBI masks and uniforms. Daydream carried a steel battering ram as he, Black, and Nightmare headed for the back of the house.

"Go Time!" said Vision as he and Déjà Vu jumped out of the cab and headed toward the living room window. They both launched flash bangs through the window, which muffled the sound of Daydream slamming the battering ram into the back door.

Vision ran over to the front door and as he raised his leg to kick it in—

BOOM!

An unexpected explosion came from inside the house that sounded as if a grenade had gone off.

After three kicks, Vision and Déjà Vu were in the living room, where they found that Black had Haans at gunpoint in his recliner. Two other people were laid out on the couch but it was obvious that they were high and completely oblivious to what was going on.

"What the fuck was that explosion?" asked Vision as he ran towards Black.

"I was gon' ask you the same thing," Black replied.

"You fuckers caused that explosion," Haans snapped, "and you probably scared my dumb-ass brother."

Black immediately began to zip tie everyone's hands, beginning with Haans.

"How many other people are in the house?" Vision asked Haans from behind his mask.

"Man, fuck you pigs," Haans replied. "Go find out."

"Jackpot!" they heard Nightmare yell from the back of the house.

"Black, watch them," Vision said as he and Déjà Vu headed for Nightmare.

As soon as they hit the hallway, they could smell an acidic, chemical odor mixed with burnt plastic. Vision continued running straight past the bathroom door, but Déjà Vu stopped and tried to open it. He could only get it open a couple inches, though. He looked through the crack he created and could tell that this was the location of the mystery explosion. When he looked down, he saw a man's body obstructing the door from the other side and figured it must be the brother that Haans had mentioned. The fumes from the explosion hit Déjà Vu like a brick wall and he stumbled back as if he had been punched in the face.

When he looked up, Nightmare was walking quickly towards him.

"Where you goin'?" he asked Nightmare.

"To get the dolly out the truck. Vision needs you in the back."

Déjà Vu made his way to the back bedroom. As he entered, he saw Vision standing next to a square floor safe. There were two large wooden boxes stacked on top of the safe, each about two feet high by two feet wide and eighteen inches deep. As Vision inspected one of the boxes, Déjà Vu went over to the bed and flipped the top mattress over, searching for the money he had given Haans earlier. Nothing. He then went over to the closet. As he grabbed the doorknob, a woman screamed from inside.

"Please don't shoot!"

He snatched the door open and found Becky, the woman who had retrieved the gun for Haans earlier.

"Please don't kill me. I have kids," she said, facing the floor as she held her hands over her head in a desperate attempt to protect herself.

"Bitch, where the money at?" Déjà Vu asked.

"He doesn't trust anybody when it comes to the money," she responded. "It's all locked in the safe."

He zip tied her wrists behind her back and closed the closet door.

Nightmare returned with the dolly and was sliding it under the safe when they heard a commotion coming from the living room.

"Fuck you, you fucking nigger!" they heard Haans yell, followed by a loud crash.

Black held Haans at gunpoint in the living room when the rest of the squad went to the back of the house.

The gun kept Haans compliant for a while, but his blood eventually boiled over and he couldn't take it anymore.

"My brother is probably dead in that bathroom. I'm suing you fuckers for taking so long to get him help. You know how volatile meth is. Let me see that fucking warrant," Haans ranted.

"Man, shut yo' pussy ass up, white boy. Fuck yo' brother," Black said.

As Black spoke, Haans noticed that he had a mouth full of gold and colored diamonds. He looked down to the hand that held the Berretta and saw that it was covered with tattoos. He also caught a glimpse of a gold Rolex.

Then it registered to Haans that he was not about to be arrested. He was being robbed. The fact that his hands were restrained in front of him meant nothing as the rage of being fooled by a fucking nigger caused him to turn savage.

"Fuck you, you fucking nigger," Haans yelled as he gathered all 250 pounds of his strength in both fists and stood to his feet, catching Black by surprise. He delivered a forceful uppercut that lifted Black off his feet and sent him crashing into a small glass-top table and the wall. Black was sliding down the wall as Haans recalled his days playing Rugby and rushed Black with his shoulder, lifting him again and slamming him back against the wall, totally knocking the wind out of Black this time. Déjà Vu and Nightmare came rushing around the corner as Black was hitting the floor.

Déjà Vu immediately snapped into action and ran up on Haans, cracking him in the back of the head with his gun. It didn't do anything to stop him though so Déjà Vu had to follow up with a second quick blow, which was enough to knock Haans unconscious and he fell to the floor.

Daydream came wheeling the safe into the living room at that point and saw Black on the floor.

"Get yo' ass up off the floor and help," he told Black as he gave him a shove with his foot.

Black slowly got himself back on his feet and tried to shake off the dizziness he was feeling. Vision walked in behind him and passed one of the wooden boxes to him.

"Fuck that white boy. We got shit to do," Vision said to Black and then headed back to the bedroom.

"Hold up, we not done with him," Nightmare said. "Daydream, come over here and help me get his ass up."

Daydream left the safe where it was and went over to help Nightmare lift Haans.

"Aight, I'm with you, but this one for Black," Déjà Vu said. "Straighten that mafucka up one more time for me."

"Don't hit my finger," Nightmare said as he and Daydream stood up an unconscious Haans as best they could.

Déjà Vu smashed the butt of the gun into Haans' grill, then twice between the eyes near the top of his nose, crushing his face. Nightmare and Daydream then let go of Haans and he instantly slumped to the floor as blood began to gush from his face. The skin was completely torn from around his nose, exposing the bone through the blood.

Still not satisfied, Nightmare stepped around in front of Haans and kneeled down by his face. "Emmett, huh?" he said, more to himself than to the unconscious man, as he slid his gun out from by his lower back. "You lucky I ain't got a gin fan," he said as he placed the tip of his gun slightly back from his temple before pulling the trigger.

"Ya'll good?" came Vision's voice from the back room.

"We good!" Déjà Vu yelled back. He looked to Daydream and said, "Get that safe out of here." He then turned to Nightmare and said, "Let's go."

Daydream went back over by the safe while Déjà Vu and Nightmare headed to the bedroom to check in with Vision. When they got there, Nightmare grabbed the other wooden box and headed out to the U-Haul with it.

"Is that everything?" Vision asked Déjà Vu.

"Yeah, that's everything."

Vision and Déjà Vu returned to the living room and found the rest of the squad talking about the best way to crack open the safe when they got it back to the storage unit.

Déjà Vu's phone rang and he looked at the caller ID.

"This Calico right here," he said to Vision.

Before Vision could reply, Déjà Vu answered.

"Cal, what up? Where you at?"

"I'm at the bus station, bro. Come get me."

Déjà Vu could tell that something was wrong by the tone in his voice. "We on our way," he said as he ended the call and turned to Vision. "It's Cal. We need to take a ride."

Vision needed to hear no more and looked to Daydream. "Let's wrap it up."

It had started to rain as Calico stood outside waiting for them to pull up. When he finally saw the Lexus, he made his way to the back door and climbed in without saying a word. After several minutes of silence, Déjà Vu decided to speak. "Killa Cal, where you been at for the last two days? You had Simone worried that something happened to you."

"Yeah," said Vision. "My sister said you left the door wide open and yo' phone was still in the house. Talk to me, man."

Barely audible, Calico finally spoke. "He chopped up my momma."

Unsure if he had heard correctly, Déjà Vu looked to Vision who cut the music completely off. "What?"

—◆—

Vision found himself staring out at the road in front of them as Déjà Vu drove and Cal sat in the back seat, reduced to tears while trying to explain his situation. The shit sounded like something out of a bad Hollywood script. Had a grown man not been crying in the back seat, Vision would have sworn it was a joke.

"So, let me get this straight, bro," Vision said after Calico finished speaking. "You killed this nigga's brother, who was yo' best friend and, in return, he killed yo' momma, yo' daddy, yo' kid, and yo' girl?"

"The savage took everything from me," Calico said as he stared down at the floor. "My family didn't have nothin' to do with this shit. My momma and daddy had to have a closed-casket funeral."

Déjà Vu looked to Vision as they both tried to assess the situation. "I gotta be real with you, Cal. I can see you havin' to kill the nigga, but robbin' him on the way out seems kind of fucked up."

"What the fuck else was I supposed to do? Them niggas got me caught up in some shit that I didn't even want to be a part of. On top of that, they gave me next to nothing… I knew Theory from the playground. It hurt me to the core to have to do what I did, but once the damage was done, I was left with no other options. I had to run. And I had nothing to run with. I don't give a fuck about the money. I barely touched the shit."

Calico sat there thinking about the fact that he had just been run out of town by the very person responsible for bringing harm to his family. He was far from a coward, yet he felt like every bit of one. There was no way he was about to stay in Memphis—hiding—while Soulless roamed the streets of Milwaukee freely. He had a proposition.

"Look, y'all. I got a quarter mil in cash. Y'all can have all of it. I just need y'all to help me get to this nigga. He runs with a few shooters who get down but I gotta have him, and I really don't give a fuck if I die in the process. I just need some assistance in getting to him. This nigga tortured my momma, man."

Déjà Vu didn't need to hear another word. As far as he was concerned, Calico was like family. *No Sleep* looked out for their own.

"Keep ya money, Cal," he said as Vision got on his phone and began to dial the rest of the squad.

20 | THE COUNTDOWN

It was 9:49:15 p.m. when he picked up the camouflaged AR-15 and watched as Calico stood there, frozen. It was a marvelous moment. Soulless trained the assault rifle on him, gave a slight grin, and pulled the trigger.

2 hours, 45 minutes, and 43 seconds earlier...

2:45:43 (7:03:32 p.m.)

It had been just under two hours since the sun had fallen out of the sky. As Calico drove the squad along I-94 in the Suburban, Déjà Vu looked up and saw a sign that read, *Milwaukee—Population 596,794.*

Déjà Vu reached into the back seat, grabbed a duffle bag, and began dispersing gloves, weapons, and ammunition to everyone. The whole squad had shown up for Calico—except Black, who had some family business to tend to. Déjà Vu passed everyone two M-17s of different calibers then took two for himself and two for Calico.

He looked over to Calico. "Where we goin'?"

"Soulless," Calico replied.

02:11:24 (7:37:51 p.m.)

Calico directed everyone to search for Soulless' blue Lexus as he circled the block in the Suburban. The Lexus was nowhere to be found. Calico pulled into the alley and parked two houses down.

Déjà Vu went into action gearing himself in a fake UPS delivery jacket and matching hat. He also had a clipboard and a small box to complete the image. "Y'all already know the drill. I'ma get the door open for us. Once the nigga open the door, I'ma step back and y'all rush him."

"Say less," Calico said as he unlocked the doors. Everyone climbed out of the truck, preparing to position themselves.

Déjà Vu made his way to the side door with the two M-17s tucked neatly against the flat of his back. He peered through the window and could see that no one was in the living room. He began knocking on the door. This was like clockwork for him. As far as he was concerned, they would have Soulless knocked off and be back in Memphis and back to his money before his heroin line rang.

"Ain't nobody here," Déjà Vu said as he noticed Calico pulling every-one away from the basement window. "You wanna kick this mafucka in?"

"Nah, I don't even want to give him the heads up that I'm back in town," Calico said. "Actually, I know where the nigga might be at."

Within seconds, they were back in the Suburban as Calico smashed off.

"Where we headed?" asked Déjà Vu.

"To Five-Seven's crib," Calico replied.

01:43:48 (8:05:27 p.m.)

"If Soulless in here, everybody in here, so be ready," Calico said as the truck sat across the street from Five-Seven's house. "We can't play with none of them at all so light up anything—and I mean anything—that move."

Calico, Daydream, Nightmare, Déjà Vu, and Vision got out of the Suburban and walked over to the side of Five-Seven's house. Calico removed his Pelle, wrapped it around his arm, and punched in a basement window. He reached in and lifted the latch to open the window. Everyone then climbed down inside the basement.

"Hit the power," said Vision. "We gon' wait to see if they come to check on the box."

As Daydream began searching for the circuit box, he noticed that the entire basement was draped in plastic. A chair sat in the middle of the room. Lined up neatly on the floor next to the chair was a hacksaw, pliers, duct tape, and a crowbar. The hairs on the back of his neck stood up.

"Who the fuck was these boys finna chop up?" Daydream wondered aloud.

When Calico finally registered the layout before him, it all became clear to him. This must have been what Glock was doing in the basement.

"Me," Calico answered in a low tone as the rage began to build.

Without saying another word, he stormed out of the basement with the rest of the squad in tow. He hit the steps by twos, rounding the corner to the last set of steps in the blink of an eye. Calico took aim at the lock on the door into Five-Seven's house and let off seven rounds before charging into the door, shoulder first. Four of the bullets had hit the lock and it was enough to weaken the frame. The door exploded open into what appeared to be an empty house.

After a thorough search of the house, the men met back in the living room to await Calico's lead.

"What's up now?" asked Nightmare.

Calico turned and headed for the door. "It's only two other places they can be—Glock's or AP's."

"Which one we goin' to?"

"The closer one—Glock's."

01:14:21 (8:34:54 p.m.)

The Suburban pulled up in back of Glock's house and Calico gave instructions.

"Give me five minutes, unless you hear from me sooner. Then, I want y'all to come in through the side door. Déjà Vu—you come with me."

Déjà Vu climbed out of the truck with the clipboard and small box in his hands. He also rocked the fake UPS jacket and hat.

They crept to the front door then rang the bell. Déjà Vu stood in front of the door as Calico stood off to the side, trying not to be seen.

Glock's girlfriend of five months, Lexus, appeared from behind the curtain in the door before she opened it.

"Is Glock here?" Déjà Vu asked her.

Her eyes grew large once she heard the name. She knew she had just fucked up by opening the door. Before she could react, they pushed her into the house. Calico called Vision's phone and directed them to come in.

Calico sat Lexus down on a chair in the living room. "Listen, we ain't got no problem with you, so we not gon' hurt you."

"Calico, Glock ain't have nothin' to do with yo' parents, yo' baby, or Tammy dyin'," she said. "That shit was Soulless—all Soulless. I don't even know why y'all fuck with him. You know he a fuckin' psychopath. He shot Glock finger off."

"Bitch, call ya man," Déjà Vu demanded, "I ain't got time for this. Ain't nobody gon' hurt him. We just need some information."

"Look, I'm gon' help y'all get to Soulless. Just don't hurt my baby."

"Okay," Cal agreed as Vision and the rest of the crew entered the house.

When she saw that there were more men with him, she became more nervous. Still, she knew that she had no choice. She grabbed her phone and began dialing.

Déjà Vu snatched the phone from her and put it on speaker.

"Whattup, bae?" greeted Glock after the first couple of rings.

"Bae, where you at?"

"Shit, I'm like four minutes away. So, check this out—warm up some chitlins and spaghetti and go look in the closet and grab the new lingerie I got you. Have it on for me before I get there."

"Where Soulless at?" she asked, looking to Calico nervously.

"Bitch, what the fuck you askin' 'bout Soulless fo'?"

"Naw, I was just askin'.... I was wondering if he was with you because I don't want that mothafucka in my house."

"You worried about the wrong mothafuckin' things. You need to be worried about them chitlins, that spaghetti, and that lingerie. One." Glock ended the call.

"You got some chitlins in this mafucka?" asked Nightmare as he made his way into the kitchen.

Déjà Vu just shook his head.

———

"Them chitlins better be ready," Glock said as soon as he stepped into the house. He removed his jacket and shoes, ready to eat and get his rocks off.

As he made his way into the living room, he saw that Lexus was standing with her back to him as she faced the TV.

"Bitch, you hear me?"

When he came into full view of the room, he saw four men in his house—one sitting on his couch, one leaning against the wall eating, and two pointing guns at him. Another appeared out of nowhere and advanced towards him.

"Calico?"

"Bitch-ass nigga—you was gettin' the basement ready for me?!" Calico didn't wait for an answer as he covered the eleven feet between them in less than half a second.

His running start had given him enough momentum to jump into the air and come down with a Superman punch into Glock's grill. Glock was blinded by the impact of the punch, but still tried to swing back. His efforts were to no avail as Calico grabbed his head and jumped up, delivering a vicious, jaw-cracking blow to Glock's head with his knee. Glock dropped on the spot.

Vision and Daydream zip tied Glock's hands together to the front then walked him over and pushed him down into a seated position on the couch.

"Y'all said y'all wasn't gon' hurt him," Lexus said, now sitting in the love seat.

Nightmare continued leaning against the wall, eating Glock's chitlins.

"I don't know what you bitch-ass niggas think gon' happen, but this ain't that," Glock said as blood poured out of his mouth.

"Where the fuck is Soulless at?" Calico asked.

"Bae, just tell them," Lexus said from the other side of the room.

Glock shot her a look as if she had lost her mind. "Bitch, fuck these niggas and shut the fuck up."

Glock watched as Calico grabbed his wrist, causing the zip tie to cut in deeper. He immediately became shaken when Calico's other hand quickly retrieved a gun. Before he could protest, Calico sent a slug through the same bandaged hand that Soulless had shot. Both Glock's and his girl's screams merged into oneness.

"Where he at?" Calico asked again.

"Stupid-ass nigga," Lexus cried. "Tell these mothafuckas where Soulless ass at before they kill us. I ain't dyin' for yo' stupid ass. You tryna protect that animal when he almost killed you. He don't give a fuck about you. He ain't yo' mothafuckin' friend."

"Bitch, would you shut up?! And I ain't telling you shit, Cal. If you want him, go find him," Glock yelled out through his pain.

"Cal, just kill 'em both," said Nightmare, snacking on another chitlin. "We'a just find him at the next stop."

"Man, just let her go," Glock pleaded. "She ain't got nothin' to do with this."

"What?" Calico asked. "My mother didn't either."

Calico walked over to Lexus and grabbed her by the hair, forcing her down on all fours, then dragged her on her knees like a dog. He placed her in front of Glock.

She looked at Glock with pure terror in her eyes. She shook uncontrollably, causing her teeth to chatter as she begged, "Baby, please tell these mothafuckas where he at. Tell 'em, baby." Tears fell from her swollen eyes. "Please...tell 'em!"

Calico put his pistol to the back of her head and looked Glock in his eyes. Glock could see that the Calico he once knew was missing. He saw murder in these new eyes. "Please, don't," Glock pleaded.

"Nigga, is that what my momma said?"

BLAHH!

The slug pierced the back of her head, wreaking havoc as it travelled through her brain, and crashed out the front of her dome, creating a golf-ball-sized hole as it exited her face. Blood sprayed out and covered Glock.

Glock heard his girl gasp her last breath as the bullet burst through her face and lodged into his leg. He hadn't even registered the pain in his leg as he found himself stunned by what had become of her face. The hole just above her left eye began to ooze blood mixed with fleshy gray material, which Glock knew was her brains.

Calico gripped her spiritless 146-pound body tightly by her hair, not allowing it to fall. He emphasized his words as he gestured with her head. "Nigga, you think I'm playing?" Calico placed the barrel of his gun back against the lifeless head and squeezed once more.

BLAHH!

He sent another slug through her head and into Glock's stomach this time.

Glock yelled out in pain. "Okay, okay, Cal! You got it, fam." Glock found himself reduced to tears. "They at Soulless house, man. I just left 'em."

Calico just stood there, holding the lifeless body by the hair and looking at Glock with venom in his eyes.

"You lyin'. We was just there a hour ago and the house was empty," Calico seethed.

"You just missed us. We got there around eight. I swear," Glock said through tears.

Vision took control of the moment by walking over to Glock and snatching his phone. He started scrolling through as he asked, "Nigga, what's the number?"

"Just call AP, man. Soulless ain't gon' answer his shit. They all there, man." Vision found AP's number and called it, then put it on speaker.

When AP answered, they could hear a game system playing loudly in the background. "What's to it, playboy? You just left this mafucka—what you want?"

"My...my wallet. Did I leave it there somewhere?" Glock stammered.

"What the fuck you mean, yo' wallet? Nah, yo' wallet ain't here."

"Ask Soulless or Five-Seven if they seen my shit."

"Soulless, is dawg wallet here?" There was a pause before AP spoke again. "Man, Soulless in his own world, fuckin' with his phone. He ain't tryna hear that shit."

"Ask Five-Seven."

"Five-Seven! You seen this cat wallet?"

"Hell, nah!" Five-Seven yelled from the background. "If I find it tho', I'ma take the money out and throw that gay-ass wallet in the trash. Matter of fact, tell that nigga I got his shit and for him to come get it but stop at Wendy's first."

"Tell him to get me two bacon double-cheeseburgers before I shoot him in his other hand," a third voice ordered.

Calico immediately recognized the third voice. His heart stopped momentarily, causing his left hand to lose grip of Glock's girl's hair and her torso dropped. It was Soulless.

Glock pushed back a little deeper into the cushion of his couch as his girl's head fell into his lap.

"Aye," continued AP, "pick up some Frosties, a couple of baked potatoes—"

Vision ended the call.

Without saying a word, Calico tucked his gun in his waistband and headed into the kitchen in search of the largest knife he could find. When he found one he was satisfied with, he made his way back into the living room. "Y'all meet me in the truck. I'a be out in a minute."

Calico walked over to Glock as everyone else exited.

"Calico, man, I got sixty-seven bands under the floorboard in my room. It's yours. Just let—"

Calico moved his hand over Glock's mouth and used his knee to knock the girl off Glock's lap before placing his knee and all his body weight on Glock's zip-tied hands.

Calico looked Glock in his eyes and said, "My mother was many things to many people..." as he slowly inserted the nine-inch blade into Glock's stomach.

Glock went crazy trying with everything in him to move but Calico pushed his head back firmly into the couch, immobilizing him. He twisted the blade in Glock's stomach before slowly pulling it out halfway and continuously repeating the process from different angles. Glock shook as though he was having a seizure, with tears flowing down his face in streams.

Calico muffled Glock's screams with his hand as he continued, "...and she should have been left out of this." Calico pulled the blade from Glock's stomach and moved it up to his neck. He pushed the blade against Glock's throat, just under his left ear, then dragged it across his neck, slowly slicing Glock from ear to ear, nearly decapitating him.

As Glock's body went limp, Calico became aware of the scent of copper in the air and the warmth of Glock's sticky blood on his arms and body. It was at this moment that he realized what he had done and he no longer recognized himself. Soulless had driven him into the abyss. Calico paused a moment, then collected himself and walked out to the Suburban.

Déjà Vu looked to the passenger's seat as Calico climbed in, covered from his chest to his knees in blood. He knew there was no turning back for them now. "Which way?"

"At the end of the alley, make a left," Calico answered as his mind wandered back to the plastic-covered walls of Five-Seven's basement.

He grabbed a cigar from the dashboard and realized as he tried to roll it that his nerves were completely shot. Daydream, who had been watching from the back seat, saw the blunt break in Calico's trembling hands and said, "I got it, Cal."

"We suitin' up before this one. Shoot first and we'll figure out the rest on the way back to Memphis," Vision said to everyone as he passed out the FBI gear.

Calico handed another cigar over his shoulder to Daydream without even looking back. He was caught up in the depth of betrayal that he was experiencing. They knew he loved Theory. He had done time for him and he was certainly no enemy. Water was thicker than blood when it came to him. They all knew how Theory moved. They also knew that Cal did something that he was forced to do. Still, they wanted to serve him up like a meal to that savage, Soulless. A tear of rage rolled from the corner of Cal's eye, down his cheek, and fell to his blood-soaked T-shirt.

00:06:40 (9:42:35 p.m.)

AP and Five-Seven sat in twin recliners, captivated by an intense game of Madden on Theory's Xbox. Soulless was off studying a video on his phone of what looked to be a UPS delivery man standing at the side door of his house before knocking, looking around, and walking off. This was yet another alert that was slow to catch up to his phone and he didn't get until after it happened.

As Soulless began adjusting the app's settings, he thought about his brother's persistence on installing the security system and syncing it to their phones. Soulless was never a fan of it. Theory, however, insisted that one day it would save their lives. The irony was that Soulless knew there was a good chance that Theory used the system when he gave Calico entrance to their house the day he got killed. It was too bad the system couldn't detect malicious motives. If it could, Theory's life might have been saved.

Soulless watched AP and Five-Seven enjoying themselves as if shit was all good, as if his brother's body was not ashes. They couldn't even pretend to be ashamed or remorseful of the fact that they had allowed Theory's killer to get away. The sight of them was enough to make his blood boil. How could these bitches laugh and kick it while Calico was still breathing? It just went to show that no one loved his brother the way he did. They had no love for him or his brother.

He had grown so angry from watching them that he hadn't even realized he was gripping the trigger of his .357 Judge. He wanted both of these niggas dead. He wanted to put a slug in the back of Five-Seven's head and watch as AP struggled to understand why.

With the two of them manipulating the controllers as if their lives depended on it, Soulless reached between the couch cushions and pulled out his preferred gun—his Draco.

He decided to let the video game determine their fates as they headed into overtime. A grin began to spread across Soulless' face as the plan took shape in his mind. He wasn't interested in sports and didn't know much about football, but he knew that overtime was also referred to as "sudden death." The terminology was perfect, but with his own spin. *Winner dies sudden and loser dies slow,* he thought to himself as Five-Seven offered to raise the wager with AP.

The two were so caught up in their game that they almost forgot about Soulless behind them. They were completely oblivious to what was about to happen.

After a couple minutes, Five-Seven scored the first touchdown, winning and ending the game. Soulless clutched the wooden grip of the Draco and stood to his feet, aiming the gun at the back of Five-Seven's head. The grin still blanketed his face as he anticipated how AP would react once he put half of his clip into Five-Seven's medulla.

Milliseconds before pulling the trigger, the alert from his security monitor went off on his phone again, causing AP to look up and notice the gun pointed at Five-Seven's head. AP froze momentarily as he and Soulless locked eyes.

Soulless had no shame as he slowly lowered the weapon and checked his phone. He hoped it was Glock so he could save a trip and have all three of them where he wanted them. The moment he tapped on the notification to see what was happening outside his house, he went into a frenzy.

"Oh, fuck no!" Soulless yelled as he watched men in FBI vests and masks jump out of the back of a dark blue Suburban that was coming to a stop in his driveway.

"What the fuck is going on?" Five-Seven asked, jumping to his feet and peeping the Draco partially pointing in his direction. He quickly drew his .44, unsure of what was about to go down.

Five-Seven could see that the man was breathing hard as he began to silently pace like a caged lion. Five-Seven made his way to the window and saw what he had been hoping to dodge for the past decade and a half. It was the feds. "Oh shit."

"I ain't goin' to jail," Soulless warned AP and Five-Seven. "This shit finna go down right here."

"Fuck it then," AP said and grabbed the 32-shot .45 that he had set down on the coffee table. "We get sentenced right here, my nigga. Fuck them."

"Calm down, y'all," said Five-Seven, even though he knew there was no way to calm Soulless. "If they come through the door, we just gon' handle our business. They probably ain't even got a warrant anyway."

BANG! The flash at the front door caused everyone's ears to ring. Then the shots commenced.

Daydream sneaked in through the back door and was the first inside the house. He came in with an M-17, but quickly wondered if there were too many niggas to subdue. His only job was to plexicuff everyone on sight until Calico confirmed the face that he had come for. Before Daydream had a chance to think any more about it, Soulless emptied his 50-shot clip in less than six seconds into who he thought was a federal agent. He struck Daydream nineteen times in the vest, seven times in the face, and three times in the neck, inflicting twenty-nine piercing wounds from an automatic chopper.

As Soulless dropped the young nigga, he noticed that there were more shadows coming through the back. The front door blast must have been a diversion. *Nice,* he thought to himself as he found that he was growing erect by it all. They were now in his world, and he was going to make this a situation like writers wrote books about and movie directors made movies about. Dropping the Draco, he pulled out his Judge and in one swift motion let out all six shots at the main light in the living room, knocking it out and cutting visibility down by sixty percent. He jetted for the stairs, hoping that they would follow him.

"Daydream!" Nightmare began blasting at the sight of his brother-from-another falling to his face, dead on the spot.

AP got off eight rounds before taking one to the chest that barely slowed him. As he stared at the man in the mask, he tried raising his gun again. He could barely pull the trigger before Nightmare put three more shots into his torso.

Among the confusion, Calico entered through the back door in his FBI gear and remained low to the ground as he navigated through the house, glad that he knew the layout. He too had seen Daydream go under, but now was not the time for regret. He had come for one person and he was not going to stop until he got his man.

As he turned the corner to move into the living room, Calico locked eyes with Five-Seven from behind his ski mask. He quickly fired four shots at Five-Seven, but missed the man entirely. Next thing he knew, a host of rounds fired from behind him as Five-Seven was trying to take cover behind a couch. He pivoted to look back and found Vision and Déjà Vu sending shots at Five-Seven's body.

Calico then looked to AP on the floor, somehow still clinging to his life, and saw that he had taken aim at Vision. Before Calico could do anything to stop him, a round blasted out of AP's .45. The bullet crashed into Vision's forehead and shred through his brain before flying out of the back of his skull and lodging into the frame of a painting of Soulless, Theory, and Teresa.

Calico wondered how he was going to break the news to Simone that her brother was dead as he fired five shots into AP, finally killing him.

00:01:28 (9:47:47 p.m.)

Calico heard movement upstairs. He left Five-Seven to Nightmare and Déjà Vu as he quickly ascended the stairs, only slowing down as he reached the top. He pulled up his mask so it wouldn't obscure his vision at all. As he peaked around the corner, he found that the hallway was eerily empty. His gut was telling him that Soulless was in one of the closets waiting for his moment to strike.

Calico crept toward the linen closet in the hallway then snatched it open as he prepared to fire. It was empty. He then made his way towards Teresa's bedroom. As he entered, he saw that her bed was still neatly made and all of her belongings sat perfectly in order, just as she had kept them when she was alive. Knowing that Soulless hated the woman, Calico could not see him cowering in mommy's room like a bitch. There was only one other place where he could be.

As he rounded the corner into Theory's room, Calico found Soulless standing in front of the closet, staring at something inside as he strapped on a Kevlar vest. He looked to be so caught up in what he was doing that he had forgotten all about the gunfight downstairs.

"Aye, Solstice."

Soulless had been studying the white and gray tundra-camouflaged AR-15 and blue steel Mossberg pump leaning against the wall in his brother's closet. He still had not made up his mind about which weapon to use. When he heard his name, he looked up and saw Calico standing in the doorway. He could not believe that—of all people—Calico was standing there.

"You workin' with the feds too?" Soulless asked him, trying to make sense of the situation.

Calico steadied his weapon as he stared at the man. He knew that Soulless had it in him to go for one of the heats and he was not about to chance the nigga getting the ups on him. Calico squeezed the trigger.

Click...Click

Soulless frowned in confusion until he realized that the nigga was out of ammo. Allah had forsaken his ass and he was about to make him pay for such a rookie mistake. A satisfied grin came over Soulless' face as he finally made up his mind and delivered some last words to Calico.

"And the Lord looks down from Heaven and sees the whole human race and from his throne he observes..."

00:00:00 (9:49:15 p.m.)

He picked up the camouflaged AR-15 and watched as Calico stood there frozen. It was a marvelous moment. Soulless trained the assault rifle on him, gave a slight grin, and pulled the trigger.

Click...Click

Soulless opened up the door to his house carrying all of Li'l Greg's merch. He went straight to the kitchen, high and hungry. He tossed the gold Breitling, canary-colored diamond earrings, compact .40, jar of pills, ounce of soft, and the AR-15 onto the kitchen table. He took the blood-caked cast-iron skillet to the sink, washed the blood and gray matter off it, then placed it on the stove and turned the burner on. He then grabbed some eggs and prepared them with seasoning.

As he ate the eggs, he looked at Li'l Greg's merch and decided to give all that shit to his brother, except the compact .40. When he finished eating, he took everything upstairs to Theory's room. He placed the watch and earrings on the dresser, then counted out seven g's of Li'l Greg's money and set it on the dresser next to the jewelry. He placed the jar of pills and ounce of soft on top of the money. He was going to lay the AR-15 on the bed, but decided instead to put it in Theory's closet. He leaned it against the wall next to Theory's pump. It would be a nice little surprise for his brother the next time he went in there.

—

BLAHH! BLAHH! BLAHH! BLAHH! BLAHH! BLAHH!

Soulless couldn't even believe it. Of all the dumb shit that could have happened, he had made the mistake of thinking that even a fake-ass nigga like Li'l Greg would always keep his weapons loaded.

I knew it wasn't nothin' but a fuckin' fashion show to his bitch ass… Damn, I shoulda went for the pump, he thought as he found himself catching round after round in his upper body. He cursed himself for forgetting one of the original rules: always keep it locked and loaded.

Calico wasted no time pulling his other pistol from his waist and using it to walk Soulless down like the dog he knew him to be.

The shots were rapid and powerful as they slammed into Soulless' chest and stomach, causing him to fall backwards to the floor as the bullets beat up the thinly-plated vest. A few missed the vest and hit Soulless in his bicep and the side of his neck.

Calico walked right up to him and kneeled down. He observed the grin on a still-breathing Soulless' face and began hammering away with the pistol, trying his damnedest to remove the grin and break his face. When he realized that Soulless was unconscious, he placed the tip of the gun into Soulless' left eye socket and pressed it in. He pressed in with the fury of a mourning son, a mourning father, and a mourning husband. He could feel the bone fragments crack and chip as the eye itself popped out, making the sound of a raw egg hitting the floor. He thought of how terrifying it must have been for his mother to die such a slow and unimaginable death at the hands of this monster when he should have been there to protect her.

Before he even realized it, the barrel of the gun was a full inch inside Soulless' face. Calico began firing round after round into his head as the slide of the gun jumped and jerked, causing blood and brain matter to spew out all over himself and the room.

Eleven. It was a number that Calico would never forget, as it was the number of rounds it took to slay a beast among men. He stared at Soulless' mangled face and realized that the feeling of satisfaction was only short-lived. At the end of the day, he was still alone in the world. Soulless had lived up to his name and Calico was sure that he had shown the man far more mercy than Soulless had ever shown any of the people he had wronged in the world. He stood to his feet and slowly headed for the stairs as he wiped blood from his face.

The second he reached the bottom of the stairs, he was greeted with two shots that narrowly missed his head by inches. He had been so zoned out from everything that just went down that he barely even flinched. He scanned the room and found that Déjà Vu was the only man left standing.

Déjà Vu quickly lowered the weapon as he realized that it was his man, Calico.

"My bad, bruh! You good? I thought that nigga killed you up there. What the fuck was all them shots?"

Calico looked at Déjà Vu's shirt and noticed blood coming from his shoulder. It was evident that he had just survived a battle. He looked around the house and saw that Nightmare had not made it. Five-Seven's body was stretched out over the couch as Vision's and Daydream's bodies lay sprawled across the living room floor.

"None of it was supposed to happen like this," Calico said, shaking his head in disbelief as he assessed the carnage.

Déjà Vu looked to his fallen homeboys in complete remorse as the thought of returning home without their bodies entered his mind. As much as he did not want to, he knew that he would have to leave them in Milwaukee to be unidentified for the moment. Their creed had always been *no man left behind*, but he was sure that they would have all wanted him to save himself.

"We gotta get up outta here, Cal."

Calico knew that the police were probably already on their way. The ShotSpotter sensors positioned throughout the city were enough alone to alert the authorities. He looked at Déjà Vu and wondered if he would be okay to make it back to Memphis.

"You good?" he asked him.

The truth was that Déjà Vu had suffered a shot in the collarbone and one in the calf. Now that his adrenaline was slowing, he was beginning to feel the pain. Still, he knew that he had to get home.

"Shit, I'a be good once I get the fuck up outta this hot-ass house," he told Calico.

As the two men headed out to the alleyway behind Soulless' crib, they heard sirens in the distance. As much as they both hated to admit it, they were as good as sentenced if they remained together. Déjà Vu knew that with his bloodstained clothes and slight limp he would be more of a burden for Calico than anything else.

Calico also knew that the boy would be a hindrance to his getaway, but, at the end of the day, he had made a trip halfway across the country to aid Calico in something that had nothing to do with him. Calico knew he would be completely out of bounds if he didn't at least try to get the boy to safety.

As they both stood there searching for the least conspicuous path, Déjà Vu spoke first.

"Fuck it, Cal. Don't worry 'bout me. I'm a eagle. I'll find my way."

Calico looked at him and wanted to protest, but knew that it was the only option they had. The man was in a foreign city with no resources and two gunshot wounds. Yet and still, he chose to rely on his own grit to get him back to where he needed to be.

Before Cal could say anything, Déjà Vu spotted a bike leaning against an adjacent garage and began moving towards it.

"In a minute, homie," Déjà Vu said as he hopped on the ten-speed.

"Be careful out here, man."

"Don't worry about me, my nigga," said Déjà Vu as he began to pedal. "I'm goin' home."

EPILOGUE

Three and a half years later...

The champagne-colored BMW 745Li pulled into the car lot at a snail's pace as a young, redbone cutie sat in the driver's seat, nervously navigating the high-end luxury sedan. "Where you want me to park it?"

"Pull up next to the nigga in the suit talking to that woman over there."

As she made her way past a few potential car buyers and focused hard on not crashing into any of the other cars on the lot, she wondered if she needed to take a selfie behind the wheel once she was parked, as if she hadn't taken enough already.

"Right here is good."

As she eased the car to a stop, Calico, who sat low in the passenger's seat, lowered his window and smiled at the man in the suit before speaking.

"What would the boss say if he saw you out here fraternizing with the customers?" Calico asked.

Déjà Vu smiled as he gave a farewell to the caramel cutie he had just negotiated a good leasing deal with. "You lookin' at the boss, homie."

Calico climbed out of the ride and embraced his boy.

"Go walk around and look at the cars," Calico told the girl. "We won't be long."

Calico and Déjà Vu headed into the building that now had *FOR EAGLES ONLY* painted in big letters on the front of it. Shit had been looking good for the two of them over the past two summers. Déjà Vu had managed to open his car lot in Atlanta with the dope money that he and Calico had bled from the streets of North Memphis. His car inventory was of the high-end, previously-owned sort for now, but he was well on his way to securing an authorized dealer contract with Lexus and Toyota.

Calico funneled all of his cash through the dealership to clean it and was doing so well that nearly every night of his life was a party. He switched women like he switched shoes, and he had pretty much been to every popular scene in the A.

After what happened with her brother in Milwaukee, the relationship between Calico and Simone was never the same. As sweet as she was, there were times when he knew that she resented him for what he had gotten Vision into. The tension between them eventually got so bad that Calico decided to pick up and leave Memphis behind him for good. Before he left, he made sure that Simone and her son were safe and would always be financially sound.

It was then that he followed Déjà Vu to Atlanta. The town was poppin' and he loved the nightlife. No matter how hard he partied, though, he knew deep down that no amount of liquor and weed could fill the void deep within his soul. He had never fully recovered from the havoc Soulless had brought down on him, although it may have looked quite different to anyone who was unfamiliar with his story.

"Bro, what I tell you about lettin' thots push the whips?"

"Come on now," Calico laughed. "You know these bitches gon' be the death of me."

Déjà Vu shook his head as he eyed his homeboy. The shit they had been through together had only bonded them tighter. They were brothers.

"Anyway, man," Déjà Vu said, "I got a guy who's throwin' a bachelor party at Magic City tonight. He invited Phoenix thick ass to come through and you know she put bitches like Cherokee Da' Ass to shame. I know you down with it, so be ready at about eleven-thirty."

"Off top," Calico confirmed, "but, check it out. I don't like the way the BMW ride, so I'ma just grab the Audi for the night, bet? Bet."

Before Déjà Vu could say anything, Calico headed for the glass cabinet where the keys were kept. Believing that none of his success would have been possible without him, Déjà Vu never cared if Calico placed a few miles on the vehicles from time to time.

"Whatever, man. Just be ready. And, if you let one of them bitches crash my whip, I'm takin' the ho' to court."

Calico waved his boy off as he made his way for the exit. "Come on now, Déjà Vu. You know I got you. Besides, these ho's ain't got no money. I'm the one keepin' red bottoms on they feet. Anyways, what's up with that thick-ass redbone? You still fuckin' with that?"

"Naw, bro. She too used to fuckin' with small-minded niggas. I got bigger dreams," Déjà vu said, dead seriously.

———

Later that night, Déjà Vu and Calico found themselves sitting in the midst of nothing but big asses, thick thighs, and cute faces as dollars flew all around them. The club was packed, but they shared the VIP section with Déjà Vu's homeboy, Lip, who was known and respected throughout Atlanta as a rather wealthy socialite. Lip had his hands in all sorts of things, from drugs to the stock market.

It felt good to be among players who shared similar statuses, as it eliminated the thirst element that was the root of most bullshit in the game. Calico looked down to see if his cup was empty and, by the time he looked back up, he was greeted by a chocolate cutie who had bent over at the waist and began to wobble her backside in front of him as she looked back smiling. He slapped the girl on the ass with a dollar before flicking a bunch more bills at her.

"That's a beautiful thang right there," said a middle-aged cat who looked to be in a rather fortunate position, judging from the jewels and designer gear he wore.

"I hear you," agreed Calico, continuing to tip.

"Just think, we promised fifty of these beautiful creatures when we reach paradise."

The statement was simple, but peculiar enough to catch Calico's ear. It had been a long while since he heard such speak. "You practice Islam?"

The man smiled. "I certainly try to remain on my deen, but you know we all fall from grace every so often."

"I hear you on that," said Cal as they both eyed the chocolate temptress before them.

"Are you a Muslim?" asked the man.

Calico thought back to his days in the cell with Asad, then about all that had happened to him upon being released. "Once upon a time."

"Nah," said the man, "Islam is forever. It's not a phase, so you either a believer who has slipped in his walk, or an infidel."

Calico was in no mood to talk religion, mainly because he had not been true to his faith over the past couple of years. "Check it out, homie. I came here to enjoy the women and congratulate the bachelor. I really ain't in the mood to debate about the Quran right now."

The man smiled, unable to blame him for his reluctance. He rose to his feet and set his sights on a few strippers on the other side of the VIP section, but he did not leave without a few parting words.

"Allah is the most high and benevolent. Talk to him. He'll always find a way to bring you back home."

At that moment, Calico spotted perhaps the baddest chick in the club. She was headed towards him wearing a g-string and garter belt as her eight-inch stilettos carried her across the marble floor. She was a light toffee-complexioned chick with a petite frame, but more curves than the average chick her size. Her face was beautiful, and he could tell that she would have looked even better without the makeup.

"Goddamn, baby. Where you been all night?"

"Don't I know you?" she asked as she stopped just a foot short of his lap. "Do you be on the East side?"

"Naw, baby. I ain't from around here. I don't think we've met."

"You sure? You look vaguely familiar, like I mighta seen you somewhere before."

"I tell you what," he said, looking to his right to see that Déjà Vu was occupied with a few gorgeous girls of his own. "Let's dip up outta here and talk about it."

Calico entered the keycard into the door of his suite on the seventeenth floor of the W Hotel in downtown Atlanta. Cherish, the toffee-colored, Cardi B look-alike stood patiently behind him. He had come to the hotel so much over the past few months that the concierge and most of the staff knew him by name. They always gave him the same suite every time.

As he walked into the room, he hit the lights and made his way to the wet bar to get them a drink.

"Where's the bathroom?" Cherish asked as she removed her jacket and gently placed it on the large bed.

"Over there to the right," Calico said, pointing her in the right direction.

Cherish went into the bathroom and stared into the mirror as she took a deep breath. She pulled out her phone and began scrolling through it. Before long, the tears began to flow. She placed the phone down next to the sink, then went into her purse and pulled out a small pill bottle. She opened the bottle and tapped out a portion of the powder it contained onto the counter next to her phone. She lined it up with her fingernail, then bent down and snorted. Every speck of it went into her nose as her nostrils began to drain. She looked back up and stared at her reflection again in the mirror.

By the time she picked her phone back up and stared at it, the narcotic was beginning to take its effect, sending her into a world of memories....

—

"Ms. Pennington, you still haven't turned in your paper on Social Conflict Theory and I'm concerned that, without it, your grade might slip drastically."

"I'll make sure to turn it in," she promised as she rushed out of the classroom, feeling overworked and overwhelmed. She was so tired of dealing with the pressure from school that she simply wanted to break down and cry. She had no time for friends and she was barely retaining any of the information she received from lectures. She was ready to be done with it all.

As she headed back to her dorm room, she pulled out her phone and called her boyfriend. As usual, the tears were rolling from her eyes.

"Hello?"

"Bae, I can't do this shit no more. I'm done. It's too much and I'm fallin' behind."

"What? What the fuck you mean, you done. We got a goal, remember?"

"I know, but I can't—"

"But, nothin'. Get it together."

She could hear him talking to someone in the background.

"Who you talkin' to?" she asked.

"Nobody...my guy, Calico. Remember when I told you about my nigga who took the case for me?"

"The one who you said you needed to send some money to?"

"Yeah, he a real one. Hold on..."

Moments later, she found herself receiving a picture of a somewhat handsome-looking fellow with his hands up as if he were trying to keep from having his image captured. She quickly saved it to her phone before placing it back to her ear as her man continued to speak.

"Back to the subject at hand. I don't wanna hear no more about you dropping out of school. Bitch, don't tell me I'm wasting my money on tuition for nothing."

"No, bae. Damn. Don't I got the right to fall apart sometimes. I just needed to vent. I'm good now."

"Well, then you better hit those books."

She ended the call and smiled to herself as she realized just how much she needed this man. Without him, her life was nothing. He had gone out of his way to put her through school and she was on her way to getting a degree in pre-law. She owed it all to him and she was glad that he had it in him to stand on her the way he had. She loved him and there was nothing she wouldn't do for him.

Kim, who now went by "Cherish," snapped out of her daze and stared again at the image on her phone. As sure as the sky was blue, there was Calico in a failed attempt to block his face. Had it not been for this photo, she would never have known what had gone down with her man that night.

After Theory was murdered, Kim's world was turned upside down. She tried to stay in school, but the stress of studying, taking tests, and trying to keep up with tuition on her own was too much. Her mother and father had always told her that she would be nothing and Theory was the only one who ever told her that she had the potential to be much more. She knew that he knew of her past as a stripper, and not once had he even mentioned it. He never judged her and simply supported and cared for her when there was nothing in it for him. He wanted her for more than her body. This was what made her love him more than any man she had ever met.

She was raped by her uncle on numerous occasions when she was twelve and she never told anyone, which made it especially uncomfortable to be with family on holidays. By age fifteen, she had met a man who called himself pimping her, which led to stripping.

Theory was the one who had decided that, rather than investing in her ass and titties, he would invest in her brain. She had never had a man speak as highly of her as he did.

After Theory died, she had to go back to stripping to keep up with tuition and, before long, she found herself wrapped back up in the world. She slowly began to develop dangerous habits. Percocets became Oxycontin as she struggled to numb herself of a pain that could not be alleviated. After a while, college became nothing more than a dream of the past as she eventually found herself doing whatever it took to get the paper. She had even been the victim of another brutal rape, which led to a pregnancy that she had to abort. In her mind, all of what she had gone through was Calico's fault. She hated his ass and she needed her retribution.

She did another line before she put the heroin back into her purse and pulled out a compact .380 Taurus. She made sure the safety was off then cocked it to make sure that one was up. Justice needed to be served. Kim grabbed her purse and looked into the mirror once more before taking yet another deep breath. She then reached for the doorknob and made her way out of the bathroom, gun in hand behind her back.

"What you like to drink?" asked Calico, who had been busy searching for the right cocktail. He was glad to see her finally emerge from the bathroom. As she approached him, he noticed that her mascara was running. She had been crying and there was a look of fury in her eyes. "What's wrong with you?"

THE END

AFTERWORD

While *Soulless: Dead Bodies Don't Bleed* is a work of complete fiction, it's really the story of a young, Black serial killer growing up in the inner city of Milwaukee. When people think of serial killers, they typically picture white men like Jeffrey Dahmer and Ted Bundy, but never someone like Solstice Smith. I intentionally avoided using the phrase serial killer in the book because, where I come from, they are called animals, savages, goons, goblins, and even friends.

ABOUT THE AUTHOR

I am a poet and a painter. I'm originally from a small town that I love—Marked Tree, Arkansas—where my father, brother, and beautiful sister reside. I grew up in Milwaukee, Wisconsin with my beautiful mother (whose eyes are far too virtuous for this book so she better not be reading it) and my wonderful stepfather, who has always been a father figure to me. I also have two handsome sons, who I love very much. Over the past four school years, I have mentored at-risk kids during school seasons.

DISCUSSION QUESTIONS

*** Warning: plot specifics are included below. ***

1. Was the amount of money that Theory gave Calico for the use of the hatchet sufficient?

2. Was Calico wrong for taking Theory's and Soulless' money before leaving town?

3. Did Tammy make a bad choice by picking who she thought was the better man to raise her son, rather than telling Soulless he was the father?

4. Soulless' mother used torture tactics on him, masked as discipline based on religious dogma. How did this affect his relationship with God and his views about the Bible? Was this the fuel added to the rage within his heart?

5. Soulless memorized the majority of the Bible by age 12. He never felt the need for anyone to guide his understanding, leaving room for a strong belief system built on the words of the Holy Bible alone, rather than an outside doctrine from religion. Did this help or hinder his development?

6. When Theory questioned Soulless about the fires he set in the neighborhood, including the one that killed three people, what did Theory's reaction to Soulless' silence tell young Soulless?

7. When young Soulless explained to Theory that he wanted to see the cat's voice box, did he have misguided curiosity or did he do it simply to inflict pain on the animal?

8. Could Theory have done more to prevent what was happening to young Soulless at the hands of their mother?

9. If Soulless' mother showed him the same kind of love and respect that she showed Theory, would that have changed who Soulless became or was his outcome inevitable?

10. On his way back to Milwaukee, why did Calico give up his faith completely when faced with a similar situation as Asad, his mentor in prison?

11. What separated Déjà Vu from other characters in the book that allowed him to find another path and start his own business? Was there a cost to him for being a survivor?

12. Was Soulless a victim of his childhood or simply an evil person?

COMING SOON

Tango: Bodies in the Walls
(excerpt from the prequel to *Soulless: Dead Bodies Don't Bleed*)

The loud gunfire filled the house as 16-year-old Li'l Bro and 17-year-old Money sat in twin recliners playing a James Bond video game.

The house was practically bare, aside from the 52" television, surround-sound system, and the somewhat expensive furniture that sat in the living room. Li'l Bro had gotten a deal on everything from a junkie who was being evicted. The house was simply used as a dope spot, which was ironic in a sense. Money often spent the night, even after Li'l Bro warned him about the perils of being off his square. The way Money saw it, there was no need to leave. He was in mode.

When the doorbell rang, Money turned to Li'l Bro. "It's yo' turn, nigga. I answered it last time. Pass me that blunt, too."

"Cool, I got you," promised Li'l Bro, completely ignoring Money's request as he lit the blunt and walked out of the room with it.

After making his way down the stairs from the top flat of the duplex, Li'l Bro opened the door and was greeted on the back porch by Jack, the neighborhood dope fiend.

"What you need?" Li'l Bro asked.

"Man, you gon' love this," Jack said as he stepped into the small hallway.

Jack went into his jacket pocket and produced an all-black .40 before handing it over. "That's fresh out the box," he oversold. "At least a nickel."

Li'l Bro was impressed by how beautiful the gun was, but there was no need for Jack to know that. The 16-year-old spit six Ps of crack from his mouth and said, "This all I'm givin' you for that."

"Man, I need a hundred, Li'l Bro! I coulda got $250 fuckin' wit dem niggas around the corner. I came to you because I fuck wit you. At least give me ten Ps."

Li'l Bro reluctantly spit three more Ps into his hand. "Come back tomorrow and I'a give you a wake up, plus the one I owe you."

The last thing Jack wanted to do was walk away from the transaction feeling as if he had been played. However, nine dime-bags of what he knew to be good dope was far too tempting to pass on.

"Aight, Li'l Bro!" Jack said. "I'ma be back for my shit tomorrow."

As Jack made his exit, Li'l Bro closed the door and started to rush up the stairs, excited to show off his new heat. Halfway up, he noticed how light the gun felt so he removed the clip to check if it had any bullets in it. It was empty. He shoved the clip back in and rushed up the rest of the stairs. He knew that Money would flip when he found out that he got a pistol for next to nothing. He could not wait to rub it in.

As he reached for the door, Li'l Bro thought about how funny it would be to scare his homeboy. He kicked the door hard as he entered.

"POLICE!" he yelled as he moved to the back room where Money sat. He pointed the gun at Money as he approached him and unconsciously squeezed the trigger. BOOM!!!

The bullet ripped through Money's chest, knocking him back against the couch. Before Li'l Bro could even make sense of what happened, he saw Money's eyes widen.

"You shot me?" Money struggled to say before blood began spilling over his lower lip. Seconds later, his eyes rolled into the back of his head.

"Fuck! Fuck! Fuck!" Li'l Bro screamed before dropping the .40 and rushing over to Money. Unsure of what to do, he began applying pressure. He could feel the warm blood as it began to ink his fingers. He reached into his pocket and grabbed his cell phone. Money was unresponsive. Li'l Bro knew that his boy needed help, but he could not bring himself to call 911. A possible murder rap was too much of a chance. He dialed the only other number he knew he could. After a few rings, he got an answer.

"What's to it, Li'l Bro?" answered his 31-year-old brother.

"Bro, Money shot in the chest. He bleedin' bad. What should I do?"

"Who shot him?"

Li'l Bro paused before speaking. "It was an accident, Bro!"

Big Bro grew nervous as he hoped his little brother wasn't saying what he thought he was saying. "How the fuck did he get shot?! Who shot him?"

"I shot him, man! It was an accident!"

"Did you call the police?"

"No! I called you."

"Is anybody else there?"

"No! What should I do?"

Big Bro sighed as he tried to decide for his little brother. "Aight, li'l nigga. Sit tight and don't answer the door until I get there."

Li'l Bro ended the call and continued to apply pressure. In the back of his mind, he knew Money was already gone. Selfishly, he wanted Money to live for his own sake, but he also couldn't bring himself to accept that his friend had died by his hands. How would he explain this to the hood? How would he explain this to Money's family?

It only took minutes for Big Bro to show up, but it seemed like forever to Li'l Bro. After hearing the signature knock at the door, he quickly ran from the back room, down the steps, and answered the door. Big Bro calmly walked in and closed the door behind him.

"He's dead, bro! I ain't try to do it! It was an accident, man."

"Where he at?" Big Bro asked, hoping to make sense of it all.

Without saying a word, Li'l Bro dashed up the stairs and towards the back room with Big Bro right on his heels.

Big Bro walked into the room and spotted Money on the couch, slumped. Immediately, he went into his pocket, pulled his car keys out, and tossed them to Li'l Bro. "Go open the trunk."

Big Bro stared a moment before he tried to find the hole in Money's blood-soaked shirt. The boy's eyes were closed and it was obvious that he was no longer breathing. How could his little brother have been this stupid?

Big Bro walked over and effortlessly picked Money up before tossing him over his shoulder and heading for the door. As he made his way down the stairs and out of the house, he looked around to see if they had any eyes on them. Luckily, the back yard was boxed in by tall wooden fences. He rushed out to the car and placed Money in the trunk. He then climbed into the driver's seat of the black on black box Chevy as Li'l Bro climbed into the passenger's seat.

Big Bro began dialing his phone as he backed out of the yard and smashed up the alley. After one ring, he got an answer.

"Speak," his right-hand man, Tomorrow, answered.

"Where you at, homie? Li'l Einstein done got in a li'l trouble."

"What's *a little trouble*?" Tomorrow asked suspiciously.

"Let's just say I need you to do somethin' for me. Grab the keys to my Impala, take it to the gas station, get two five-gallon gas cans and fill 'em up to the brim, then meet me on 6th and Burleigh in the alley. You know where I'm talkin' 'bout, right?"

"Ten minutes," Tomorrow said before hanging up the phone.

As he drove to the abandoned house, Big Bro looked over at his brother. He was more disappointed than mad. "You average a 3.9 GPA. You're in Advanced Placement courses. You're going to be the first person in our family who makes it to college. You ain't like me or Tomorrow. Shit, if I had what you have, the streets would be my last option. You just killed yo' homie, Li'l

Bro! Do you get that your life is changed forever? You're lucky you had the smarts to call me. I'm about to save you from a life sentence, li'l nigga. Yo' ass would be on your way to Waupun or Green Bay doing convicts-to-college if you didn't call me. You know what? After I clean this shit up, I'm sendin' you to live with Aunt Lulu! That's it, that's all."

Li'l Bro was too busy being in his feelings and trying to wipe the tears from his eyes to hear much of what his brother was saying. He looked from the window to his hands and began frantically wiping them against his shirt. His homeboy was in the trunk as if he meant nothing to anyone. The guilt alone was enough to kill Li'l Bro.

Once they were on 6th Street, Big Bro pulled into the alley near an abandoned garage and killed the engine. The two of them sat in silence as they waited for Tomorrow to pull up.

Big Bro knew that his brother was taking it hard. He needed this. Li'l Bro needed to understand what he had done. He knew that he would be able to make this go away with virtually no effort, but he wanted Li'l Bro to absorb the reality that he had just taken a life.

A few minutes passed before Tomorrow pulled up in the Impala and parked near the garage. Big Bro then pulled the box Chevy into the garage and both he and Li'l Bro climbed out.

"Go get those two gas cans from Tomorrow and tell him to stay in the car until we're finished."

As Li'l Bro walked off, Big Bro grabbed a screwdriver, went back into the driver's seat, and began breaking the steering column with it. He pulled the key out of the ignition, put it in his pocket, and began jamming the screwdriver into the keyhole. Li'l Bro came back holding a gas can in each hand. The plan was clear.

"Dump that shit everywhere," Big Bro instructed as he climbed out of the car. "Inside and out."

Li'l Bro followed orders and began dumping gas all over the interior. He knew that he was going to have to go into the trunk, but he did not want to. The smell of the gas was making him feel lightheaded and his eyes were burning from the fumes.

He tossed the empty can and looked to his big brother. "We good?"

"Hell nah, we ain't good, nigga! Dump the second can on the outside. Hit the trunk, too."

Big Bro stood there watching as his little brother went to work dousing the car in gasoline. He went into his pocket and pulled out a zippo lighter before walking out of the garage in search of a sewer. Once he found one, he walked over and dropped the keys to the box Chevy into the grate.

When he got back to the garage, Big Bro handed the lighter to his little brother. "Light it up."

Li'l Bro did not even want to think about it. He reluctantly walked over to the car, struck the flame, reached in the window and set the driver's side headrest on fire, then quickly dropped the lighter on the seat. As the car went up in flames, Li'l Bro stepped back and watched.

Big Bro stood with his brother a moment longer to ensure that the car was completely engulfed. It was then that he heard something.

"What the fuck?" He looked to his little brother before stepping closer. "Did you hear something?"

"Nah, man," said Li'l Bro. "What the fuck you on?"

Before he could speak again, Big Bro heard the muffled cry being called out louder than before. He looked to his little brother again and it was clear from the look in Li'l Bro's eyes that he now heard it too.

"Money?!" Li'l Bro said in shock.

"Help me. Help. I can't breathe!"

Li'l Bro stood frozen as he looked to his brother for a clue. The fire had yet to consume the trunk.

Big Bro ran over to the car, reaching into his pocket, only to realize that he no longer had the keys. "Fuck!"

They heard Money's screams evolve into a bloodcurdling pitch. He desperately began kicking from inside the trunk, knocking out the back left taillight, which allowed his words to become even clearer.

"Li'l Bro, pleasssse! Don't let me die like this!"

At that moment, something within the dashboard exploded, causing Big Bro to react. He shoved his little brother out of the way as Money continued to kick from inside the trunk. "Head to the Impala."

As Li'l Bro nearly tripped over himself trying to get out of the garage, Big Bro paused, hoping that Money could kick himself free—to no avail.

"Lord God," Big Bro said quietly to himself as he stepped outside of the garage. He thought about the tortuous death that Money was enduring as he reached up and took hold of the handle to the garage door.

"Please forgive me." He then brought the heavy door down with a SLAM!

Also available where books are sold:

B'S IN DA' TRAP
B'S IN DA' TRAP PART 2: REIGN OF THE GERMAN PRINCESS
SHE DID DAT

by Vision Marques